SURVIVING ANNE

SURVIVING ANNE
A Novel

Gustavo Dessal

Translated by Daniel Tunnard

KARNAC

First published in 2016 by
Karnac Books Ltd
118 Finchley Road
London NW3 5HT

British Library Cataloguing in Publication Data

A C.I.P. for this book is available from the British Library

ISBN-13: 978-1-78220-322-3

Typeset by V Publishing Solutions Pvt Ltd., Chennai, India

Printed in Great Britain by TJ International Ltd, Padstow, Cornwall

www.karnacbooks.com

For Iago

INTRODUCTION

I'm not entirely sure, but I think the first time I saw Anne was the same day Judge Delucca called to ask me to personally take care of interviewing that African American woman. Shanice Tide had been detained the previous afternoon and brought before the magistrate on charges of vandalism of state property. She'd thrown a tin of yellow paint over the city's most prominent statue and caused a major rumpus, especially among those shocked tourists who were splattered with paint. Delucca recognised signs of mental disturbance straight away, and decided to send her to our service before taking any other action. Besides, the fact that she was a member of the black community and that the statue represented the role of the blacks in the Civil War added a touch of social and political sensitivity that called for kid gloves. Delucca was pretty old by then, and I had a good, friendly relationship with him from years working together. He'd got through the inevitable storms a judge faces in a long professional career with considerable honesty, and as he was on the verge of retiring he hadn't the slightest interest in giving himself any headaches with a rash sentence. But he was also aware that our city's more conservative elements weren't going to let Shanice Tide, crazy as she might be (and she was), walk free from a felony that many considered an unforgivable affront to civic values and the sculptor's painstaking art.

The media had already splashed the news in full colour, and even the social networks were bubbling with debate, lit up by an event that spiced up the everyday soup, at least for a couple of hours. I have to say that I'd never liked that statue of the black soldiers enlisted in the Union army, bravely fighting to build a country that, once it had discharged them, repaid them with a century of renewed scorn. That was precisely what Shanice had been thinking, although I of course abstained from confiding my opinions in her, and limited myself to asking her about her motives for this strange act.

"I don't have to answer your question," she said, polite but firm. She was thirty-five, diminutive and pretty slim, and held my gaze with an air of dignity, even pride. She wore her hair down, straightened, not too long, and wore cream pants and a pistachio green polo neck. It was clear that she fully condoned what she'd done, and wasn't prepared to recognise her crime or show the slightest regret.

"Of course, you have the right to refuse. The judge has requested that I examine you to find out whether you're responsible for the act you've committed, and whether you should be judged as someone in her right mind or whether you've followed an impulse you cannot control, which is pretty much the same thing. This distinction in what motivated the felony makes all the difference to your sentence. I'm sure you know all this very well, but it's my duty to inform you. All the same, you can refuse this examination if you so choose."

"Is there really any difference?" she asked, staring at me with unblinking eyes. She let out a long sigh, and added, "I don't care about this legal and psychiatric subterfuge. Of course I'm responsible. I am anyhow, and now it's down to me to say that deep down you know that too."

She smiled triumphantly, waiting for my reply.

"Well, it would be dishonest of me to deny what you say. I totally agree. If it were up to me, I'd change a heap of laws, in fact I'd change a heap of things in the spirit of our laws. So let's leave the motive out of this. What can I do for you?"

"Tell the judge to lock me up without further delay."

"I see. Are you taking any medication?"

"I've been trying to get some for a long time. The social services haven't given me any solutions."

"Solutions to what?"

She hesitated a few seconds, then answered the question.

"I've had these ideas going round in my head for months, they won't leave me be. I'm scared I'll hurt someone, I'm scared of doing some real damage, you know? Now everyone's up in arms over a bit of paint on that fucking statue that they should've pulled down years ago, but they have no idea that there are far worse things than throwing yellow paint."

Throwing Agent Orange, I thought, but didn't say. I was surprised that she'd suddenly said a curse word, at odds with the educated language she'd been using. It was like a paint stain on the noble bronze surface.

"You're right. There are far worse things you can do. From what you're saying, I get the impression that no one has ever really paid much attention to your fears."

"That's right. No one. The social workers referred me to health services in my area, but they just told me to do some kind of sport to keep my mind off things and stop thinking about ridiculous stuff. Do you think anyone can be up for sport when they know they're about ready to shoot someone, or throw themselves out of the office window?"

"I still don't know what you do for a living," I lied, as it said on the court report.

"I'm a high school teacher."

"Aha. What do you teach?"

"History of art."

"History of art. Must be a beautiful thing to be able to do something like that for a living. These ideas that are tormenting you, have they been with you long?"

"About a year. My brother died, and then I had to look after my father by myself, he was really sick. My mother passed away years ago. Since my brother died, a voice has been talking to me."

"Can anyone else hear it?"

"No, I guess not. It just talks to me, and I know very well that I'm hallucinating. As you might say, I am *informed*," she added, with a sarcastic emphasis on the last word.

"Well, I think I understand your reasons for messing up the statue. It's preferable for you to be locked up for that before they lock you up for killing someone, or the firefighters scrape your corpse off the sidewalk. It makes sense."

"Will you give me medication?"

"Sure, I can get that for you. I can even get Judge Delucca to give instructions so that after sentencing, you can come and see me and we talk about what's been going on with you since you lost your brother. That'll be just as important as the pills. But if you want to talk to me, you've got to help me convince the judge and the DA that you need to be heard."

Shanice Tide fell silent. Finally, she answered.

"That'd be a happy ending, right? I'm sorry, I don't like those endings. I admit that I'm doing all I can to get locked up. But I'm not going to give in. I'm not going to carry on taking the abuse and humiliation I've been getting for the last year. A year of moral torture is a long time." As she spoke, she moved her head from side to side, closing her fist tightly, her words bursting out heavy with rage.

"You've told me nothing yet about that abuse."

"It's the sculptor's descendants, they make fun of me. They've started a campaign against me. They heard me teach at school that the statue doesn't represent the historic truth at all, that it's a real insult to African Americans. Neither I nor any of my black brothers and sisters have to stand for that. I demand that the authorities remove the statue. I also demand an official apology from the mayor. Otherwise the actions will continue. And I won't be the only one carrying out this mission. Yesterday was just the start. Many will come, we will be thousands of brothers and sisters ready to teach a lesson to all those who have humiliated us for centuries."

Now Shanice Tide was really showing her craziness in all its splendour. She abandoned her air of aloof indifference as her face filled with passionate hatred. She spouted her words in a foam of fury, the same fury with which she had thrown a tin of yellow paint over a statue that represented the sacrifice of the blacks for the cause of a freedom that would end up being betrayed. She was crazy, no doubt about it, but her craziness dragged history along with it, which gave her a large measure of authority.

"There are no pills that will help all that," I admitted, "no words that can repair the damage. I can't promise you that the authorities will listen to your request to remove the statue, even if it is a legitimate one."

"I have nothing else to say, then."

"Maybe you're right, but at some stage you've got to put a stop to this endless war."

"And why should it be me who takes the first step? It's they who should ask forgiveness."

"Why you? I can think of just one good reason: because you've seen the truth, and in doing so, the truth means you're involved, even if you refuse to admit it." I improvised the most high-sounding answer I could come up with at the time, because I realised that Shanice expected to hear something in keeping with her demand. And I was right.

Her fists loosened, her face relaxed, and she looked at me as if she wanted to figure out whether I wasn't hiding some new trick.

"All right," she said. "All right. You win. Tell the judge that I'll go see him. Can I go now?"

"You can go."

I put out my hand, but she didn't shake it. She just nodded goodbye. Outside, an officer was waiting to cuff her and take her back to the court. The heat was so oppressive that not even the air conditioning could dispel it. I saw Shanice walk away and a second later Delucca's secretary called me with a new assignment.

"I'm sorry, Dr. Palmer, I don't know if it's the heat or what the hell is going on lately, but we're off our feet. It's like they opened up all the town's asylums," she joked. "Would it be possible for you to see this woman today? She's real worked up."

I saw Anne that same afternoon. She really was worked up. Like Shanice Tide, she had her reasons, too.

"And you managed to talk round that black woman with that argument?" Judge Delucca asked me the next day when we spoke on the phone. "Amazing, Doctor."

"Yeah, it's amazing that there are still people for whom the word 'truth' still convinces them of something," I laughed.

ONE

The duty officer hung up the phone, grunted, and looked at his watch. It was four in the afternoon. He'd been taking calls for over six hours. He took a sip from the coffee that was languishing lukewarm at the bottom of the cup, pressed the button, and spoke to the car that the computer screen indicated was the closest available to the area of the report.

"Attention, we have a code 507 at 359 Fuller Street. White woman, about fifty, obese, wearing a mustard-coloured tracksuit. Doesn't appear to be armed. She's been causing a scene in the street for the last hour. Threatened her husband and daughters. Call was made by the husband, and some neighbours, too."

The officer grunted again. In another time he could have said, "Attention guys, some jerk called, fucking faggot pussy scared 'cos his wife's threatening him from the street, and the guy wants us to scare her off. Gimme a break. Sorry guys, go after the crazy woman and see what the hell's wrong with her. White, fat, about fifty. From what the jerk said, she's wearing a mustard-colour get-up, I think that's what he said, so it might be worth taking a photo." Sadly, all conversations were recorded now, and you couldn't let off steam with your workmates whenever you wanted.

Officer Andrew Miles put his foot on the gas and headed south without sounding the siren. He was a few blocks from the place, and when he got there he didn't need to look too hard to work out the reason for the report. Positioned opposite number 359 Fuller Street, a woman of medium height, several pounds overweight, wearing a jogging suit of an unlikely colour, something between French mustard and duck diarrhoea, was screaming like a woman possessed as she threw all kinds of clothes from various supermarket bags up at the windows of the building. Some neighbours stuck their heads out of their windows, not many, as it was still early and most probably hadn't got back from work yet. Several pedestrians crossed the street to avoid her and looked back as they walked away. Curious drivers slowed down for a few seconds, as long as the impatient traffic would allow. The woman was moving angrily from one side of the street to the other, waving her arms and shouting with a voice so loud that it seemed to be coming from a megaphone. Her tone was a mix of desperation and resentment. She screamed the names of two women, begging them to return to her. She alternated her supplications with anger, as if she were playing the role of two different people who had nothing to do with each other. Her voice even seemed to change, like a ventriloquist's trick. At times it resembled the roar of an enormous moribund animal, and when Officer Miles and his partner Sarah Farrington came into view it changed to a wordless whine. She kept throwing the clothes up, and when they fell she threw them again, but this movement grew slower as she began to wear herself out. She could hardly bend over anymore, until finally she fell in a heap on the ground, her face sinking in her hands as the whining continued. She was surrounded by jeans, jerseys, colourful skirts, women's underwear, trainers, and high-heeled shoes, scattered all around as if she'd looted a department store. The officers approached her slowly, keeping their distance so as not to startle her. Sarah Farrington spoke to her softly.

"Anne? Are you Anne Kurzinski? Please, I need to talk to you. I can see you're very upset, but I need you to listen to me. You can't go on like this, out here in the street, with this attitude, do you understand? Can you hear what I'm saying, Mrs. Kurzinski? Please, answer me."

But the woman just sat there, crying with her face hidden, still moaning like a foghorn in the middle of a storm. To make matters worse, a light but insistent drizzle was starting to complicate matters. Officer Sarah Farrington was accustomed by her trade to seeing all kinds of things of different size, colour, shape, and condition, so when she saw Mrs. Kurzinski surrounded by clothes scattered on the ground, slowly getting damp, as if she were about to melt under the dull light of an inky sky, she turned around to look for a help signal from her partner. Officer Andrew Miles in turn looked back at her with the same expression of amazement and impotence, so Officer Sarah Farrington had no other choice but to get closer to Mrs. Kurzinski, her rain—and tear-drenched body shaking convulsively, and after a moment's hesitation put her hand on that woman's immense, fleshy shoulder. Despite her huge size, the woman now seemed like a lost little creature abandoned in a city recovering its indifference amid the rain and the silence.

All Officer Farrington's professionalism proved futile in preventing her being caught off guard by Mrs. Kurzinski's unexpected reaction. When she felt the contact on her shoulder she reacted as if she had a piston mechanism, and suddenly threw Officer Farrington to the ground. The scenario changed in a fraction of a second, as the officers found themselves wrestling down and attempting to handcuff a furious two hundred pound mass that put up a fight like a wild beast, while at the same time spewing all kinds of insults and threats against the same names she continued to invoke. For a few minutes the officers considered the possibility of requesting backup, but pride proved greater than need, and they eventually managed to get Anne Kurzinski into the patrol car and take her to the emergency ward at Carney Hospital. By then the woman had stopped shouting and was babbling unintelligibly, her body shaking spasmodically as if a fit were imminent.

The duty doctor managed to get a few words out of her and administer an injection of Haloperidol while officers Farrington and Miles gave their report to the chief. Mrs. Kurzinski liked doctors, and that young man inspired immediate trust in her. Half an hour later, Anne was sleeping in a hospital bed. Her laboured breathing and a slight facial twitch were evidence of the violent state of excitement she had been in, but at least now she would remain calm. A tube in a vein in her left hand slowly issued a cocktail of medications that would ensure that she remained sedated. The doctor talked to the officers to find out who he should contact. The police didn't have any information about the detainee, except that the report had been made by her ex-husband. Officer Sarah Farrington could have pressed charges for resisting arrest and assaulting a police officer, but she had no intention of doing so. It seemed to her that the woman was down on her luck enough as it was, and besides, the punch she had managed to land on her was insignificant. Now that she was asleep and under medical attention, there was no reason for the officers to stay.

Under medication, Mrs. Kurzinski remained stable throughout the night and was discharged the following day. Since she hadn't been carrying anything with her when she was arrested, not so much as a bag or a coat, and no one was expecting her or had taken any interest in her (with the exception of Officer Farrington, who had dropped in at the emergency ward early in the morning to see how she was doing), the outgoing doctor gave her a twenty dollar bill so that she could take a taxi home, but Mrs. Kurzinski flat-out refused, and said she'd walk, that it would do her good to walk a while to order her thoughts.

"I bet that twenty dollars that I can guess what she's going to do," the doctor said to one of the male nurses leafing through the paper in the rest room as he drank a large cup of coffee.

The nurse didn't look up from the newspaper, and nodded with a slight snort.

"Sure, it's obvious. No one can get him out of her head."

Anne Kurzinski walked for some time, trying to work out where she was. When she finally recognised the streets and managed to get her bearings, she sped up and headed as fast as she could to her home, or rather, what used to be her home, which was now occupied by her husband, or ex-husband, whatever he wanted to call himself, he was her husband to her, the great son of a bitch who had kicked her out of her home and kept everything that was hers, including her two daughters, those two ingrates who betrayed her despite the enormous sacrifices that she'd made for them, but she wasn't going to give in, she wasn't going to accept defeat like this, and for them to deprive her of the most important role in her life, the role of being a mother, because that was what she was destined to be in this world, a mother, and if they couldn't understand that the easy way, then it wasn't her fault if she had to resort to force. When she arrived, she rang the doorbell insistently but no one answered. She crossed the street to have a better view of the windows, but she couldn't see anything. So she started to walk round the surrounding area, until she found Richard's car parked in another street. It wasn't actually Richard's car, but she was totally convinced that it was. She even thought she saw one of those sports magazines he used to read on the seats. Her breathing and her pulse sped up. She tried to open the doors, but they were locked. She kicked the side of the car, which caught the attention of a passer-by. Anne looked around her and her eyes lit up when she saw a pile of cement paving flags that city hall contract workers had left to fix the pavement.

"The next thing I remember is what you already know. The judge took my statement, and told me I had to come and see you."

TWO

"It was all that asshole's fault," said Anne, searching for some sign of complicity in me. Since the first day I saw her, she'd used all kinds of strategies to get my approval. Often, to move me, she would come across as a defenceless animal, and on other occasions she would try to guess the effect that her stories would have on me. At each of our meetings, and regardless of the matter we were dealing with, it was evident that I was the privileged recipient of her story, a witness to her life, someone who would vouch for the truth that came from her mouth. I had to be submissive in this mission I'd been given, and at the same time ensure with the greatest tact that I remained outside of the friendly intimacy in our relationship that she wanted to achieve at all costs.

"I felt really betrayed, you know? I gave that man the best years of my life. I tried to be a good wife and a good mother. And how did he repay me? By sending me packing, and to top it all he's managed to talk the girls into abandoning me and going to live with him. Now that was a low blow. I can't stand it. I was starting to accept the separation, but since the girls left my side, I've lost everything. That's exactly what I feel: that I've lost everything, that there's no sense in fighting it anymore. I suppose it's something that happens to people when they reach the conclusion that there's no one left, that everyone's gone. I've been left on my own, I'm so alone. Sometimes I go whole days without speaking to a single person, so I call the number of the gas company, or the power company, or the cell phone company, one of those numbers that has a prerecorded voice that asks you stuff. It used to drive me crazy to speak to those machines, but now it's comforting to hear a voice, even if it is a recording, a voice that doesn't even know I exist. I call and they take me on a tour of all the recording, you know how hard it is to get to speak to a real person, but it's good enough for me. It's as if someone were keeping me company, and I feel less alone. My daughters don't want to talk to me anymore. I imagine their father's told them about me. We were very close when they were young. They were the most important thing in my life. I've always said that being a mother is the only thing that makes sense to me. And I'll keep saying it. Sure, there's my job, there's that of course. I've worked a lot. Not lately, of course. I have problems. I find it hard to get out of bed. I swear there are days when I can't move. I open my eyes and stare at the bedroom ceiling. If I had a television screen on the ceiling, it wouldn't be so bad, but even then, no, I'm not interested in TV, either. When I'm like that, kind of dead, or floating in the air, I can't do a thing. Have you seen those magic tricks, where they make a reclining person float without touching the ground? Well that's how I feel on those days. I don't feel a thing, I don't even perceive my body. I'm not hot or cold, hungry or thirsty. All I can do is think."

"What do you think about?" I asked in a brief pause. Anne spoke hurriedly, garbling her words and barely pausing for breath. It was clear that it was impossible for her to hear herself, there was no time for it, but all the same she was perfectly alert to the way I followed her story. I got involved in her monologue, I stayed glued to the chair as if wanting to assure her that I wouldn't move, that I wouldn't abandon her like everyone else had done.

"What do I think about? I think about my whole life. My life passes before me at those times like a succession of broken images, pieces of memories that spin on themselves. Sometimes they move so quickly I can't make them out. All I know is they always appear."

"They?"

"My parents."

"Are they alive?"

"Yes, you could say that."

"That's a strange answer," I said, surprised.

Anne breathed out, and for the first time in half an hour she was silent. It wasn't a normal silence, the kind of silence I'm used to, when people lose the thread of what they were saying, or think they've exhausted the subject they were talking about and expect me to pick up where they left off, or they're reluctant to go on advancing in a given direction. This silence suggested something else, as if the woman had reached the edge of the abyss, and in front of her there was nothing more but a deep void, an immense nothing, utter darkness. We'd reached a very dangerous limit, and now it was necessary to step up the caution, advance with great care, because the ground could crumble apart at any given moment to reveal an enormous crevice below, concealed until now.

"We don't need to talk about that today," I hastened to add.

"Yes, we do. Today, next week, it's the same. I'm going to have to do it sooner or later, so the sooner we start the better. They're pretty old now. My parents, I mean. My mother never leaves her house. As far as I can remember, she's never left her house. When I was young I couldn't understand why my mother never set foot in the street, or spoke to no one but us, I mean my father, my sister, and me. And she couldn't stand anyone coming to our house, so we could never have friends or schoolmates over. Our house was almost always in silence, because my mother needed to be surrounded by silence. When we asked our father why all that was, when we started to realise that there was something strange about her, that out mother wasn't like our neighbours' moms or our schoolmates' moms, then my father would take us out for a walk and explain that mom was very anxious, that something very serious had happened to her when she was young, something that he would tell us about when we were older. He begged us to be patient, said our mother was a very good person, that she loved us with all her heart, but that she was sick, very sick, and that she needed a lot of care, and that the best way to care for her was by not bothering her and behaving ourselves. We, my sister and I, didn't say a word and obeyed him. We loved our mother, but above all else we adored our father, and it was enough for him to ask us to do that, or whatever, and we would redouble our efforts to behave ourselves. We achieved this to the point of annulling our own existence; we became a couple of spirits who went unnoticed so that she wouldn't get in the least upset. Even so, most of the time she was shut up in her room, with the lights out and the curtains drawn. From time to time she'd get up, come into our bedroom while we were doing our homework, and stand at the door a little while, her eyes full of tears, whispering in German, "Oh, meine Kindern! Entschuldigen Sie mir! Meine arme Kindern!" "Oh, my poor children." She hardly ever spoke Hebrew, just German. My father on the other hand has always spoken to us in Hebrew. But my mother spoke to us in German, even though she never wanted to know another thing about Germany. In my house, that word and anything related to it was prohibited. The world, or rather, our world, didn't include that country or its inhabitants."

"But it did include the language."

"Yes, it included the language. Weird, right? Or maybe not so much. Actually, it's not true that Germany doesn't exist to her. On the contrary, there's nothing else. She still lives there, she hasn't been able to get out, she hasn't managed to escape. She's still a prisoner, captive to the horror of the memories that never leave her, night and day. That's why she could never be with us, because she was very far from my father, from that house, from those daughters, meaning us. In his way, my father managed to save himself, but she didn't. The Germans killed her."

She paused, but this time I had the impression that she could go on safely, at least for now. She even seemed to have calmed down. She no longer spoke like a river flooding its banks, but considered her words, retaining them softly before sending them out, and didn't seem so obsessed with ensuring my attention. She knew I was listening, that I was listening with ears wide open to this strange and fascinating woman who began to spell out a story that would strike anybody dumb. Fortunately, my profession allowed me to conceal myself in silence. Once I'd managed to get those who came to see me to throw themselves head first into the game of words, I didn't have to say much else. I just had to limit myself to setting it all in motion, and then I could sit back and watch as the players went along, leaping over obstacles, and finding their way to their goal. From time to time it was necessary to help a little, stop them from losing their way, or encourage them to go on when they felt let down or that there was no point to the game. But that didn't happen all the time.

"Of course, this isn't something that can be told in a single day, I imagine," I said to somehow assure her of my presence.

"No, you can't imagine. You can't imagine this story. No one can. We tried, but it was no use. Even when we were older, and we knew what had happened, we still couldn't imagine it. There were things we'd glimpsed in dreams, or rather in nightmares. Figures in the shadows, blurred names. Bodies. Screams. Flames. But despite all that we couldn't put together a legible picture. Even today, all I can do is repeat what I was told, as well as everything I've read about it, but I can't imagine it. It's impossible to imagine. It's just far too big to get your imagination round."

As if she'd shifted up a gear, she gave her account a sudden turn and returned to the same tone she'd used at the start. That made me think that I wouldn't need to worry about the time, protect her from her own memory. She alone, when the time came, would know when to put a full stop, say see you tomorrow, move on to something else, to then pick up at the place where she had broken off. It wasn't necessary to reward her, or ask her anything, or hurry along the reconstruction. Nor was it necessary to try to make her forget, or shield her from the pain of her memories. She was too far ahead to need that kind of help. Too lucid.

"How could he have spurned me like that? My husband, I mean. The worst thing is that he keeps saying he had all the patience in the world with me, that it wasn't his fault, that it was I who turned our married life into a torment with my nervous crises, my constant attention-seeking, and my need to be a mother. He accuses me of being a possessive mother, of not letting my daughters breathe. Do you think he can blame me for being a possessive mother? The very expression just sounds pathetic to me. Possessive mother! What a stupid language! Possessive because I took care of them day and night? Possessive because I hung on every minute of their lives? Possessive because I lived on the air they breathed, because I cried for their sorrows and laughed for their joys? Can you reproach a mother for that? You must know. You're a doctor, or psychologist, whatever, but you have experience, you know what life's like, what people's minds are like, what it's like to be in your right mind or lose your mind completely. Do you think I've lost my mind? My husband thinks I have, and he's managed to persuade my daughters too. My daughters! He's set them against me. He's set two daughters against their mother. Isn't that losing your mind? Isn't that a greater madness than mine? Isn't that a crime worse than mine? You tell me what my felony is, what the offence is that I'm accused of. Do we live in a world where we mothers have become beings you have to be protected from?

Do we pass on some disease to our children? Is that it? Is that what you psychiatrists and psychologists and therapists teach people? To get away from their mothers? I knew what it was to have a distant mother. I knew what it was to have a mother who we couldn't touch, who we couldn't hug, who we had to watch from a distance, in case she'd have insomnia again that night because of us and scream out in horror! Is that better? You tell me if that's better than what I've done!"

I no longer spoke. She was sitting up in her seat opposite me, yelling at the top of her voice, her face ablaze and her arms circling in the air. She threatened me with her fist, not me personally, of course, but everything I represented at that moment: all the injustice of the world that she had to face every day, a world where she didn't fit in, that cast her out over and over again, a world where it was impossible for her to find mercy. In time I discovered that the best way to calm her was to keep quiet, and obviously not try to convince her of anything. Then, once her anger had reached its limit, and she'd noted that I could take it, that I was willing to take on that role she'd given me, little by little she regained her self-control. She would sit back down, the swelling in the veins in her forehead would decrease, and she'd open her bag to take out a tissue and dry the sweat from her neck.

"I know, I know. You have to excuse me. Sometimes I can't control myself. He's taken advantage of that, my husband, to kick me out of his life. Taken advantage of my rage attacks. I have to tell you something, because you have to know this. I'm worried because lately I've left him various messages on the answer machine. I'm really embarrassed talking to you about this, but I suppose there's nothing can be done. Some nights, when I can't sleep, I have to do something, something to keep from going crazy, or because I'm scared of throwing myself out of the window. So I write letters. Long letters. But on some occasions I've left messages on my husband's answer machine. I think I've been … a little rude. I don't remember very well what I've said, but I don't think I was right to do it. I'm worried he might report me, and I wouldn't be able to stand it if I was arrested again. Plus, there's the risk of losing my job, you know? That would be terrible. I can't allow that to happen. You've got to help me, you've got to help me keep my job. What would I do? I'd have to move back in with my parents. Can you imagine what that's like? Will you help me? The problem is that no one's ever been able to help me. All the psychiatrists and psychologists who've seen me have done nothing but abandon me. That's the root of my illness. I'm alone, too alone. Loneliness makes you useless for life. You gradually lose ... what do you people call them? Social skills, that's it. You turn weird, you feel like others treat you like a rare species. I notice it all the time. I always live with that feeling that I'm making a mistake, that I'm going to do exactly what I'm not supposed to do, that I'm going to put my foot in it, that I'm going to lose control. I do everything I can to hold it in check, but sometimes, several times, maybe, I can't do it. And I've done worse things than leave messages on my husband's answer machine. I can't tell you about them now, but I've done them. The thing that saves me is that I'm a survivor. Always have been. My parents told me that since I was a girl. I'm a survivor. Deep down I know they won't get to me, that I'll be able to get through it all. I'm a survivor, like my father."

"And like your mother," I added.

"No, she isn't one. My father managed to survive, but she didn't make it."

"Even though she's alive?"

"She isn't. She's like a ghost. People think that ghosts don't exist, that they're figments of our imagination. People say a lot of stupid things. Of course ghosts exist. There are people everywhere who seem to be alive, but they're dead inside. They move, speak, eat, but that doesn't matter at all. They're dead all the same. Who knows, maybe I'm one of those ghosts myself, don't you think?"

THREE

I could actually have retired but that's not in my plans just yet. I came to an arrangement with the hospital and they've let me stay on a while longer. Everyone knows me here: I've been working for the Psychopathology Service for nearly forty years. When I first got the job I was young and enthusiastic about the reformist school of thought coming across from Europe from those who were determined to preach reconciliation with madness. I'd had the opportunity to spend a year in Paris, which really shook up how I thought, and when I came back I knew that something had changed in me for good. I understood that my place was among people who one way or another rebelled against normal life, and that I had everything to learn from them. Over the years I've done nothing but prove to myself I was right about my choice, to the extent that I've never been interested in normal people, people who follow the rules and don't tread where they're not supposed to, people who do what's expected of them. Those people haven't taught me a thing. On the other hand, if there's something I've learned from practising this strange profession of word hunter, I've learned it from those other people, those who do everything backwards, those who can't love but love regardless, those who don't know how to live but live regardless, those who don't hunker down and fall flat on their faces against reality, those who get up in the morning and go to bed at night wondering what reason they'll have to come up with the next day for carrying on in this world.

I'm a word hunter. It's a job like any other, but it requires a certain amount of attention. People open their souls to me, let out hundreds, thousands of words that are captive, and I have to observe their flight, recognise now and again one of great significance. Then I catch it in the air and give it back to its owner, convince him that he'd do well to check out that word that he didn't even know was in him, take a look at it, because it's one of those words that's been feeding off his blood for a long time, like a little vampire. The result is usually surprising, because most of the time people prove me right by letting loose another flock of words, and I have to go on hunting a few more, until all those words that were feeding on their blood let go of their prey and go away for ever. Of course, I never manage to hunt them all down. But I teach a trick to the people who come and see me, and after a certain time I manage to get them to tear out the words that devour them themselves. Other psychologists prefer other methods. They consider themselves wise, and therefore they feel they have the authority to pontificate. They recommend what has to be done, what has to be chosen, what's for the best, what's good for one's health and harmful to one's spirit, which thoughts have to be strengthened and which have to be discarded through quack remedies, positive thinking, and other similar potions. Unfortunately, I lack all wisdom on life. At my age, I'm still trying to work out why life is so devilishly complex, and why we're condemned to incurable unhappiness. That's why I envy those psychologists, because deep down they don't have my thankless task of reconciling everyone I hear to the idea that I don't have a single solution for anyone, and that I can only offer them my services as a refuse collector, which is another way of explaining what I do for a living. That's why those other psychologists look great, dress well, and keep their distance from their patients. They open the manual at a given page and read the corresponding chapter. I on the other hand spend the day sifting through the trash. The trash is full of treasures. Sure they stink, and you have to really work up a sweat to fish them out, but I think it's worth it, because I've always thought that man has to learn to live with his own garbage. Of course, I don't have many followers in the professional world, because I'm not profitable, nor do I represent the values of modern society. I don't promote self-esteem, or competitiveness, or assertiveness, or optimism, or the spirit of self-improvement. I don't believe in figures, or balance sheets, or questionnaires, or statistics, or risk-prevention, or re-education. I go against anything that puts itself forward as life skills for adapting to one's surroundings. I have no idea what anyone ought to do, and therefore I abstain from expert imposture. Of course, it isn't a comfortable position these days, when they'll have us believe that a definitive and ideal model of existence has been found that we must all imitate to be happy. But I'm still standing despite all that, and they haven't finished me off yet.

As Anne might say, I'm a survivor too.

* * *

"The telephone never rings. No one calls me, except my father. He calls me every two or three days, asks me how I am, whether I need anything, he even offers me money sometimes, but I never take it. He asks me about the girls, and I have to lie to him, I tell him they're out, that they're at some friend's house, or something like that. He knows perfectly well that it's a lie, that they're with their father and aren't speaking to me, but he acts like he doesn't know. It's a kind of pact we have, him and me, an arrangement that came about without us having to agree on it. I don't understand why my daughters don't call my parents either. There's no reason for it, although I'm sure my husband's poisoned that relationship too. It kills me to lie to my father, even if it isn't a lie, it's a bit of theatre we both do, a prolongation of the play we've always had to act in. At home we all acted like nothing was going on. Mom was very sick, she could hardly do any household chores, and she barely looked after us. Dad made a superhuman effort to make up for her as much as he could, and hide the fact that we had a major problem. We loved him so much that my sister and I were willing to play along and make out like nothing was up. We knew that mom loved us too, she loved us with all her heart, but she was incapable of coming back to life. The Germans had torn out her soul, tortured her until they'd destroyed her. She'd seen everything and more than a human being can stand."

"Your father suffered the same."

"Yes, but somehow he managed to survive. You must have an explanation for this mystery. Two people are thrown into the flames of hell: one survives, the other doesn't. Is it a question of resistance, of strength? Is one weaker than the other? I couldn't say. Nor do I know exactly what each of them went through. Over the years, I found out that survivors don't tend to say anything about what happened to them. We grew up with very little information about my family, about what had happened to them. All we knew was that my mother and my father were the only ones left alive. There were no photographs to be seen, and I remember I found one once of my mother when she was young, with her parents and brothers and sisters, hidden at the bottom of a drawer. I didn't dare say anything, and my father asked me to put it back, saying that he had lost his parents and all his brothers and sisters too. What we never knew is how the two of them managed to escape. We only found out that for almost a year they wandered in the woods, terrified at the possibility of being caught, always on the verge of exhaustion and death, suffering starvation, fever, pain. Nor were we very clear on how they managed to emigrate to Israel. They got married there and we were born."

"Your parents never told you about their escape? And you and your sister never asked them about what had happened?"

"It sounds strange, but that's the way it was. We grew up wrapped in a silence that soaked us to the bone. No one ever told us that we shouldn't ask questions, it wasn't necessary for that to be put into words. Even that was part of the silence, of everything that was tacitly imposed on us as something natural. Every day the curtain went up and we played our part, read from the script we'd been given. The only one who didn't play act was mom. She didn't have to act, because we all knew she couldn't play any characters. She was allowed to be who she was, and no one argued with that, because we loved her. My father loved her all his life, and we felt so sorry for her that we forgave her everything. We weren't taught to respect her inability to look after us. Not at all. It was something we assumed straight away, like one might assume being born into a poor home, or with a blind or paralysed mother. It was natural, she was part of our life, and we accepted it without any complaints. That wasn't the problem. The problem was that my father, just as he does now with my daughters, made such a great effort to try to cover up what was going on. He supposedly kept up this sham for us because he thought that would help us to live, and we went along with it because we thought that he needed our help to keep up that pretence. Deep down, we were all doing it for her. She was the wounded baby, prostrated by grief, and we looked after her and protected her like one cares for a defenceless child, a baby who has been snatched from her mother. Now I realise that it was that well-intentioned farce that did the most damage."

"And who looked after you and your sister?"

"My sister is six years older, and as soon as she was old enough she started to spend as much time as possible away from home. That was part of the deal. Someone had to stay at home so as not to leave my father on his own, and that someone was me."

It was notable how at times Anne was capable of talking about herself with the serenity and lucidity with which one refers to someone far away or unknown. She was still emotional, but she expressed a feeling of deep resignation, as if she was perfectly at peace with her family history. Her voice softened, the words flowed more slowly, and the temporary withdrawal of anger made her look more transparent. Suddenly, it was another woman sitting in front of me, a woman with hardly any resemblance to the one who had come that first time. But they both continued to coexist, except they showed up in shifts, as if they didn't know each other at all.

* * *

"Then something came up fortuitously, although I now wonder if that was really the case, or whether I should acknowledge that it was a way of distancing myself, of fleeing from all that. When I was twenty-two, I was offered a year's scholarship to come and study here, in the USA, and I took it. As often happens, I met a man, and ended up marrying him, living in his country, and having my two daughters. I still call them daughters because a mother forgives everything, although the truth is I should disown them. How could they be so evil? How are they capable of behaving like that with me, their mother? Because I am their mother, and will continue to be even though they ignore me! This week I've called them several times every day, but they won't come to the phone. Sometimes their father picks up and he says they don't want to speak to me. It's a lie! It's he who has kidnapped them, and has murdered them from my life."

"Murdered them from your life? That's a curious expression. I've never heard anything like that. I suppose it expresses what you feel well."

Now it was the other Anne who had the floor, and she shifted up the gears.

"He's a murderer. Of course he's a murderer! He's done away with them, he's killed my children. But I'm going to get even, I swear I am! I'm not afraid to go to prison, I'll do a long stretch if I have to, but I'll destroy him."

She backed up her threat by banging her fist on the table, and all her voluminous body seemed to grow even more, as if she were swelling and about to burst into a thousand pieces.

"I may remind that you've asked me for help so that you don't do anything that puts your work in jeopardy."

She stood up, staring at me in silence, breathing laboriously. She was a wounded animal in her death throes, an animal with an arrow stuck in her heart who can't go on fighting, and stays still, panting, conscious that she must give up and accept defeat.

"Yes, yes. I know, you're right. I get carried away by the impulse. I have to calm down. I have to reflect more on all this. Please forgive me. I wasn't like this before."

"Before what?"

"I don't know, I used to be different. I didn't have these outbursts. Or maybe I did, I don't remember so well. I'm confused. Richard says I've always been like this, but I don't know if I believe him. Maybe it's true. Can I go?"

"Of course you can. I'll see you the day after tomorrow at the same time. OK?"

"OK. Would you mind if I occasionally write you? I can't sleep at night sometimes and I need to write. Would that be a problem?"

"Not at all. You can write me all you like. Here's my email address."

"Thank you," she said with great humility.

When she thanked me for listening to her, she did so with a feeling of profound and total gratitude, as if I'd given her something priceless. For the first time in her life she had the chance to surrender herself to her madness in front of someone who wouldn't call her crazy. For the first time in her life she could let the hatred and the guilt fight it out in the open, like they'd never done before. She understood this, and knowing it was a great comfort.

FOUR

It's very late at night, although I don't know what time it is exactly. It's hard to sleep, very hard. I've gotten used to that, but it keeps getting worse. I know why it happens to me, but it keeps happening. Knowing that doesn't cure it, nor does it cure my lying awake all night. It happens to me because it's at night that I have to be most alert, more awake than ever. I can snooze during the day, I can live a little lethargically, except when night falls. Then I have to keep my eyes wide open to stop them from coming. They come all the same, but if I'm awake it's easier to take.

I see everything with absolute clarity. It's night time, we're asleep, and suddenly we hear the screams. More than screams, they're cries of horror, it's a sound I can't describe. It's the sound of someone going through something that has no name. There are no words to express it. The whole house shakes, the ground shakes, the furniture too, and my father is behind her, trying to calm her. She's seen something, but she can't talk, she can only make those shrieking noises. Then she comes into our room and stands there, howling. Eventually she speaks, but her voice sounds so strange that we can hardly understand what we're hearing. She shouts things about the fire, about the bodies. Yes, something about the bodies burning. "They're burning the bodies, they're burning the bodies!" she repeats, and we are paralysed with terror. My mother is a ghost in the middle of the night, a ghost that howls as if she were being torn apart alive, and in fact she is, she is being ripped apart alive. Finally my father manages to get his arm round her and lead her back to bed. After a while we can only hear a whimper, a sob, and shortly after the silence returns, but it's impossible to sleep now.

It happened a lot of nights. The strange thing was that at those moments I had the impression that my mother was coming back to life, abandoning her daytime paralysis and getting up on the stage. It might sound incomprehensible, but that's how it was. When my mother was alive that's what she was, a nocturnal creature being prey to terrors. During the day she was pretty much dead. Which did we prefer? It's hard to answer that question. It's easier to say that we would've preferred a mother like the others, like our friends' mothers, like Emil's mother, or Esther's, or Bertha's, simple women who smiled and went out into the street and talked to everyone. Mothers who didn't mind if their children brought friends home, mothers who were there to instil courage and shoo away any fear of life. Our mother was none of those things, and yet we worshipped her. I can't get out of my head the image of her kindly face, marked by indelible grief, grief that surrounded her like an angel's halo. My mother was that, an angel fatally wounded by the devil's hand, who could never fly again.

Once, when I was five, I had to play a small part in a performance at the end of year party at school. I was terribly excited, and at the same time I was terrified that I wouldn't do it right. By then I knew that my mother wouldn't leave our house under any circumstances, but on that occasion I begged my father to do all that he could to persuade her. My mother agreed to come, and when I went out onto the stage I saw to my great joy that she was standing by the door of the assembly hall, proudly watching me. But after a few minutes she couldn't take any more, and asked my father to take her back home. I never found out why she did it, whether it was the chronic fear she suffered when she was forced by some circumstance to go out into the street, be with other people, or the emotion of seeing me act in that performance. When I realised she'd left, I couldn't go on, and I had a crying fit in front of all the parents sitting in their chairs. It was a terrible experience, because for the first time I felt hatred towards her, hatred that I would experience again later, and which ate me up inside, filling me with guilt and shame.

Only on one occasion did I dare ask her what was wrong with her. It was the only time that I decided to bypass my father, who would inevitably have stood up as mediator between her and the world. We never spoke to her directly, but through him, her spokesman and agent, a protective role that he'd taken on with total devotion. He wouldn't let anything or anyone do her any more damage than what she'd already suffered. But then I asked her why she couldn't stand people. I was a teenager, and starting to stick up for my right to have friends over, and not have to make up excuses all the time to explain why I never celebrated my birthday. Her reply was so blunt, that it stayed with me for the rest of my life. "You know," she said, "when I was your age something terrible happened to us, and at the time we had no idea what the consequences would be. We were left alone. We Jews were left completely alone. One fine day, everything that surrounded us pushed us aside, removed us from view. We became a blemish, a disease that had to be quarantined, the same way that people with the plague are quarantined. We were abandoned by friends, neighbours, local acquaintances. They all turned away, averted their eyes, and left us alone, delivered us to our fate. You know what that fate was. We became surplus to the world, and the world became something that had lost its sense for ever to us. That's why I can't stand anyone else but you two and your father. Beyond these four walls there is nothing for me, nothing I can trust, nothing I can love again. I'm very sorry, but I haven't found the strength to forgive."

My sister thought up a way to get away from all that. She was very smart, and she soon stood out in life. She had a special gift, an ability to not succumb completely to the influence of that atmosphere of permanent mourning. Because that's what my house was like, an eternal funeral in which we restlessly kept vigil over the departed, who at the same time could not be named. The departed returned nearly every night, and it was logical that they should, because time and again they kept demanding atonement for what had been done to them. And although I hadn't met any of those unfortunates, I inevitably felt that I had been born deformed, like I was missing something. I too had been deprived of part of my life.

No one wants to hear that story nowadays, just as no one wanted to hear it when it happened. All the interest, debates, and the sincere or phoney indignation that those atrocities aroused, all that was no more than a brief ray of light in the perpetual darkness of ignorance. A fleeting exception to the human tendency to sidestep the truth. How long did the shame of the German people last? It should've lasted the thousand years they proclaimed for the Third Reich, but that didn't happen. They calculated the amount of shame in economic compensation for the victims, and realised that so many years wouldn't be necessary. They're very handy with their accounts. They're very efficient with handling numbers, and used them to wipe away the blood and ashes a little so that Deutschland would look clean and tidy again. Now they're the new pride of Europe. They're so proud that they're starting to consider themselves the master race again. Deep down they never stopped believing that, but it's true that for some years they acted like they regretted that idea.

Was I born with something broken, or did it break later? I still ask myself that. I couldn't say. Do you know? Since I was very young I've known that my head wasn't right. I've always tried to get round that, and do the same things everyone does. I was a really observant girl, copying what the others were doing. I laughed when I saw them laugh, and shut up when I saw them shut up. It's so simple. When you've no idea how life works, when you find yourself completely lost, the trick is to sneak a peek at what's around you and imitate everyone else. That was a great help to me in the early years, to the point that no one ever realised what was happening to me. Not even my father. Or maybe he did, who knows? Maybe he did, and that's why he took special care of me. The order of the hierarchy of those who enjoyed his protection was this: first my mother, then me, then last of all, my sister. It was a reasonable order, as my sister was the least vulnerable. I don't know why that was, what makes one individual in the herd stronger than the others. Not all those who survived the annihilation have done so in the same way. Some, like my mother, were left forever incapable of picking up their lives. Others, like my father, managed to at least get a residual part of it back, enough to move the machinery of everyday sustenance. He probably used his devotion to my mother as a reason to go on in this world, a world that had dealt them a cruel fate, a world in which God had fled in horror. In any case, my sister didn't need looking after so much. My father shared out his concerns according to a standard that in the long term proved about right. From time to time, to ease my loneliness, he'd take me out for a walk when he got home from work. Despite her fragility, my mother would have no qualms about our going out a while and leaving her alone. She didn't ask anything of us, nor did she ask us where we'd been or what we'd done. Maybe it was all the same to her, or maybe she respected the intimacy of our little escapades. They were nothing special, a few blocks of the neighbourhood, my father asking me about school and life in general, and me answering him, striving to overcome my embarrassment and shyness. My father was extremely tactful when he asked his questions, trying to work out how I was handling the situation with my mother, but I preferred to avoid giving any answers. She was something that completely overwhelmed me, and at the same time I understood the crucial importance of not complaining, not even about the slightest thing, because I knew instinctively that it was deadly serious, a matter of life and death even. We were living on brittle ground that could crack open under our feet at any moment, so soon enough walking on tiptoes became the fashionable way to get about. Besides, complaining would only have made my dad even more anxious, and guilty too, for allowing us to be born into a home that wasn't fit to receive us. Often I wondered why, despite everything, they had bothered to have children. Why my mother had wanted to be a mother, carry life in her womb and then remove it one day and set it to walk. Perhaps she thought that in those duties she would put a full stop to the grief that dogged her days, but that didn't happen. On the other hand, I always knew that I would have children. I couldn't have gone on without having them, that's why I understand women who are capable of doing all that it takes to become mothers: travelling to faraway places, withstanding interminable waits to get an adoption, subjecting their bodies to all kinds of twists imaginable to fertilise it, or sex. Sex I don't understand, except for having children. For everything else, I've never needed it. It just isn't me. I probably wouldn't have got married if it wasn't the way to have kids. I never deceived Richard about this. I never told him that I was in love with him, although for years I was very grateful to him for giving me the chance to become a mother. In those years, one couldn't imagine any other way. Now, with all these inventions, I probably would've had children by myself. Or maybe not, I'm not all that sure. But what I am sure of is that sex is just something that doesn't interest me. I always had problems with that, and I remember when I was a teen my friends at high school were very excited and didn't do anything but blather on about sex, which always made me especially uncomfortable. People think sex is so important, that it has to be, and we're bombarded everywhere with messages and tips. You know, those campaigns that try to convince us that sex prolongs your life. Why does the world insist that things have to be the same for everyone? When I was young, people would look at me like I was a strange fruit. None of the boys wanted to date me, would hardly even speak to me, because I was the problem girl. Didn't they have problems? I always had to carry around this reputation for being disturbed. I've had that everywhere. Even today, at the school where I teach, most of my colleagues take me for a crazy woman and whisper behind my back, keep me off all the projects, think I'm "difficult". Is someone difficult just because they're different from others?

It's four in the morning, and I haven't slept a wink. Tonight I tried to talk to my daughters, but I couldn't. They wouldn't come to the phone. It's the eldest's birthday, and I think it's their obligation to be with their mother, at least on a day like today. Have you ever heard of a mother not spending her daughter's birthday with her? When they live in the same city, just a couple of miles apart? It's an outrage, it's an insult to human dignity, that's why I'll never forgive Richard, because it's him who's turned them against me, he's poisoned them, he's murdered them from my life. I have to tell you something else about Richard, something that no one knows except me. It's something I've suspected for many years, but I didn't dare say it. Now I'm ready, now is the time to say it, but I want guarantees, legal guarantees that he won't try and get even. I'm scared that I'll talk and he'll kill me, or have someone kill me. I don't trust him at all. Deep down he fears me, he does, because he knows that I have a lot of information, enough to have him locked up for life. I realised very early, shortly after Karen, my eldest daughter was born. At first I didn't want to give it any heed, I thought it was my imagination, but little by little I became convinced that what I saw was true.

This is why I have to tell you personally. I don't want it down in writing.

You never know.

FIVE

Anne arrived for her appointment two hours early, carrying the enormous bags that she never let go of, and whose contents were part of her mystery. The secretary tried to calm her and persuade her to stay seated in the waiting room, but to no avail. She was agitated, speaking in an irate voice, shouting, refusing to tone down her behaviour. I heard her kicking up this racket while I was attending to another patient, but at first I assumed that the secretary and the nurse would be able to contain her. In the end I was forced to interrupt the session and leave the office. Anne was wearing her usual long, stridently coloured skirt and one of those t-shirts that tend to get given away in advertising promos. She paid no attention to her personal grooming, and even abandoned elementary hygiene at the most critical times. She could go weeks without showering, and on one occasion I had to act directly to advise her that she couldn't go on with that attitude.

On seeing me, she wriggled out of the argument with the secretary and waddled over to me in a way that was starting to become familiar.

"Dr. Palmer! Praise the Lord, thank you for coming! Imagine, that bitch insisted that it wasn't my time and that I had to wait. I have a lot to tell you today," she shouted, possessed with a sincere joy, her face sweaty and lit up.

At those times she was completely oblivious to everything around her. She felt the need to see me, and considered it the most logical thing in the world to show up at the service without delay or formalities. The other patients, the secretary, the nurse, any possible commitments I might have, none of that mattered to her in the slightest. Very soon I got an idea of the kind of complications her behaviour caused her, and in time I managed to understand some things. Anne's life was real chaos, a constant storm that she triggered without the slightest awareness of what she was doing. The result was always the same: incapable of seeing that she was directly responsible for the major problems that weighed down her everyday life, from her relationship with her daughters and her ex-husband, to the void she was being pushed into at work. Everyone preferred to avoid her company, condemning her to the same solitude of which she ceaselessly complained.

"All right," I said, soft but firm. "But the thing is there are other people before you, and I have to respect all their appointments. You'll have to wait. You can wait in the waiting room, or if you prefer you can go for a walk and come back in an hour. Now I have to get back to my office, because I've left another patient there."

Anne stood open-mouthed for a few seconds, as if she'd seen something extraordinary for the first time in her life. Then she looked at the floor, and a feeling of great shame flooded her from head to toe. Her mood was utterly erratic, capable of swinging from euphoria to tears in a matter of seconds. When she finally understood something about her behaviour, an intense guilt mixed with self-pity absorbed her completely. There might then ensue a long period of absolute paralysis, a kind of state of hibernation that confined her to her bed for days, without moving or eating.

"I thought you'd be pleased to see me," she said in a childish voice, trying to prolong the conversation.

"Of course, I'm delighted to see you again. It's just that your appointment is a little later. That's all. By the way, I read your email!" I added as I turned to go back to my office. "We'll talk about it later."

This seemed to placate her a little. She waved at me, just like a little child, and docilely trotted off in search of a seat in the waiting room, where she fell into such a deep sleep that when her time came she had to be woken up.

* * *

"Do you want to talk about your email?" I asked her.

"It's very important that I tell you everything. It's terrible, but I suppose you'll be used to hearing this kind of thing. My husband and Karen have a very strange relationship. I've known it since she was born."

"What do you mean?"

Anne looked to her left and to her right before she went on, as if we were being watched. Almost in a whisper she answered, "It isn't an appropriate father-daughter relationship."

"What you're saying is very serious."

"I mean it. Of course it's very serious! Why do you think I spend whole nights awake? I've spoken to the social services about this on many occasions, even to the judge who handled our divorce, but no one listens to me. Richard is very crafty. He's managed to get everyone's complicity and convince them that I'm crazy. I might be, but that doesn't mean the other thing isn't true. Richard's always preferred Karen, that was perfectly clear from the beginning."

"Preferred Karen to your other daughter, you mean?"

"No, preferred her to me. Why else would he have tried to make her my enemy? The worst thing was we then had to have Karen hospitalised. He manipulated it all to put the blame on me."

"Wait a minute. You have to explain what this is about. When did you have to have your daughter hospitalised? What happened to her?"

Anne breathed out, and then breathed in all the air as if she were preparing for a lengthy immersion in the depths of the sea.

"When she turned sixteen, Karen started to have eating problems. A kind of anorexia. She refused to eat, it was a terrible time. I lost control of the situation. I never thought that something like that could happen in my home. I'd put all my heart into raising my two daughters, and there was nothing that would make me feel prouder, happier about myself, than being a good mother. I've always been one, I swear. I don't know what they put on the reports, or what they've told you, but I say this with all conviction. I am a mother, that is what I live for, and I'm not going to give up my rights for anything in the world. The psychiatrist who started treating Karen insinuated that I was to blame. She accused me of creating a rejection of food in her because of the way I swamped her with my care. She went as far as to say that I was smothering my daughter, and things like that. As you can imagine, I reacted by declaring war on her. I wasn't prepared to stand that woman questioning my role. I admit that I'm not worth two beans, but I'm fully conscious that as a mother I have done nothing but look out for my daughters' happiness day and night. No one can deny that, and if they deny it it's because they've been drugged, or they've been brainwashed somehow. That's why I want justice done, I want them to acknowledge that a great crime has been done unto me. I soon realised that the psychiatrist and Richard were in cahoots: it was clear that he agreed with her and backed up every odious thing she said. I reached a point where I couldn't stand it any more, and I threw myself at her, tried to throttle her. I would've done it, I swear, I would've strangled her with my own hands, if it hadn't been for Richard and a hospital security guard who dragged me off her. After that, when we got home, something strange happened to me, because I couldn't eat. I went nearly ten days without eating a crumb, locked up in my room, lying still like a corpse. I couldn't even go back to the hospital to visit Karen. After one week I was so weak that Richard had to have me committed, and I spent a fairly long time in the psychiatric hospital. Something must have happened then, because when I got out I noticed there'd been a major change. My daughters weren't speaking to me, and Richard was cold and distant with me. The three of them whispered behind my back, exchanged messages with their looks, and excluded me from their conversations and their plans. They'd turned me into a stranger in my own home, someone who was surplus to requirements, and I could never understand why. Then I reached the conclusion that there was something awful going on between Richard and Karen."

Anne's face changed strangely when she reached this point. Her gaze turned cloudy and unfocused, as if she were distancing herself, and her voice became heavier and deeper. Also, all this business about her husband and Karen remained wrapped in an ambiguity that I couldn't quite work out. Anne spoke through allusions, but at no time did she dare to call things by their name. Her comments suggested incest, but she never managed to express this directly. Perhaps deep down she had her doubts, or perhaps she held back because she feared that those ideas could arouse in me a psychiatric opinion of her. It's quite common for people with delusions to keep quiet, to avoid being taken for insane. They come to be perfectly conscious of the disbelief they can arouse in the listener, even when they are completely sure of what they think and feel. As for me, I had no intention of asking her for any kind of detail or clarification. The exceptional and distorted character that Anne saw in the relationship between Richard and Karen was probably a displaced figure from the relationship that she herself had maintained with her father, to whom she was joined by a bond that mixed love, tacit complicity, and a deep and bitter guilt that tortured them both.

"Did what happened to your daughter make you doubt at any time your actions as a mother? When children have problems, many parents tend to blame themselves and search for an explanation in what they have or haven't done. Aside from that psychiatrist criticising your behaviour, did you yourself feel in any way responsible?"

"No way! I've always been a perfect mother, I told you so and I will repeat it until the day I die. Or don't children have any responsibility themselves for what happens to them?"

Anne reasoned with the skill of a sophist, and there was no sense in casting any doubt on her identity as a mother. The conviction of being in that indisputable and deserving position of absolute recognition was one of the few elements that grounded her in life. I soon understood the importance of respecting her conviction and overlooking all the evidence of her spectacular failure as a mother. She had desperately wanted to restore the cracked image of her own mother, but she couldn't do so, or rather, she only succeeded in increasing the destructive power of that figure, and her daughters ended up painfully throwing back in her face her failed efforts to shower them with love.

"So for the first time I thought about suicide. I couldn't stand what they were doing to me. Imagine, for a moment, that this meant that in my home, my daughters, my own flesh and blood, were turning against me. For the first few days I tried to figure out what was happening, but I didn't understand a thing. I only felt pain, a pain that I can't describe. I remembered then what my mother had told me on that occasion: "We were left completely alone." I understood then what that meant. I understood what she had felt. I relived that immeasurable pain, and thought that was a way to pay homage to her. I had to rule out suicide as I was a survivor, and I couldn't forget that for anything in the world. That's what my parents taught me, and thanks to that I've always been able to get by, get through all adversity. Do you understand? One night I ran away from home, I went out into the street and started walking aimlessly. Actually I was told about this, I don't remember it. Apparently I was in a very strange mental state, as if I'd lost my memory, and the police found me two days later. I'd walked several miles without stopping and my feet were messed up. I've had trouble walking ever since. I think I must have injured my feet or my hip; anyhow, I can't walk right any more. But I don't care, because I can take it. I can take it all, no doubt about it. No one in my place would've taken it all. I told you, I'm a survivor, and I owe that to my parents. My mother always used to say it over and over. She said I'd save myself."

"Is it easy to live with that?"

"Sure ain't. You hit the nail on the head there. No, being a survivor isn't easy at all. Leaving my home and forming my own family was much more than a natural act, a normal move as part of the law of life. It was a desperate measure to not die a prisoner to my mother's sadness and my father's sacrifice. But at the same time it meant abandoning them, leaving them behind like the herd does when one of its number falls sick. Richard couldn't understand that. It was real easy for him. I was coming to live in his country, he didn't have to suffer any kind of separation. It was I who bore the burden of leaving my parents on their own, or even worse, leaving them to the terrible memory of what had happened to them, leaving them in that house besieged by ghostly creatures that returned at night, the bodies, the smell of burned flesh, the sound of the whips, the boots, the shouting, the hunger."

"The hunger. One way or another, we always come back to food!" I pointed out, intrigued.

"It's true. I'd never noticed that!" she exclaimed with a look of surprise. She was very expressive with her feelings, and transmitted them straight away in her face muscles and multiple inflections in her voice, which alternated between whispers and shouting, impetuousness and stammering.

"That comes from way back," she added. "Mom had serious problems with food. It was very far removed from today's fads, bulimia, anorexia, that stuff. No, she wasn't that. But I can't explain it."

"You can't explain it?"

"It had something to do with horror."

"Horror?"

"Yes. She had these really weird rituals with food. At home, we couldn't eat anything canned, or fried. She couldn't eat meat, and the rest of us had to eat it where she couldn't see us. Sometimes dad would take my sister and me to a restaurant, so we could try something different. My parents ate the same thing all their lives, day after day, invariably. My father could try other things, but he respected the limitations that my mother imposed, and went along with her. We couldn't watch TV either, except a few minutes a day, during which mom would shut herself in her room and plug her ears with cotton wool. The sound of the TV upset her nerves terribly, but we never found out why."

"The sound? The TV also gives you information on what's going on outside."

"Maybe it was that. She preferred to live in isolation from anything that wasn't her little family refuge. She only felt safe inside the house, and although she knew it was impossible for us to be by her side permanently, she found it hard to take whenever we went out. Everything was a cause for concern, and when we crossed the threshold of the door to go into the street, a journey filled with innumerable perils began. My sister handled it better, she was braver, but I succumbed to my mother's influence, and my mind was full of fears. She managed to pass them on to me, even to this day, and I've always fought so that they wouldn't bring me down completely. I've only half succeeded."

"You think? Personally I think you've succeeded and then some." She smiled slightly, lowered her gaze, and looked at her hands, which she kept clutched together. Then she opened them, the palms facing up, and stayed silent for a while. Despite her voluminous humanity, at those moments she took on the appearance of a little girl.

"It often happens that I experience a terrible weakness," she went on. "It's not fatigue, but something deeper. It's the sensation that my body's most elemental strength has abandoned me, and that all my body's mechanisms are depleted for ever. When that happens, I have to lie down on the bed and stay like that for hours, sometimes days on end, because I'm incapable of getting up. The surprising thing is I don't even feel hungry or thirsty. And I have no way of knowing what it is that brings me down, nor have I figured out why I feel good again. It can happen after a few hours, or after two days. My body starts to get back in the rhythm, my heart beats again, blood runs through my veins, my breathing quickens. I feel like my brain gets its vitality back, and then I get up and pick up my life again at the point where I left off. It's like a parenthesis, a short circuit that leaves me on the sidelines."

"You say you don't know why it happens, but have you ever thought about *when* it happens?"

"I haven't, but I'd say it comes after I have an attack of the nerves. The last time it happened when Karen wouldn't come to the phone on her birthday. First I went into a fit of rage. I lost control, and the phone company had to change my phone because I smashed it against the wall. I lied to them, and told them I'd dropped it. I don't know if they believed me, but they didn't ask any questions. In the afternoon, when I realised there was no point in trying to talk to my daughter, my body started to grow weak, and I had to sit on the floor so as not to fall over. This time I couldn't even make it to bed. I lay there as if I'd been shot, and I stayed like that all night and the next day, until I was finally able to stand up and drink a little water. The worst thing is that this problem makes me miss work, and that really scares me. Now I'm on leave, but any day now I'll get a letter telling me I've been fired and that'll be the end of me. No one will want me anywhere, they all end up kicking me out, one way or another."

At times, Anne gave the impression of understanding the extent to which she was directly responsible for the complicated problems she got herself tangled up in time and again. But at the same time that didn't stop her from maintaining the absolute conviction that she was a victim of a universal injustice done unto her. When she got to this point that ultimately went back to her parents' tragedy, her persecution mania intensified. Then the phone calls to her ex-husband, the verbal threats to her daughters, and the messages on my answer machine rapidly multiplied.

"Dr. Palmer? It's Anne, Anne Kurzinski. Do you remember me?"

"Sure, Anne, of course. It's hard to forget you, given that you call me several times a week."

"I'm sorry, I know I can be really annoying sometimes. It's just that I remembered something very important that I forget to tell you in this morning's session."

"Go ahead. It's three in the morning, but I was writing. What is it?"

"I lost control again. Yesterday afternoon I ran into my mother-in-law in the supermarket. She tried to avoid me, but I stopped her. I asked her about my daughters, and she tried to make me believe that she didn't know anything, that she didn't see them either. I know that's not true, and I told her so. We argued, and in the end I pushed into her with the trolley. She fell into a shelf of bottles of beer and it was a terrible scene. Security came, took down my name, but nothing else happened. My mother-in-law wasn't injured, and she left without saying a word. I'm very scared, and I think perhaps the supermarket might report me, or that the judge might intervene so that I never see my daughters again. I've been obsessed with that all day."

"Calm down, Anne. Your daughters are adults. No judge can intervene in that. They're the only ones who can decide if they want to see you or not. The courts don't have any business in this. We'll have to think up a way for you to recover your relationship with them, but you won't get anywhere if you force it on them. You can't force someone to eat, or to love."

"What you say is very good, Dr. Palmer. Yes sir, it's very good. You have no idea how grateful I am to you for answering my call. I think I'll finally be able to get to sleep now. I'll see you on Thursday."

"Yes Anne. See you Thursday."

* * *

"Dr. Palmer? It's Anne, Anne Kurzinski. Sorry to trouble you again, but as soon as I hung up I wondered if forcing someone to eat referred to me. Do you think I forced Karen to eat when her anorexia started? I was only trying to look after her, Dr. Palmer. You know that as a mother I'm always very concerned for my daughters' health."

"I have no doubt about that, Anne," I said, cursing myself, because it would've been enough to say, "You can't force anyone to love." "Please, we both need to sleep."

"You're right, and I doubted whether I should phone you, but I wanted to clear up that point. Thank you Dr. Palmer, thanks again."

SIX

After I graduated in medicine, I decided to put my feet up for a year and think about what specialisation I'd follow. At the start of my degree I was convinced I'd be a surgeon like my father. Naturally, he wholeheartedly encouraged this idea, and dreamed that one day I'd take his place in the hospital where he worked. He'd take me to watch his operations whenever he could, and I can say that even before I'd completed half my degree, my theoretical surgical knowledge exceeded that of many experienced surgeons. But something happened that completely changed the path that seemed to be set out for me. One night I borrowed my father's car, and took out a girl I'd been dating for a few months. She was a physics student who I'd met at the campus cafeteria, and promptly asked out. A real beauty, my classmates were green with envy when they saw me around the campus with her. That night she was acting strange, and after a short while she admitted that she'd taken lysergic acid. She offered me a tab, but I'd never taken drugs and didn't have the slightest interest in that kind of experience. We argued, and in the end she asked me to take her back home. She was terribly upset, and I couldn't understand why she gave so much importance to the fact that

I didn't want to take acid. We stopped seeing each other, and she disappeared from the university.

A month later I found out she'd died of an overdose. She'd been found in a disco bathroom, where she'd choked on her own vomit, like so many young people who back then were experimenting with various drugs for the first time. I had a tremendous breakdown, and the sadness overcame me in such a way that I even needed pharmacological treatment. The psychiatrist, an older man who'd trained in psychoanalytical psychotherapy, offered me the chance to lie on his couch and sail that stream of associations and fantasies. It was the start of a strange and captivating experience, one that carried me much further than I'd imagined at the beginning. My friend's death had untied a badly-tied knot, and over several years Dr. Rubashkin helped me to inquire into my life and my history. Then I realised that I wanted to do that for a living, instead of surgery. Although my father discreetly lamented my decision, he still gave me his full support, and when I finally concluded my medical studies he willingly agreed to pay for a year in Paris so that I could attend some courses and seminars. Back in the Sixties, Paris was bubbling with new ideas. The May '68 protests, anti-psychiatry, and Deleuze and Guattari's experiences at La Borde clinic had created the background for a debate that took on far greater force and commitment than anything I'd seen at American universities. When I got back home, I was sure that I wouldn't follow in my father's surgical footsteps, and that I would devote the rest of my life to psychiatry and analytical therapy in the public health area. Aware that at the same time I was giving up a life of prestige and fortune, I dived into five years of hard study to get my doctorate. I never regretted my decision, although I continued to frequently attend my father's operations until he retired. Although I wasn't going to work in surgery, there was something in the technique, in the act of opening, cutting, suturing, that seemed to me close to the art of calligraphy, and also to the art of my own profession, in which we do similar things with words. That's why I liked to see my father leaning over a body, making an incision with a godlike movement, sweaty face and steady hand, aiming at his goal.

"Surgery is like cutting diamonds," he used to say. "A diamond and a body only allow one perfect cut. Any error is unforgivable."

Although I never came close to his precision, I've always endeavoured to remember his example.

* * *

Those first years allowed me to establish two fundamental things that the books taught and the poets had shouted from the rooftops for anyone who wanted to listen, but whose value I didn't fully realise until I was able to see them with my own eyes. The first is that we human beings aren't hardwired for happiness, but rather the contrary, and that we persist quite remarkably in the pursuit of our own doom. The second, which is to some extent an extension of the first, is that we are incapable of learning anything from experience. Of course, we can learn many things, but none are of any use in eliminating the universal principle of self-destruction. These two things quickly alerted me against the gospels of learning and rehabilitation, and I took the caution of distrusting all those who pursued normality as the essence of wisdom. Normality not only tends to be one of the most common vehicles of hypocrisy, but is also the favourite food of spiritual and moral mediocrity. I deplore the mental health prevention prophets, the self-esteem apostles, those who give out prescriptions and formulas to achieve the greatest pleasure in life. I have given up on curing anyone of anything, save their inability to live on better terms with their illness. Nor do I attempt to persuade anyone to come and see me, and I even take pains so that those patients who do come to me, harried by court orders, can nonetheless find their own impetus. Anyone who comes to me is free to leave when they please, whether because I am of no use to them, or on the contrary, because they've managed to get what they need.

I'm fully aware that the days are numbered for this handful of principles. The current world trend is heading in quite a different direction: nowadays, sugar-coated happiness pills are dished out in the way conquistadors handed out glass trinkets to the natives of the New World. If back then it was easy enough to trick those wretched souls, now everything is even simpler, since the glass trinkets have become so sophisticated that the gods are no longer needed to guarantee their appeal. Man today is more inclined to believe in molecules than words, has more faith in neurons than speech, and in the same way that not believing in tragedies brings tragedies, not believing in dreams leads to belief in reality, precisely the most ambiguous and false thing that has ever existed.

As the years passed, a growing pessimism about mankind has allowed me to better practise my profession. The only dignity people have lies in their drama, in the fact that their existence is always a failed project, a truncated encounter, an unfulfilled desire. I have proved it in winners and losers, in the rich and the hopeless, in gifted geniuses and idiots. No one is safe from this inexorable law that beats us everywhere we turn. All those who imagine they are exempt from this fatality are deceiving themselves. And the more they do so, the more they bang their heads against an impossible brick wall. That's why the defeated and the weak are better prospects, those who admit failure, because at least they have the courage to ask themselves the reason for this set of senseless actions that makes up their lives. Those are the ones who end up thanking me for what little, or more, I can do for them. They know I haven't tricked them, haven't promised them joy, a happy ending, or a pot of gold at the end of the rainbow. At most, I teach them to stay afloat in the uncertain storms of each day.

I have many powerful competitors. First is modernity, striving to liken our unhappiness to the tormented brains of mice on which wise men in laboratories experiment. Traffickers of happiness compressed into pills, self-esteem preachers, self-help merchants, specialists in whatever, opinion experts and professional charlatans, physicists and metaphysicians, well-intentioned counsellors, know-it-alls and convinced optimists, cynics, believers in universal harmony and behavioural psychologists. Each one separately, and all of them together, waving their banner of faith in achieving balance, moderation, and personal improvement. Given that I preach no particular good, most bureaucrats and many of my colleagues consider me socially unprofitable, an ideological oddball. So I stay in my place, shrug my shoulders, and wait. The disillusioned of the system, the tortured of thought, the unsatisfied and the anguished, the sad and the suicidal who for some reason have survived the curse of magic recipes, questionnaires, and positive strengthening, end up coming in one by one, and they soon feel relieved when someone finally takes them in without wanting to turn them into the people they should be.

Now that I'm old and I've seen and learned a few things, my aspirations have become increasingly modest. I admit that human beings do not easily give up suffering, and that on many occasions this is because they find in their pain a fellow traveller, without whom they wouldn't know how to cope. Terrible marriages, senseless sacrifices, absurd acts of perseverance, conscientiously fabricated failures, love turned sour, and all kinds of unhappiness make up the entertaining palette of sadness to which people cling with real obstinacy, as if this were their most valued possession, the one private treasure they don't want to be dispossessed of. That's why I smile when I hear the self-improvement and self-belief preachers, the spokespeople for the progress of the will and other songs of similar sirens. They are the same ones who end up getting irritated with the anorexic who won't see reason, with the drug user who neglects his health, with the woman who always returns to the bed of the man who torments her. Incredible though it may seem, the whole history of mankind and clinical experience put together are not enough to convince them that desire and reason walk irreconcilable paths, and that human beings have never been guided in any of their actions by what is sensible and right, whether these actions are insignificant or grandiose. If the Argonauts' motto was "Sailing is necessary, it is not necessary to live", then modern man embodies this in his own way. For him too it is necessary to sail, and for that very reason he does so silently towards his own shipwreck. It isn't that he doesn't know, but there is something stronger that drives him to stick to the course he insists on sailing.

One could argue that the human being is also a creature capable of clinging tenaciously to life even in the most unimaginable conditions, and that his desperate determination to survive allows him to adapt to everything and use up every last drop of energy and courage. That too is true. However, it is best not to over-admire the fight for pure survival, given that it is inevitably the enemy of the moral conscience, which leads us to the terrible paradox that it is highly unlikely that one may safeguard one's own life and ethical principles at the same time. Furthermore, man deploys all his wit and strength in defending his life from outside threats, but he hasn't the slightest scruple about attacking himself through innumerable and often ingenious procedures, some imperceptible and others manifestly grotesque. Jealous protector of life when nature or his fellow sorts jeopardise it, he does not hesitate to spurn it when it depends on his own hand. But there aren't many people willing to admit these long-held truths. Most find bliss in ignorance, a narcotic far more powerful than any other substance discovered.

Nor do my conclusions distance me from people: on the contrary. On the one hand, I feel neither freer nor more exempt from all that I find in them. Also, familiarity with what has failed in a human life brings me closer to that life, and puts me intimately in tune, predisposed to listening better to the broken fictions that people take out of their pockets. Those who truly distance themselves are the philosophers of the right joy, the defenders of spiritual correction, and all that legion of social engineers who fabricate a correct measure of normal man.

My critics say I complicate things too much, that I don't educate my patients in relaxation techniques or teach them to prize positive thoughts.

It's true.

I was quick to reject the road to stupidity.

* * *

Shanice Tide wasn't easy to deal with. From the start she distrusted me for being white. As she had good knowledge of political philosophy, after a few meetings I decided to counterattack.

"Although you are a terribly reactionary person, I'm making a real effort to listen to you," I said, feigning offence in my tone of voice.

Surprised, she sat there open-mouthed a few moments, and then defended herself furiously:

"I'm reactionary? How dare you say that? I'm a woman who belongs to the feminist black left! I've been reading Audrey Lorde for as long as I can remember. I've been in the BFM, I've published several books about the liberation of black women. And you're trying to say I'm reactionary?"

"You're wrong. I'm not trying to say it, I'm saying it openly. I think it's a facile argument unworthy of an intellectual that you should want to focus our differences in terms of black and white. I have no trouble in admitting that you may not like me. But I'd feel happier if I could base it on something more solid."

"The race difference doesn't seem solid to you?"

"Not at all. In the context in which you and I are meeting, I think it's banal. I've read Audrey Lorde too, and I very much doubt that you can use her as a pretext to reject my work. You are facing a problem considerably greater than the colour of my skin, and I couldn't give a damn about the colour of yours. All the same, we can assign you a black therapist, if you prefer, especially if you think that is the right criteria for selecting the kind of help you need."

"Sorry, but I don't believe for one second that you've read a single word of Audrey Lorde," she said with a laugh.

Not only had I read her, but I was also able to recite several of her poems, until I succeeded in getting her to back down, astonished. From that day I became someone she could trust, and the sessions changed noticeably. Then it wasn't very difficult to start to rummage through the debris of her life and find in her relationship with her stepfather one of the fundamental roots of her hatred.

"Strange though it may seem, that guy was a black preacher who hated blacks with all his might, and called me and my brothers and sisters the same names white folk called us."

"Unfortunately I know those cases well. Racism can lead to that kind of aberration. Was it just name calling?"

"If you mean sexual abuse and that stuff, he wasn't into that. But he was convinced we were all perverted, and that we sold our bodies in the street to anyone. He particularly watched over my sisters and me, but he'd attack my brothers too, accusing them of sodomy, incest, all kinds of perversions. He had this incongruous radical discourse, as he hated blacks and at the same time proclaimed the purity of the black race. He was obsessed with the idea that we might have some white in us, and spent hours, days at the registry office archives looking for information on our ancestors. I've just realised that you were right a few weeks ago when you said I was a reactionary. I was conscious of it, but I've lived under a cruel influence."

"I don't doubt it."

"My stepfather wasn't happy with just preaching at mass, he did it all the time. Living with him meant having to listen to a constant sermon from morning to night, a torrent of fury coming out of his mouth in the form of moral diatribes, warnings, threats, and invocations of the wrath of God. God lived among us, he was everywhere, and since I was a little girl I had the feeling that he was watching me, watching over everything I did. I think the moment came when I couldn't clearly tell God and my stepfather apart. Seriously, they both got mixed up in my head and in my terrors. When I was fourteen or fifteen, I started to hear voices. At first I couldn't figure out what they were saying. Then, little by little, I started to make it out. At first I thought they came from God, that he was talking to me to reprove me for my sins. I worked hard to follow the Ten Commandments, but it made no difference, because the voices accused me and mercilessly spilled out their reproaches. Later, I thought I heard my stepfather, and then I didn't know what to do. I ran away a couple of times, but the police found me and brought me home. Both times my stepfather greeted me with a disconcerting attitude. Bathed in tears, he took me in with infinite mercy, and blamed the influence of the whites for all that was happening to me. He'd yell that school, with its non-segregation of the races, encouraged the creation of an impure, mixed teaching, a sullied teaching, stained by the degeneration of the white race, which was a race unworthy of God. As the days passed, his behaviour gradually changed. He'd come to consider me an accomplice of the whites, accused me of bringing that race's virus into our home. He then stopped me from going to school, and when social services came with the court order, he believed that I'd called them. So then he accused me of being "like that black trash that fought in the white man's army". My head started to go to pieces, and I lost all notion of who I was. I no longer knew if I was black or white, or an impure mix of both. More than that, I no longer even knew what I wanted to be. The idea that I was carrying an infection started to disturb me, and I did all I could to figure out what I could do about it. Then I read *The Human Stain* by Philip Roth, and that totally freaked me out."

"I've read the book. Why did it affect you so much?"

"I didn't know that people could exist who were apparently white but were really black. That confused me, to the extent that I imagined that the opposite was also feasible, and that I myself, despite the colour of my skin, might really be a white woman. In the end, I slit my wrists, because I thought that that way the doctors would analyse the blood and could figure out what was wrong with me."

"How old were you when you did that?"

"I was sixteen, and I remember it well because it was the day my friend Berenice turned twenty. My stepfather had his eye on her, because he considered her a bad influence, and wouldn't let me go to her party. I locked myself in my room, and that was when I thought about suicide."

"The dates don't fit. The book was published in 2000, a long time after you turned sixteen."

"I'm sure it's like you say, but I remember it differently."

"Had you thought about suicide before?"

"Never. It all happened so fast. The voices reminded me of the virus, and suddenly it occurred to me that the solution was for the doctors to study my blood. Maybe, if they didn't find anything, my stepfather would leave me alone."

"So it wasn't really suicide, but rather a desperate attempt to find a solution. What you really wanted was to be free of this supposed virus."

"Looking at it like that, I guess you're right. But it was all a waste of time, because the doctors' opinion only served to encourage my stepfather's idea that I was possessed by a demon."

"What did the doctors say?"

"That I needed help, and I was receiving an inadequate upbringing."

"You haven't said a word about what your mother thought of all this."

"My mother? She couldn't say anything, she'd been dead for years. Besides, I doubt she would've done much if she'd been alive. My big brothers remember that she was totally under my dad's thumb. I don't even have a memory of her."

"Carry on. What happened next?"

"What happened next was I met Trayvon."

"Trayvon?"

"Trayvon Kendrick Alliston Jefferson Jr."

"Sounds imposing."

"He was. Almost seven feet and two hundred pounds of pure black race, who I bumped into coming out of a store. He helped me get away from home for good, as I was an adult by then, and when my stepdad tried to make me go back, Trayvon grabbed him by the neck and threw him through the window of the café where we'd met up. It was unforgettable, because from that day on I never heard again from that repugnant man."

"What about your brothers and sisters?"

"All scattered in the wind."

"That's very sad. What happened to the voices?"

"They went away for a few years."

"Does that mean they came back?"

"Yeah. I can never be totally free of them."

SEVEN

"My paternal surname was actually Kurczynski. My grandparents came from a farming region in Poland, and when they moved to Germany they changed the spelling of their surname, making it Kurzinski, more German. Being *Östjuden* was a source of shame, even for Jews themselves."

"Why?"

Anne stared at me and smiled sadly.

"Because they were poor. Jews from the east, from Galicia and Slav regions, tended to be very poor. You know how it is: the poor are not welcome anywhere, and the Jews themselves snubbed these wretched semi-literates who only spoke Yiddish and smelt of radishes and salted fish. Those who managed to climb a couple of rungs socially tried to hide their background. Changing the surname was the first thing. It's funny how people should feel obliged to cover their tracks like animals, disguise their smell, hide in the thicket so as not to be caught out, camouflage themselves like those insects that you can't tell apart from the leaf they're clinging to. I've lived like that all my life. First my mother's illness, that forced us to cover up our own existence, so as not to upset her with our worries or our good news. We'd talk quietly, swallow any kind of emotion, good or bad, so as not to upset the fragile balance that my father tried to strike every day. And then, when I grew up and got married and I thought that I could finally start to stick my head out, my husband accused me of being crazy, and blamed me for everything that happened to my daughters. At work people looked at me funny, so I had to go back into my hiding place, but for some reason it was no longer possible. I'd been branded, as if my prisoner number were tattooed on my arm. Everyone thought they knew who I was just from looking at me. It's true that I sometimes lose control, but that's not the same as being crazy, is it?"

"Of course not. But you were talking about the history of your surname."

"You're right. That always happens to me, you know? I lose my thread when I'm talking, I can't stay on track. I go off the rails, go along the sides, run here and there, and then I don't know how to get back. It happens to me especially when I'm nervous; I need to talk, it's as if a torrent of words were welling up in my mouth, and if I don't open it I'll burst. But then I can't stop that torrent. The same thing happens in my head."

"In your head?"

"It changes from day to day, from one moment to another. There are times when my thoughts build up so much that they form a knot, like a train crash where one carriage crumples into the next. But the opposite also happens, my thoughts disperse, break up into tiny pieces that shoot off in all directions. It's very hard to stop that, and I have to take more pills, or get drunk, until the fuel runs out and the engine comes to a standstill. Then I stay completely still, maybe for a few hours, maybe a few days; I just breathe, I don't eat, I don't drink, and my head is empty. What were we talking about?"

"How they changed their surname."

"Of course, thanks. Don't you think that's something serious? I mean, changing your surname, feeling ashamed of your own name? That can't be good, that's got to cause harm, a lot of harm, because it's like denying yourself. I'm sure that was where something very bad began to brew, something terrible. My grandfather committed a great sin, and here is the price we've had to pay," said Anne, pointing at her chest.

"Hang on, hang on!" I interrupted her. "I don't think your grandfather committed any sin. In any case, the sinners were those who made him feel so bad about where he was from. As you say, that probably caused profound damage, but the others were to blame."

Anne looked at me with that look of concentration on her face that she tended to wear when she understood what I was saying. She always took a few seconds to reply, leaning forward a little, her head to one side to listen better and soak up the meaning of what she was hearing, weigh it up, before then picking up her thread. She'd look up, straighten her hair with a nervous tic, and finally speak again.

"Yes, I think I understand. Sometimes I think that my head works completely backwards. I can't understand what I'm guilty of, and I blame myself for things that have nothing to do with me. It's true what you say. My grandfather had to get by as best he could, we all did. My mother never spoke about that, but my father told us that they were forced to do terrible things to escape and survive for months, hiding in the woods, eating roots, and drinking melted snow. They slept in holes that they'd dig with sticks so as not to die of cold, like animals. I think that's why my mother had so many issues with food. Maybe you go crazy when you're about to die of starvation. Do you think that could've influenced my daughter? One fine day she decided to stop eating, and my husband accused me of driving her crazy. I get it all mixed up, Dr. Palmer. I don't know if it's me, if it was the Germans, or whether my daughter inherited her illness from my mother. I just wanted to raise my daughters, care for them as the most important thing in my life, but my husband was jealous, you know? There was something strange going on with him with my daughter, I realised that straight away. Everything changed very quickly when the girl was born, and nothing could ever be the same."

"Didn't you change too?"

"Maybe. I don't rightly remember. Did I change? Let me think a minute," she said, closing her eyes. "Yes, I remember that when I got back from the hospital after giving birth, those first days I felt very strange. Maybe I needed my mother's help, as happens to most women who have their first baby, but my mother couldn't come and see me. If she was practically incapable of leaving her house, imagine if she'd had to fly from Israel to America. It was unthinkable, and I couldn't expect my father to visit us either, as he couldn't leave her side for even a second. The worst thing for him was when he had to be absent during work hours. He'd call on the phone two or three times, and would often go and see her in his lunch hour, so he'd go back to work without eating a thing, because there was only enough time to take the bus there and back. He'd open the front door, go into the room my mother usually locked herself up in, and check that she was calm, or on the contrary if she was having one of her bad days. Then he'd stroke her head, barely saying a word, and go straight back to work. He did this reluctantly, he had no other choice, but he would've liked to stay with her all the time. I was always aware of how little they talked to each other. They'd communicate with signs, looks; my father could guess what she was thinking, what she was feeling, what she was imploring without saying a word. He knew all that because he loved her with all the strength he could muster, and because he'd taken the decision to make up to her at least a little bit of what had been snatched away from her. My father never asked for anything himself, and yet they destroyed him mercilessly too. I could never understand how he was able to go on loving, trusting in human beings. She, on the other hand, couldn't. Once I read that certain things can break for ever our ability to believe in others. Is that true? I think that was exactly what happened to my mother. They massacred her soul, and no one paid for the crime. I think about it all the time, I think that no one pays for the crimes they commit. Do you know how I imagine the world? As a huge lie, revolving around an infinite injustice."

"I really can't object to that image. But we have to find the way to live, even despite that."

"Is it necessary? Is living imperative? Has it never occurred to you that that philosophy might be false?" she asked, suddenly changing her tone. Her face could contract and fill with fury in a fraction of a second.

I looked out of the window. In the hospital garden the trees were turning golden in the autumn sun. I stayed silent for a moment.

"Of course. I've thought about it many times. I still haven't reached a definitive conclusion."

EIGHT

"What do you think?"

Shanice avoided my gaze. She sighed and was silent for a while. I waited for her to decide to speak.

"It's bullshit."

"I thought you'd be pleased. Personally I was worried that the sentence would be harsher."

"It's humiliating. That's what they want. To humiliate me, as they have always done to our people."

"What is it you find humiliating? The five hundred dollar fine or the court order that you clean the statue yourself?"

"Both. I have no intention of doing either anyhow."

"I see. What's the alternative? Jail? In that case, we'd have to stop our sessions. I'm too old to go and visit you there. Plus, I doubt they'd let me see you."

Shanice couldn't help but smile.

"I know you take me for a real crazy. Even though you're professional, I can tell. But I'm not going to be any less than Angela Davis."

"Angela Davis? What does Angela Davis have to do with it? I think you're taking it too far. I totally supported Angela and everything she stood for, back in the day, but these are different times. You're a lot more use to the African American cause if you're free and teaching at your school than locked up in prison."

"You don't understand. At the school my message has no impact at all. But from prison my case will be known all over the world. You know, social networks and all that. I need my message to reach millions of people. Africa must awake from its lethargy. The world has to apologise to black people."

"So you want to become a martyr? Is that it? Have I got that right?"

"You got it."

"I thought you'd had enough of history. In the end, after all that, you're going to end up a fanatic like your stepfather."

Shanice took my words like a kick in the gut. She was about to burst into tears, but she held it in. She was tough, real tough, because she'd saved her skin by surrounding herself with the armour of everything she was certain of. Sometimes madness can become a survival force. Not always, it doesn't happen to everyone who's crazy, but there are some who are made invulnerable by their madness. That's why I had to hit hard too, aim a blow at a place that would hurt enough to make her doubt. After that, there were two possibilities. Either I'd get her to change her mind or, on the contrary, I'd push her to total defiance and everything would go to hell. The consequences of this reckoning cannot be known in advance. There are no rules, no protocol to follow. No glass to break in case of fire. Ultimately, the glass might be the glass in the window, and there's no fun in that.

Shanice recomposed herself and smiled.

"You win, Doc. You always win. Fine. What you said is fine. A wise guy, yes sirree. A word juggler. Ingenious. I can't deny it. And will I have to clean that statue in front of everyone?"

"I hadn't thought about that. Maybe I can do something, but I'm not making any promises."

"Listen, I'm perfectly aware that you've done your best. I'm not questioning that. I just want you to understand that this is a person, you know, who has a very particular pride."

"You don't say. Everyone has a very particular pride. Didn't you know?"

"OK, OK! All I'm saying is she won't recognise that this is a light sentence. She's taking it as a humiliation, and I've had to bust my ass to stop her from being a rebel and going to prison."

"Look, Doctor, I've got all kinds of problems on my head. Seems folk have decided to make my last months of work before I retire a nightmare. So I can't waste time on the sentimental problems of some wacko black woman who, by the way, I'm doing a favour by giving her the lightest sentence that can be applied to the felony of damaging historic property in this state just because you ask me to. So if she wants to go to jail, that's her business. What more do you want me to do? Buy some rubber gloves and a stepladder and clean off the paint myself? Is that what you want?"

"Come on, don't get pissed with me now. It's precisely because it's a wacko black woman, it would be dumb to turn her into a Facebook hero. Imagine: 'Judge Delucca enrages city's black community.' I'm trying to work out an alternative. She'll pay the fine, but she doesn't want to be seen. She doesn't want the TV cameras there while she cleans the statue. That wouldn't be great publicity for you, either."

"Aha. Will she do it at night? Would that fix the problem?"

"The best thing would be to surround the statue with a tarpaulin, so she isn't recognised. Some plain clothes police officers could take her there. This can be done discreetly."

"Sure, sure. Very discreetly. You think five hundred bucks is going to cover the cost of all that? You gonna make up the difference? You know what I say? I say I can't believe I'm having this conversation. I can't believe that with the career you've had you're wasting time on this kind of thing. We're two old men talking crap. I don't know who's the craziest of the three."

"The three?"

"Yeah, the black woman, me, or you. You're unbelievable, Dr. Palmer. Unbelievable. I've met some stubborn people, but you're the champ. You always have to win. So fine, you win. Now leave me alone for a few days. I don't ask for much. Just a few days. You think you can do that?"

"You have my word, Al. You have my word. Thank you. I knew you'd understand."

"A few days then?"

"Word of honour."

* * *

I kept my promise, but on this occasion it was Al who had to go back on his word and call me the next day. Turns out, problems respect no man, not even an honourable judge on the verge of retirement.

"Hi Dave. Long time no speak, right? Hey, how are you fixed for time?"

"Bad, as usual. You know how it is. I take on more cases than I should. I thought you didn't want to hear from me for a while," I added in a mocking tone.

"Well, you know. Circumstances beyond my control. Besides, you owe me one, so shut your mouth and listen to what I've got for you. A gift on the house, yes sir. White, Latina, twenty-nine years old. Detained yesterday at a branch of Walmart for attempted abduction."

"Abduction? Did you say abduction?"

"You heard right. Abduction of a ten-month-old baby. The mother was looking at the prices of something on a shelf, and had her baby boy sleeping in the buggy next to her. She was distracted for a moment, the defendant took advantage, took the kid and ran for the exit. The mother's screams alerted the security guards, who chased the kidnapper across the parking lot. They caught her in no time. The boy wasn't harmed. Seems he didn't even wake up. The mother was taken to hospital with an attack of the nerves, and the defendant has refused to make a statement. She's under arrest and under surveillance, because they suspect she might be a suicide risk. In fact she had to be transferred to the infirmary because she headbutted the wall. She's sedated and tied to the bed. What do you say if I order a transfer to your hospital so you can take a look? I've just sent you the report. It's on your computer."

"Wow, not bad," I said leaning over the screen to check my mail. "Yes sir, got it here. Baby snatcher. What do we know about her motive?"

"We got nothing, Doc. Not a word. Just a summary of her record. But she's refused to make a statement."

"Have you seen her?"

"Yeah, just a few minutes. She made quite an impression. I couldn't tell you why."

"Really? Well I don't want to miss this. Tell them to bring her in tomorrow. Women are beating all the records just lately."

"No doubt about that. Are there no more serial killers like in the old days? Real tough guys? The world is changing a lot, Dave, I swear. Now women dominate everywhere. You had any interesting men in your office lately?"

"One or two. An Asian who tried to poison his wife."

"That's pretty good. And did he?"

"Seems the woman suspected him, and switched her husband's plate when he wasn't looking. He almost went blind from ingesting strychnine, or something. Very small amounts."

"I see. Asians have infinite patience. They have a very special feeling for time, don't you think? Anyway, we're not going to debate that now. I'll send you the woman tomorrow. Her name's Brenda, or Linda. One of those names, whatever. How's your black woman doing, the artist? Tell her from me to put on her next event in another town, in another state, even, if it's not too much to ask. They fucked up the blacks a whole lot more in the Carolinas. I'm sure there are heaps of statues to screw over."

"Oh, she's pretty quiet lately. She's going to keep her part of the bargain, and come to therapy. She's gone back to work at the school. No complaints about her."

"That's great, real great. You really got a knack, Dave. I don't know how you do it, but you really got it. I'm curious about this case tomorrow. Keep me in the loop, if you can get a word out of her."

"Sure. Will do."

There are times when I wonder whether the cases I take on are isolated stories, or whether there is a secret thread connecting them all, as if each one were in fact a chapter in a great book written by that evil genius whom Descartes had imagined. The really hard thing for someone like me, who doesn't even trust God, is to be able to conclude that it's all one enormous tall story. Life often turns out too weird for me to believe it.

NINE

Not Brenda, not Linda. Jessica. Jessica García. American. Twenty-four years old. Daughter of Nicaraguan immigrants. Works for an office cleaning company. Had worked in the laundry at the maternity ward, but was fired for strange behaviour. She was caught in the nursery without authorisation. She was warned about her conduct, and then did it again two days later. The hospital board sacked her without pressing charges, because no criminal intent was proven. The nursery workers stated that the young woman had on two occasions been seen by the cribs and incubators, vacantly watching the babies. She put up no resistance when ordered to leave the room. What most concerned the staff was that she didn't say a word, and that she walked like a robot. One of the nurses ventured the impression that she might be schizophrenic, and alerted her supervisor, who in turn spoke to human resources, who decided they no longer needed her services.

For two years she bummed around in different jobs, mostly cleaning. Poor background. Never finished elementary school. Estranged from her family for some time. Lived on the street for some spells, or in charity shelters. In the last year her situation had improved when she'd found work cleaning offices. Her employers were satisfied with her, and were very surprised when the officers investigating the case told them what had happened. According to their statement, the defendant is a quiet woman, shy by nature, hardly speaks, but a responsible and efficient worker. They don't believe her capable of harming anyone.

I don't believe she is, either. One look at her was enough to rule out any criminal motive. This isn't a kidnap attempt. There are women, like Anne, who can only imagine existence if they have children, and are convinced that life owes them at least one. Since life didn't keep its side of the bargain, Jessica just decided to take matters into her own hands and get a child any way she could. She's never contemplated the possibility of having it like most women. She hasn't known love, not even casual sex. She's a virgin. She only intended to keep the baby to look after him, to have someone to look after, someone who needed her, someone who would make her feel there was some kind of reason for existing.

It wasn't at all easy to find all this out. Jessica wasn't exactly a communicative person.

* * *

"Hi, Jessica. I'm Doctor Dave Palmer. Do you know why you're here?"

Silence.

"I've read the police report, and the district attorney's report too. You've gotten yourself into some serious trouble. You can hide away inside yourself, but that's not going to make this problem go away. It would be good if you and I could talk a little, see if we can work out what's happened to you."

Silence.

"You know something? I'm really used to silence. I can live with it no problem. I can sit here in this chair, putting up with your silence for days, weeks even. I can sleep a while, get up to go to the bathroom, order in some food, and keep waiting. I've spent my whole life waiting for people to speak. Sometimes they decide to speak from the get-go, others take their time, but everyone ends up saying something. You need to say something too. I have to know what's happened to you, and more importantly, why it's happened to you. I won't get you off a sentence, but the conclusions we reach might make it lighter. That's not a promise. It's just a possibility."

Silence. Something told me that this woman's feeling of guilt was so intense that she'd surrendered herself to being punished. She didn't want to defend herself, or be defended. I've seen a lot of cases like this, people who declare themselves unfit for life, and do everything in their power to reach the abyss. Once they get there, they throw themselves in without hesitation. They can't be stopped. It's a blind race to hell, to the worst kind of suicide, dying without killing themselves.

"How old were you when your mother died?" I asked like someone firing a shot into the air to see what came down.

"Eight," she replied without making me wait. Bingo.

"Hmm. Eight. And how did she die?"

"She threw herself under a train."

"Do you know why she did that?"

"Yes. My little brother had died, he was one year old. He died from some fever, and my mother couldn't take it. She mourned his death for nearly two years. She couldn't think of anything else or do anything. She barely ate, and she'd lie on her bed and not get up again. My father had to work, and my other brothers and sisters and I looked after her. My dad loved her very much, but he couldn't give up working. We had to live."

"How many brothers and sisters do you have?"

"There are five of us. Well, four, really. I can't count Brian any more."

"Are you the eldest?"

"No, the eldest is Thomas. He was twelve when my mother died. But I was the one who spent the most time with her.

Thomas took care of helping the others with their homework, and I spent all my time with my mother. She didn't talk. She'd sing something, a kind of lullaby. I can still hear it. It's stuck in my head, that song. It was what she used to sing to Brian, and I guess all of us when we were little. She'd lie on her bed, singing that song again and again. We couldn't get her to say a word. She was locked up in her own world, she couldn't get out. Or didn't want to."

"She couldn't get over it."

"Sometimes she'd talk, but only in her sleep."

"In her sleep? Can you remember what she'd say?"

"I only remember one thing: 'Bring me Brian'. She'd say it drowsy like, in a real quiet voice, but I heard her, because I slept next to her."

"Why did you sleep with her?"

"I don't know. That's how things were. Maybe she preferred it, or it was my father's idea. I can't answer that."

"'Bring me Brian.' And what did you think when you heard that?"

"I couldn't answer that either. Sorry I can't help you more, but I don't remember."

"Sure, it's perfectly understandable that you don't remember. It was just a question. But tell me one thing. What do you think about that now, now that you're telling me about it?"

She was silent for a moment. It was clear that she was making a great effort to gather in her head all the pieces of broken memories, like someone trying to stick together the pieces of a vase that's smashed against the floor.

"I think ... I think that we kids always obey our parents."

"Well, not all do. But in your case it seems to be true. You've always been a very obedient girl?"

She nodded her head. Her gaze had withdrawn from the conversation, and was looking for a point on the horizon. Given that it was our first meeting, I decided that that was enough. More than enough. Jessica had explained everything with great clarity. All I had to do was follow her attentively, make her feel that every one of her words was a great treasure, that her story, chewed and eaten up by pain, had a reason.

"Do you think we could carry on this chat next week?" I asked her as delicately as possible. "I'll give you an appointment, and if for any reason you want to cancel it, you can do so. Personally, I'd like for us to keep on talking, but you're the one who has to decide."

"Why? I'm very interested in this point, Dr. Palmer. Why did you decide that you didn't have to insist or press the patient to return?" asked one of the resident doctors at the weekly clinical seminar I gave to discuss cases with a group of young psychiatrists and psychologists who were interested in the way I worked.

"That's a very good question, because to be honest I was about to do that. But luckily I held back. Do any of you want to answer? What do you think?"

Deborah Chester, a psychiatrist who I would've fallen in love with if I'd been half my age, shot her hand up. At my age, I was happy just to look at her, without this being noticed too much.

"It's clear. The patient converted her mother's desire into an imperative that obsessed her for the rest of her life. It would've been a serious mistake to make her feel a 'I want you to come back'. That's how I see it, anyway."

"Exactly. That's it. You've interpreted it perfectly."

"Yes, it's very interesting what you've just said, Deborah," added one of the other members of the group. "But all this is very tricky. How do you know when to say one thing and not the opposite?"

"I'm not saying it isn't tricky. We're practising a cure with no prescriptions or a user manual. A major part of the training necessary to understand that consists of learning to put up with it."

Deborah gave me an approving look and I told myself that I was a total liar. Even at my age I could fall in love with her. And if I hadn't already done so, it was because I let common sense beat me.

TEN

"I have to tell you something, Dr. Palmer. I've been trying to for some time, but whenever I make up my mind the shame is too much. It's something awful, an idea that comes to me again and again. I'm convinced that it's just an idea, that I would be incapable of doing something like that, but I still can't get it out of my mind." Anne seemed shaken. It wasn't anger, but some other kind of trouble, the kind that leads to extreme anguish. I'd learned to tell her emotional states apart. Anger tended to come out in a volcanic eruption. Her face would burn up, and her body mass seemed to double in both height and girth. Bathed in sweat, she'd stand up, look me straight in the eyes, lean into me as far as she could, and her voice would come out like that of those fanatical preachers who harangue their masses of followers, a threatening fist in the air. Sometimes she'd bring it down with all her might on my desk, making papers and pens leap up. Anguish made her tremble a different way. Her body would get smaller, to the point of vanishing, her voice like that of a child drowning in fear, and she couldn't look me in the eye. I found her mood swings fascinating. She was capable of making every human fibre sing, and her repertoire of emotions, the different timbres of voice, the way she managed to transform the impression her physical presence had, made a real artist out of her, except this term didn't have the sense of a simulation, on the contrary it had the sense of an amazing capacity for identifying absolutely with all her masks. She was each and every one of those personalities, and authentically so, in such a way that one couldn't decide on the real person acting.

"Shame. It's a very dignified sentiment," I said, adopting a philosophical tone. "I tend to distrust anyone who doesn't experience it. Don't you?"

"Yes, I agree with what you say. But it's not easy to beat it. You see, I think I'm going to be able to tell you. I can do it this time. It's an idea that captivates me. I haven't always had it, no. It started a few years ago. I couldn't say how many years ago exactly, but I'm sure it's since the girls stopped talking to me. Yeah, no doubt about it. It's the result of my despair, I know that for sure. It occurred to me ... Oh my God, it's terrible what I'm going to tell you, but I need to get this off my chest! OK, OK. I'll tell you. I'll tell you right now. I thought about stealing a child."

She looked up at me, looking for a mirror in my face, a sign, something that would give her back the meaning of what she had just confessed. I just repeated her last words.

"Stealing a child. Go on, explain yourself."

"There's nothing else to explain. Please believe me when I say I would be incapable of doing that, but I can't hide what I think."

"I know perfectly well that you wouldn't do that. But we all have the right to imagine unlikely or unpleasant things."

"I know, I know. But you have no idea of the torment that this means to me. It's a double torment. It's terrible to think it, and it's also terrible to know that this is a wish that is condemned to never come true. I couldn't have a baby again. I'm too old to conceive one, even to adopt one. With my record they wouldn't let me. I have my imagination, of course, although it only serves to cause me pain. I'd like to be able to use it better, but it's become a damned obsession that won't let me go. It's got me by the neck."

"Listen. I wonder if you'll ever be prepared to face your life beyond your role as a mother. I understand what that means to you. You've made it clear since the first day we met. But you have to decide whether you're going to be consumed by that pain, or whether you're going to fight to find a new way of living. You know very well where one thing and the other leads. I can't push you in either direction."

"Isn't freedom a terrible thing, deep down? I desperately need you to give me some advice, tell me what I have to do. But at the same time, if you did I would never set foot in your office again."

"Of course," I said with a smile.

"Some nights I try to understand what went wrong. For years I thought we were a happy family. Was I wrong? I don't know any more. It's all mixed up in my head. I try to remember how things were before we had to hospitalise Karen. I still can't comprehend why she did that, why she decided to stop eating. Everything worked before. I enjoyed life, I enjoyed my job."

"But you yourself told me that shortly after Karen was born you started to have suspicions about your husband. Strange ideas. So not everything was going as well as you say."

"It's true. I sometimes forget. I have something like … two different versions of my marriage. One in which everything is perfect until we hospitalise Karen, and the other in which the trouble begins with her birth. I get them mixed up, I can't clearly see what the truth is."

"Maybe you don't have to decide between one and the other. Who knows, there might be a connection between both versions."

"Probably, but I can't see it yet. Now it feels absurd to think that I once thought myself lucky to have met Richard, and that our marriage would allow me to get away from my parents. I remember when my mother saw him for the first time. She didn't say a single word, as was her custom. My father tried to act as happy as possible so that Richard didn't feel uncomfortable, but my mother's silence weighed like a millstone around all of our necks. I'd warned him about my mother, he was aware of the tragedy my parents had been through, and the consequences, too. In that regard, he was always very considerate and respectful, it has to be said. My mother had an absent gaze, but understood perfectly what was happening, and what was going to happen. She understood that Richard's being there meant I would be leaving, but she never spoke about that. She had lost so much, she could no longer appreciate how much. At that moment I felt more sorry for my father, for abandoning him to his fate, but he never stopped encouraging me, not for one minute. It was as if he was saying, 'Save yourself, Anne. Save yourself. It makes no sense for our past to drag us all down. You and your sister aren't to blame for a thing.' You know something, Dr. Palmer? The night has been a great teacher to me. What little I have been able to learn in my life, I learned it at night. It's given me the greatest terrors, but it's also enlightened me, strange though that may sound. And one of the things that I've learned is that the past drags us all down. Pain is inherited, it's a river that can't stop. It's passed on from one generation to the next, like sin, guilt, or grace. It's a gift. You can't just say, 'Thanks, but I don't want this.'"

"You believe too much in heredity."

"Of course. You know I'm not wrong."

"I don't entirely share your sense of fatality. Not even in your case."

"But you must at least recognise that some people don't have the strength to stand up to fate."

"I recognise that. Against that weakness, there's not much can be done. But I haven't given up on you yet. I hope you haven't either."

"No, not yet. It's been a relief to be able to tell you that idea that's been tormenting me for so long," said Anne.

And it was true, as she'd stopped wringing her hands, something she used to do when the anguish would cut off her words.

* * *

That night she phoned me at home. It was nearly two in the morning, but I'd gotten used to the fact that time to her was a matter without form or duration.

"Dr. Palmer! Don't worry. Everything's fine. It's just that I didn't want to leave it until our next meeting to tell you what I was thinking. I hope I didn't wake you."

"It's OK, Anne," I lied. I'd been fast asleep for an hour.

"I think this is going to interest you. This morning's session was very important. Very important. When I left your office, I had this feeling of catharsis. I'd purified myself, I'd managed to get over that terrible shame, and let out that nauseating intimacy of my thoughts. I'm discovering that there is another way of letting things out. My way, the one I've used all my life, consists of opening up the gates of hatred and resentment and a river of fury flooding its banks. It's sudden. I can't control it. Now I see very clearly what's happened to me since I left my parents' home. Until then I was locked up in an invisible shroud, stronger than steel. Not having the support I needed because of my mother's pain and my father's sadness loosened something that was pent up in me. I know that at those moments I'm capable of destroying it all, but it's like the force of nature when it's unleashed. Nature isn't just beautiful, it's also monstrous. But with you I learn to use words differently. Not just to express feelings, but to think. I've always wondered why we think. No, it's not a philosophical question. Well, it is, but not for me. When I was a little girl, thinking was a terrifying thing. I was afraid of being found out, that everything I was forced to keep quiet would become transparent to everyone else. Sometimes I'd think terrible thoughts about my mother, and I was horrified by the idea that she could see those thoughts, guess them, read them somehow. That sounds like paranoia, I know, but it's what happened. I'm more and more certain that I'm crazy, and that my craziness comes from way back. Yes I am. Now I can think a little better, my ideas are more lucid. That's why I called you. It's very important, because I don't want to forget it. I want you to hear it right now, before it slips away. I know I could write it down, in fact I just have, but it's not the same. I also realise that reading out loud isn't the same as speaking to you. I don't quite get why, but it isn't."

"Hang on, hang on. If you don't pause for breath, at least once, it's hard to keep track. Sometimes you burst your banks when you talk, even if you're not angry. Now, you were going to tell me something that you realised after you left my office."

"Yes, that's it. As the hours passed, I thought again about what I'd told you. I know what it means to steal a child. It's what happened to me. My childhood was stolen. I can't blame anyone for that, but that's the way it is. Part of my life was snatched away. The terrible shame that I get from talking about this isn't because of the idea itself. I feel like I have no right to complain, and it's true that I don't. My parents' suffering was immeasurable, it was greater than anything imaginable. Who am I to declare myself damaged or harmed? Once my mother, on one of the rare occasions when she was able to talk to me, when I was already grown up, told me that for her the worst thing had been knowing that Ellie had died in the Lager. They killed her parents and all her brothers and sisters. But Ellie was the youngest. She was only seven. My mother literally said: 'Ellie represents all that has been lost. The universe. She is humanity crushed. They crushed her. Germans are not flesh and bone. They're something different. They emerged from the bowels of the earth. They are an infection that took over the world. Now they've returned to the depths, but they'll be back. I know they will.' And my father taking the bus home at lunchtime, just to see her for an instant, then hurrying back to work without having time to eat. Like that, year after year. Who am I to feel harmed? Richard is the only child thief. He's stolen my daughters. But I intend to get even. I have no doubt about that. I've written a letter to his boss, informing him of the abnormalities in his behaviour with Karen. His company should know what kind of employee they have on their books."

"Did you do that, Anne? I thought we agreed that you and I would talk before acting."

"In this case there's nothing to talk about, Dr. Palmer. It's a fact. I swore that Richard would pay for the damage he did to me, and I intend to see that through. Plus, I have a moral obligation to report him. As a citizen, and as a victim, it's up to me to alert the community to his behaviour," she added with absolute conviction.

With the caution befitting an incursion into a minefield, I weighed up in a fraction of a second what I had to say. Put a foot wrong, and I would be sent flying through the air.

"OK. But I'm worried about one detail."

"What, Dr. Palmer? Tell me what it is," she asked with a combination of anxiety and bitterness.

"If the accusation you submit has no proof, you could be involving yourself in a serious matter. I get the impression that sometimes you forget that you're involved in a lawsuit for damage to property, threats, and attempts to coerce."

"But all that is false! I admit that I got a stranger's car mixed up with Richard's, and I kicked up a scene in the street, but they can't consider me a criminal!"

"Listen, Anne. That's not for me to judge. You know very well that that's not my job. I just want to make sure that you'll bear in mind what I'm saying, and that you're aware of the importance of doing nothing to jeopardise your own job. It was you who asked me to help you keep it, and that's what I'm trying to do."

"It's true, Dr. Palmer. It's true. I begged you myself, but I just let myself get carried away by these impulses. In those moments everything spins around, it's a great confusion in my head. There's only one thing that sticks out with absolute clarity, and imposes itself with overpowering strength: revenge. But it's not just an impulse. There's something in there, yes, I recognise it, although it's a question I've been reflecting on all my life. Revenge. I've written hundreds of pages, I've read dozens of books. I've documented myself. Revenge was once a noble thing, as noble as the law or courage, but modern life screwed it all up. It turned us into sheep, and led us to the slaughter. We Jews were the first, but that's just the beginning. If we don't react, they'll finish us off."

"It's a little late now, Anne. And an issue like this can't be discussed lightly. It deserves to be talked about in our next session. Now we have to rest a little. You and me both."

"Of course, and sorry to have bothered you again, but I knew that you'd understand the importance of this call. I'm putting together the pieces bit by bit. Thank you. Next time I'll try to write you, so as not to wake you up. Oh, I'm incorrigible! I drive people crazy with my impatience! Richard used to tell me, poor Richard. Look at what I just said. Poor Richard! Do you see? It's incredible, anyway. ..."

"See you tomorrow Anne," I cut in.

"Yes, Dr. Palmer, see you tomorrow. I'm sorry, I'm stealing your time when you should be sleeping. You know that sometimes I can't stop the hurricane that goes off in my head. Thank you. See you tomorrow."

I hung up and got ready to get back into bed. I hadn't had any dinner, but I was too exhausted to get the strength together to rustle up anything. All the same, I made the mistake of having one last look at my email. Deborah Chester, the resident doctor, had sent me the draft of her paper for the psychiatry congress to be held in a few months. My students frequently consulted me on their articles and publications. It was part of my job to supervise not just their clinical work, but also their theoretical contributions. Although I was tired, the sender roused in me more than just professional interest, and I couldn't resist the temptation of opening the attached file. …

"If anyone especially occupied themselves with the term 'cure', to return it to its original sense, it was Heidegger. He often speaks in his work about 'care for the being', something that is directly related to what he calls the 'impropriety' of the being. What is the impropriety of the being? This is a consideration very close to us, because it refers to the helplessness and original defencelessness of the talking being, to the fact that its initial dependence on language makes it a being that initially lacks its own meaning, a natural basis. Taking it a step further, Lacan adds the complication that psychoanalysis introduces in his theory of subjectivity, a complication that, as Freud stated so many times, he did not seek out, but which he found without setting out to do so: the disharmonious nature of sexuality. So the being with which psychoanalysis concerns itself is seriously affected by the decisive incidence of three questions: language, death, and sex. The sum of these three factors, we must admit, do not promise guaranteed happiness, but rather lead us to understand that if we have to think about the cure or the care of the being, we must not think about a contingent affection, i.e., we do not lead from an idea of health that may suffer an accident, but rather that the disorder is consubstantial to the human condition, it is the background of existence, and the being we are concerned with suffers because of the fact of having to confront an inconsistent life, a life in which words confuse more than they clarify, death is incomprehensible, and sex is one way or another disturbing and disproportionate due to excess or lack, in the sense that one doesn't adapt to the ideal of the right amount."

The beginning was too good to let me be beaten by the idea that the dawn reduces distances. Language, death, and sex. Deborah Chester was a fast learner, and her language had depth. I tried to exorcise death through passion for a profession that didn't leave much free time. The vague mystery of sex remained a little further than the dawn, but not so much as to prevent me from dreaming for an instant. I fell asleep thinking rather more about Deborah Chester than Martin Heidegger.

ELEVEN

I was on the verge of thinking it was the best decision, but a decision is something that responds to a purpose. Only someone whose judgment is fit to set criteria, who can identify alternatives, risk the consequences, can decide. I decided nothing. The silence imposed itself as arbitrarily as before. My silence has no reason to be more sensible than what happened. Or maybe it is, but it's all the same.

They say that memory is good for dragging things back from their absence. I'm not so sure that it's really good for that, I actually think that it's good for nothing. It won't be long until everything is forgotten, and they begin again. It's always been that way, although never to such a degree. Maybe the degree isn't what counts the most, but knowing whether we've crossed the absolute boundary, or whether the worst still awaits. They say no, that nothing could be worst. Why are they so convinced? I have my doubts. No one can prove that there won't be a greater, more total evil.

That's why I keep my silence. And let me make a correction: perhaps my silence was a decision, deep down. I saw the place where words end. I lived those years in that place, and I saw things I shouldn't have seen. Things that should never have happened, but did. I saw the place where men are more powerful than God. I'd been told it was impossible, that there was nothing more powerful than

God, but they were wrong. I saw it with my own eyes. God saw it with his own eyes and was powerless to stop it. God is weak, perhaps the weakest and most impotent creature there is. It must be terrible to have people assume such incommensurable power in you, trust in you, and then for it to turn out to be an absurd misunderstanding. Man invented God to cover up his arrogance, but he has done nothing but laugh in his face. It's an invention that no one really believes in.

That's why I keep my silence. Because if what I saw has taught me anything, it's that one can only lie. It's a serious matter, because there's no way out. But that's the way it is. There's no possibility whatsoever of saying anything true. Even though I'm dead, I'm still lucid enough to know that this can lead to a game of whether it's truth or a lie to say that everything is a lie. I too was a student once, and the trick was explained to me. But I won't go into that game, because it's a trick that has gone on for too many centuries. It's the proof that we are easily led by words. Instead, I saw the place where the absolute truth begins, a place without words where no one lied, and where every day, at every hour, every minute, we witnessed the direct exercising of the truth. Most of us there were oblivious to it. We believed the truth was something else. But they woke us up straight away. The Germans have a saying. Something like, "What doesn't kill you makes you stronger." It's true, or almost true. It's also a lie like any other. It all depends on whether you believe it or not. In my case it didn't work, but for one simple reason. The saying very clearly says, "What doesn't kill you." I died, and that's why I didn't become stronger.

How many things one can discover all of a sudden. To be born is to enter head first into a process of domestication. If a human being doesn't speak, doesn't learn to do so, refuses to repeat the millions of silly things he will be obliged to repeat, this is considered reason for concern. It's a disease, a freak of nature, a flaw in the human condition. We all believe that, of course. It's what leads me to think how many things can suddenly be discovered. For example, what a strange idea we have of death. Correction: what a strange idea I had of death.

I mustn't assume a plural that doesn't belong. What did I believe about death, as a young woman brought up in an agnostic family? Naturally, it wasn't a matter that occupied much of my thinking back then. I suppose I believed what most people believe when they don't have the comfort of another life. I was wrong. Death can be something as simple as what is happening to me. My heart beats, I breathe by my own means, I obey the basic needs that make my body work, so that each piece of the strange machinery that makes me up does as it should. Thousands of millions of little, microscopic events occur in my body every second and, as they say, that's life. All that working in unison, like an orchestra made up of countless performers who read their sheet music and play the part they have to play, at the right time, without improvising a thing. However, I'm dead. That means that the wise men are wrong. Life must be something else, something that has little to do with the functioning of this marvellous machine that men bow down to.

The Bible tells the story that men once wanted to build a tower that would reach up to heaven, and because of that God punished them and mixed up their words so that they would never again understand each other. I was in a place where they tried it again, but differently. A tower that would reach to hell, and so that it wouldn't collapse, they suppressed every word. They were no more successful that time, but at least they weren't punished. They will try again. I'm sure they will, because now we know that only hell exists, so no time will be wasted searching for heaven. And when the moment comes to recruit the slaves, no one will remember a thing. History is this: a succession of pauses, of intervals. Am I not right to remain silent? It's hard to answer that question. I have the right, at least. I don't claim to be an example. It's just what happened to me, and perhaps nobody else.

How many things I was suddenly able to discover. You can cover the surface of existence, slip ingenuously among the things of the world, and with a little luck you get to the end without noticing a thing. It partly depends on chance, although not entirely. One fine day, I discovered that we had been left completely alone. That they had turned their backs on us. People whom I would never have expected to behave as they did began to ignore us, to look the other way, to distance themselves as if we'd suddenly become infectious. What had suddenly been revealed to me took its time. The human being is slow-witted. For something to get into their heads, you have to make them bleed. And even then it's incredible the number of arguments that can be made up so that everything fits, to maintain the belief that the world is ruled by sanity, except when an accident happens. It's very hard to convince ourselves that the accident is the norm, and that the attraction toward what is good and beautiful is no more than a brief exception to that iron law. It took me a long time to recognise it, as almost all of us did. When I realised, it was too late, and we were completely alone. Until then we had lived in a dream. One fine day, someone came and started waking the people. At first some resisted, yawned, went on dreaming. But the Alarm wouldn't stop shouting. It shouted so much that even the biggest dreamers ended up waking, giving up their sleep. We were the last ones. We thought the Alarm was part of the dream, and so there was nothing to fear, that it would eventually vanish like everything in the imagination. We were wrong: it snatched us from our sleep too, and on waking we realised that there was nobody left on our side. And that was the end. They called it a Solution. Men know how to do great things with words. With words they put us to sleep, with words they woke us, and with words they took us far away. And once we reached our destination, the words finally ran out, and no one deceived themselves any more.

I prefer silence. Otherwise, I'd have to say things that I don't want anyone to know. It's hard to speak and share out the words between what can be said and what has to be kept secret. Words are very treacherous. That's why I must suppress them. There are many things that I don't want to tell. Things that I've had to do that cause me shame. There is nothing more shameful than surviving, because it inevitably implies the price of a betrayal. That's the way it is. I don't care what other people may think about it, including all the survivors. I respect all their opinions, but no one will change my mind. To survive is to carry the weight of something unforgivable. Of course, the explanation is not as banal as saying that it's the guilt of being alive when others are not. It's not that. I am no longer alive, and yet I haven't stopped feeling that burden. It would be all the same if the sin had been greater, or so tiny that no one could reproach me for it. One survives at the price of a betrayal. But I won't tell mine. I don't want to.

I was born in a small town, north-west of Chemnitz. The name is of no importance, and besides, I hope it isn't there any more. I lived there for my first twenty years, that is, all my life. The rest up to the present is a residual effect of that movement with which it all began. We were a very happy family, and we were surrounded by good neighbours. My father worked in a furniture factory. He was a highly skilled labourer, a good carpenter, and the factory owners were very fond of him. As well as being a great worker, they gave him special consideration because they knew he was a cultured man. My father spoke several languages, read the classics in Latin and Greek. He'd taught himself the languages, by sheer willpower. Sometimes, the factory owners would have my parents over for Sunday lunch, and they would ask my father to read a few verses by French or Russian poets. He had a lovely voice.

I was the eldest of four siblings. Two boys and two girls. When they started waking the people, separating the pure from the impure, at first we didn't notice a thing. My father assured us that such things had always happened, and it wouldn't be long before we returned to everyday life. I'd started studying medicine, and had had to move to Chemnitz. I lived in a residence for ladies there. They were very simple digs, and the owner, a Croatian woman, wore her hair tied up in a tight bow and wore a grey dressing gown of a very thick fabric. The same one in summer and winter. She was prickly, but polite. My brothers and sister went to school, and piano and violin classes in the afternoons. It was unthinkable that any of us should not learn to play a musical instrument to a minimum standard, as at home music, along with books, was part of the air we breathed. It was impossible to imagine anything else.

One morning, I remember it very well because the summer had started and I felt very happy in a new dress that my mother had sewn with her own hands and posted to the residence in a parcel, I was prohibited from entering the university. There had been talk of that for a long time, but we preferred to live as if it were a rumour, something that wouldn't happen. The reality gave us evidence to the contrary every day, although humans are the only species that possesses that strange faculty of not seeing or hearing what they don't want to see or hear. From that moment, we Jews would no longer be admitted into university centres. I didn't know what to do, and decided that I ought to return home. What most grabbed me was the sudden sensation that everything had changed. The town looked different, an eerie stillness could be perceived, and people behaved strangely. Was it my imagination, or did everyone seem to dodge my presence in the street, as if I was no longer part of the same species, as if I had suddenly become an alien thing? I feverishly searched the faces of passers-by, looking for a friendly glance, a smile, a look of recognition, but all I found were masks of indifference or evasive looks. I thought I was dreaming. Could it be that in under an hour an invisible barrier had been raised that nevertheless acted like a barbed wire fence? And that was just a foretaste of what was to come. I wasn't dreaming, no. On the contrary, I had just woken from that dream we all clung to. As I walked, words echoed in my ears, the words of my parents, our friends, neighbours. All those people who shook their heads when they read the news and with indignant voices maintained that the German people would never accept the excesses of that gang of troublemakers. The best part was their arguments. They'd bring in witnesses like Bach and Goethe, as if either of them could stop what was happening. As if music or poetry could soften the Germans' hearts, make them see reason again. Music. We believed in music, in poetry, in the power of the sublime. Later we would learn that music would become the background of annihilation, and there would always be an officer reciting Hölderlin out loud as we walked in line towards the night they had built for us. When I returned to the residence, the owner watched from the door to my room as I packed my modest luggage and, without trying to conceal it at all, she smiled at me. Never, in the year and a half I'd been living there, had I seen her smile. I couldn't understand why she did so just then. I found out later, when chance, if we must call by that name the fact that we are not allowed to know our destiny, caused our paths to cross again. I was no longer in my summer dress, and she had changed her dressing gown for a uniform with leather straps. I saw that smile again several times. A smile that pointed out the next victim, and which in some cases was enough to kill that victim.

The journey home was a real odyssey. There was tremendous chaos in the streets, many people were being detained, mobilised, displaced from one place to another. The people, those repugnant slaves who avidly lick the feet of their master, had been infected with a frenetic enthusiasm. With authentic fervour they all embraced the cause to save their homeland, to clean it of imperfections and impurities, to embellish it by suppressing whatever stood in the way of greatness. Every one of them had become an officer of social hygiene, a faithful servant to the authorities, a vigilante of the new laws, an informer. With astonishing precision, the lives of men now consisted of being a mere piece in this gigantic machinery that had been set in motion. Everyone knew their role and carried out their citizen's obligations with passionate willingness. Human beings always need to obey. Never offer them freedom, for they feel real dread towards it. Take away their master, and you will see how they immediately get down on their knees and beg for the coming of a new one.

It was very dangerous to move around this changed world. I was lucky that in those days the turmoil was so great that, despite the prohibitions on Jews using public transport, I managed to slip through unnoticed and make it to my village. My family was very scared. My father had received a letter of dismissal, written in the bureaucratic language that had imposed itself as a kind of official tongue, given that most people started to use it in everyday conversations. Of course, Sunday lunches with the factory owners had been off the agenda for several months, and the foremen and bosses had stopped speaking to my father. In the last months, before he was fired, they switched him from his usual work, and his new job was to clean the bathrooms. My father was indignant and protested, tried to speak to the owners. He was convinced that they would be able to fix this aberrant injustice, but the owners wouldn't meet with him again. Shortly after, the letter came. That was a terrible blow for him, and when I arrived home I found him thin and weak. My mother was scared, and didn't know what to do. Terrible news was coming in. Hundreds of uniformed men patrolled the streets, terrorising and humiliating our people, and the villagers enjoyed the show. One Saturday morning a mob of the regime's collaborators took all the Jewish women out into the street and forced us to scrub the pavements with buckets of water and hand brushes, on our knees, surrounded by a multitude of neighbours who cackled, insulting us and spitting on whichever part we were cleaning. That grotesque laughter still rings in my ears, expanding in my brain like the ripples made by a stone hitting the water. I hear it every day, multiplied, mixed with the cries of pain and the barking of dogs, the tyrants' thundering voices, the sobbing, the roar of the flames rising up to an indifferent heaven, the shots. It's all I hear. Those sounds have silenced all the others and have left me speechless. I am a puppet whose strings have been cut, and can only hear the echo of the past howling ceaselessly. Joseph says sweet words to me that I want to answer. My daughters barely dare look at me. To them I am a strange ghost inhabiting this house, wandering in her sleep some nights, shouting out what her head hears and her eyes see. Between my eyes and life, a succession of images quickly parades past. They are so clear and so real that they don't let me see anything else. I've forgotten the faces of those who were by my side. I can no longer make them out. It's like a kind of blindness caused by the overlapping memories. By day and by night, with my eyes open and closed, I'm obliged to witness those flashes that never go out, to listen to the terrifying roar of the fevered masses, the drumming of boots marching triumphantly, and the smashing of windows that cover the streets with silver and blood. I know that behind all that are my own, those who still love me, those who survive. But I can't see them, I can't reach out and touch them, feel their kisses and their warmth. I am captive. Joseph managed to get away, but I couldn't. He was stronger than me, and managed to save himself. I stayed behind. I didn't have the guts, or the pain was too much for me. The thing is I'm still here, one more number on this frozen mountain of bodies with no clothes and no name.

TWELVE

Some nights, a sandwich and a glass of milk can come close enough to happiness for me to feel inclined to believe in its existence. So maybe that's the famous pleasure principle! After decades of study and clinical practice, I have reached this extraordinary conclusion. My heart beats with enthusiasm, and I imagine myself speaking on the issue at our next annual conference.

I go over some notes. I don't tend to write much about what my patients say. That popular image of the therapist taking notes while the patient on the coach tries to get out of the fix he's gotten himself into is not usually me. But sometimes, at the end of the working day, I'll scribble a few lines about things that have in some way touched me. It's strange to be part of so many lives, look into their intimate parts without violating them. Witness what they do or intend to do, a depository for grave secrets ciphered in words that sound innocent. All lives are unrepeatable, and at the same time form one single life: something that sparkles for a fraction of a second in the eternity of the universe and disappears just like that. We have done extraordinary things to try to make that last, for that feeling to hold on a moment longer, which have allowed us to take a few steps forward and a hundred steps back. But we never stop trying. They call it history. A curious name. At this time of the night, I wonder why no one has yet discovered the hallucinogenic properties of a sandwich and a glass of milk.

I'm surprised at the similarities between Anne and Jessica. That all-consuming fixation with motherhood, and at the same time the impossibility of being a mother. Anne threw herself into her role, breathing in her daughters' air, without realising she was smothering them to death. From a certain age, they worked out a response that their mother couldn't understand, and which since then she has denounced as a "monstrous" injustice. Jessica, who hasn't even had children, would be incapable of coping for a single minute with that complicated role for which no instruction manual is available. If she were to be given a child she couldn't care for it, she can barely sustain herself. She is also convinced that a fundamental injustice rules her existence. There is something that is always repeated, a tonal base that allows variations in every human being: the feeling that the world is not made for them, that someone took the measurements wrong, or miscalculated the proportions of the ingredients. Is that what madness is? The determined and unavoidable willingness to find the culprit who is behind such disorder? The problem with madness is that it tends to be excessively loaded with reason, too close to the truth, and everyday life is incompatible with such a closeness to the senseless bottom of existence. Living can only be withstood if we admit the incurable discord within us.

I won't be able to save Jessica from a harsh sentence, even though her schizophrenia counts as mitigating circumstances. It's not easy to convince a court that being crazy doesn't always match the commonplace we tend to use when we speak of madness. Sometimes it is something so subtle that it can go completely unnoticed behind an exemplary normality. Jessica is a reserved, shy woman, but in some way she matches the prototype of insanity. Anne is expansive, blatantly gone. You don't have to be an expert to notice the delirious tone of her experiences. She has in her favour the fact that she hasn't committed any more than a series of misdemeanours that do not constitute serious felonies. Also, although she declares herself dead, she's actually still very much alive. Her rage prevents her from succumbing to the terrible melancholy that she fed on for the first years of her life. In Jessica, the suicide impulse lies hidden, without visible signs, and possibly without warnings. I've given very precise instructions as to the close surveillance she requires, although the will to die can overcome any obstacle.

* * *

"I left home when I was seventeen. I don't quite remember what happened. I was confused, very confused. Something was going on in my head. I don't know how to explain it. Whenever I thought, the ideas formed an echo. They repeated themselves, like when you shout in a cave. Yeah, it was more or less like that. But I'm not sure I'm explaining it right."

"I think I understand. Carry on. Try to remember what happened."

"I was very worried. Now it's coming back to me. I had to find Brian. My mother had always asked me to. So one night I went out to look for him."

"You went out in the night to look for Brian? Why that night, precisely? What happened to Brian was many years before, and it was at the age of seventeen that it occurred to you to go out and search for him? I don't understand."

"I'd tried before, too, but I gave up real quick. I was only away one or two days. But that time I didn't want to give up. I kept looking all over. My mom talked to me, talked in my head, like I just explained. Her voice sounded like an echo. She was begging me, I couldn't let her down this time. I had to find Brian. I didn't go back home."

"And what happened with your father? What did he do when you disappeared?"

"By that time my dad didn't live with us no more."

"Where was he?"

"He'd gone south, for work. He couldn't get none here, and they gave him a job in Raleigh. He sent us money every month, till one day he stopped and we never heard from him no more."

"And who were you all living with, you and your brothers and sisters?"

"With my grandmother, my mom's mom. She looked after us, and I also took care of my brothers and sisters. But the social services had to step in when the money ran out. They took them away. I stayed with my granny a few months, then I decided to go look for Brian."

"You've been looking for him all these years?"

"Yeah. I have a photo of him. It's all messed up, but it's the only one I got. I'd like to show it you," she said, looking me in the eye for the first time.

"Sure. I'm dying to see what Brian looked like."

Jessica rummaged in the canvas bag in her hand and took out a very small, passport-size photograph, in which a boy of about one could be seen smiling at the camera. The image was pretty faded and crumpled, and I couldn't make out much. No one could look for a child based on a photo like that. Even though she carried it with her like her most treasured possession, Jessica was guided by a figure etched in her mind. I imagined her wandering all these years, trying to find some trace of Brian in hundreds of kids. Of course, she was completely unaware that if her brother were even alive, he would now be a young man in his early twenties. She was looking for the Brian who her mother was missing, the Brian who lived in that limbo where the dead go when people won't let them ever die.

"He was a gorgeous baby," I said. "It's awful to think that he died so young. It must have been terribly painful for your mother, and for you too. Your mother couldn't accept his death, and that's why she keeps imploring for his return."

As I said these words, I wondered how I should handle the problem I had ahead of me. For several years, the only direction that Jessica had found to guide her in life was the search for her brother, obeying her mother's pleas. Forcing her to accept the impossibility of that mission and to recognise that such a great loss was irrevocable meant tearing away the one thing that kept her tied to life, made her wake up every morning, whether in the street, in a hostel, or in a grotty flophouse, and feel that she had something better to do than throw herself off a bridge or under a train, as her mother had done. Within the complex mechanism of madness, there tends to be an element that acts as a balance, even if it is precarious and may even appear as irrational as the same thing it tries to contain. Loosening that piece means running the risk of sending it all to hell, unleashing demonic forces, provoking the volcano, and incurring the wrath of the gods. But at the same time I couldn't leave things as they were. I had to help her find another reason to go on living, although that wasn't something that could be pulled out of a magician's hat, nor taken from what the therapist deems right for his patient. How should we know what is right for someone? Aren't we made of the same stuff as the person before us? What right do we have to assume the power to know what is good and right? What kind of imposture authorises us, the presumed directors of the conscience, to point out the path to normality? It had taken me a long time to overcome the temptation to save souls, that temptation that assails any therapist on a daily basis, and I wasn't even sure of having completely achieved it. There is an inner resistance that stays alive, like an animal in hibernation, and which sometimes wakes up. It's hard not to succumb to the secret pleasure of worshipping ourselves for the good we think we do for others.

THIRTEEN

"Ah, Dave! This really is an extraordinary case. It's the only reason why I'm willing to forgive your absence these last months. Do you really think I have that much time left? We psychologists are as mortal as bricklayers or gardeners, and for some years I've been defying the laws of nature pretty successfully. But don't be too confident, because any day now you'll hear the news that I've gone straight to hell."

"To hell?"

"I guess it's the most logical place for us. Think about it. Do you think heaven would be the most appropriate place? We have to pay for the sin we commit in not letting people go back to sleep in their bed of ignorance somehow, don't you think? I've always known I wasn't going to get an award for that, no sir. But let's forget about all that and get to the point. Are you still single?"

I smiled. At ninety-two, Doctor Alan Rubashkin maintained the same curiosity I'd seen in him when I started analysis with him. Lean, always impeccably dressed, he possessed a magnetic gaze from which no one could avert their eyes, and a sensitivity that could hit the bull's eye of any soul that passed through his office. His voice was captivating, and his way of listening and intervening had an immediate impact on his patients. Even now, walking slowly with careful movements, his clinical genius remained intact, and I went to him for advice whenever I had a case before me that exceeded my understanding, or caused me to doubt about how to proceed.

A physician and psychiatrist, Rubashkin had begun his psychoanalytical training with Hans Sachs, one of Freud's most celebrated disciples, who had emigrated to the United States. In the 1950s, Rubashkin settled in Paris to complete his studies. In that period he psychoanalysed himself with the master Jacques Lacan, celebrated for breathing new life into the theories and practices introduced by Freud, and on returning to America, Rubashkin set up his own office, which caused a real stir among psychiatry and psychology professionals and psychoanalysts themselves. Some dismissed him, arguing that he was moving away from the established orthodoxy, while others, among whom I had the fortune to find myself, understood that we had the opportunity to immerse ourselves in a body of knowledge that would give us a completely new way of conceiving the human drama and how to approach it. I had also spent some time in Paris and attended Lacan's seminars, in a time of great upheaval when names like Foucault, Deleuze, Guattari, and Derrida contributed to bringing about a promising ideological subversion. Like all promises, it was a glimmer in the darkness of thought, but it left its mark on some. When I came back to the States and heard of the existence of Rubashkin and his practice, I didn't hesitate to start analysis with him. It was a long experience, to which I owe the fundamental aspects of everything I have learned in this trade, and a body of knowledge that is not measured in intellectual terms, but rather as life lessons. Dr. Rubashkin taught me the true meaning of "taking existence seriously", as he used to repeat as he quoted a phrase that his master Lacan had said on one occasion. Taking existence seriously means taking responsibility for what we usually accuse others of, renouncing the shameful pleasure of imagining that we are victims, accepting the consequences of what we have decided, and even what we haven't decided. Accepting that inaction is a form of action, that crying bad luck is an excuse that doesn't work for long, and that, given how hard and unlikely it is that one will not lie to oneself, we should at least have enough courage to ask ourselves from time to time whether we're abusing that custom.

* * *

"Yeah, I'm still single. Since Susan died, I've searched for love in vain. Now I seek company in my work, my books, and a handful of friends I can fool around with as I please, discussing national politics and poetry. They vote Republican, but at least they don't read Danielle Steel."

"What about your son?"

"He stayed in San Diego. He's now laboratory manager, and his wife's had quite a bit of success with her second novel. We see each other a couple of times a year, but we talk on the phone almost every day. How about you, getting by on your own?"

"Of course. I have Nancy, as you know, my lifelong secretary, who helps me with articles and bibliographical searches, and one of my granddaughters drops in once a week to take care of the shopping and such. For everything else I get by just fine. I miss having a woman to soap my back, but I get by with a loofah with a long pole that I got for my last birthday. It's not the same, of course, but now that I'm getting old I'm starting to moderate my aspirations. Tell me, that Latina woman, the one who tried to steal the kid, how many times have you seen her?"

"Three or four. It was quite a job getting her to talk but I got there in the end."

"Yes, you're very skilful, I know. The problem is what we're going to do with what we've found out. On the one hand there's the strictly legal question. Are you still friendly with Judge Delucca?"

"We speak regularly and have dinner now and again. He entrusts me with almost all the cases that come his way. In fact, it was he who sent me Jessica."

"That's good, maybe he can intercede and reach an agreement with the district attorney and the prosecution. Logically, it's necessary that the patient should receive some disciplinary measure for her actions, otherwise the feeling of guilt will bring her even greater problems. But you're right to worry about her. We can't deprive her of her delusion just like that. We need to channel it somehow. If she needs children, we'll have to find some. Talk to social workers, get them to find out where she can do volunteer work in children's homes. It would also be useful if she started some kind of training that would be of use in that line of work. I agree with you that the woman can't look after herself or anyone, and yet, in the framework of an institution and under the eye of professionals and other volunteers, maybe she could find a way to feel useful, and at the same time tone down the automatism of that hallucinatory voice she's been blindly obeying. I'm not sure it'll work, or what her future prospects are. It's a very serious case, with a very clear prognosis. We have to bear in mind that the family structure is atypical. It's rare for a Latin to become a bum, no matter what bad shape they're in. They're part of a community with very strong symbolic ties. They don't tend to let one of their own be left at the side of the road. They have firm principles about that, which is why we have to presume a very deep primary pathology, and not get our hopes up too much."

"Do you think she could be dangerous? With a prior of passage to the act of this calibre, it won't be at all easy for anyone to accept her as a volunteer."

"I know. The poor girl is as harmless as a daddy-long-legs."

"A what?"

"A crane fly. That insect that people get scared of because it looks like a giant mosquito. The problem is that Jessica has crossed the line that the current state of social hypocrisy considers sacred, namely childhood. Of course, it will be far more difficult to convince a jury of the dangers of pharmaceutical companies that push anti-psychotics on children, or the bastards in our union who prescribe them like peanuts. But we already know that the double standard won't allow exceptions. They're the rules of the game we have to play by. All the same, let's be patient. You've managed to get her to say a lot in very few meetings. You've been good, very good, yes sir, because you've managed to go much further than the actual event that brought her to you. I remember I once consulted Lacan on the case of a man who worked in a day-care centre, who had been falsely accused of sexual abuse. Once his innocence had been proven, he came to see me, dogged by a great depression. Lacan listened to me with his usual attentiveness, and said: 'Don't confuse legal innocence with the culpability of desire.' He added nothing more, but he helped me find the way."

"What was Lacan like?"

"I swear you've asked me that before. Besides, you met him."

"But I wasn't his patient."

"He was a curious mix of sage and comedian. His intellectual genius was astounding, as was his clinical perceptiveness. He could be charming and unbearable. He had the extraordinary faculty for seducing even his enemies. Tender, cunning, conceited, incredibly committed to his work. If he deemed it necessary, he was capable of dropping everything to run to a patient's house, holding his hand, and talking him out of throwing himself out of the window. He rather liked me, despite being American. You know what the French think of the Americans. They can't stand that it was us who liberated them from the Nazis, and they laugh at our customs. Of course, then they all dream of making it here, and Lacan was no exception. But our lot didn't pay much attention to him. He didn't try too hard to make a good impression either, at least that was the impression I got when I went to one of his lectures in Baltimore, the last time I saw him. There will never be another man like him, and I'm afraid the locals were not ready at that time to understand the meaning of what he was trying to get across. The neuroscience ideologues had already started their ascent on their way to conquering language, and Chomsky, who was among those present at that lecture, even came to consider that Lacan was a nut. That didn't help much. Lacan at the time was an unknown here, while Chomsky enjoyed great respect as an intellectual. But Lacan loved James Joyce, he identified with him because he was convinced that his work would also feed several generations of university students, and he was right. He didn't live to see it, but American universities now worship his teaching, as you well know. By the way, and before I forget, who's monitoring this patient's medication?"

"I've medicated her myself, and I hope that in the detention centre they're following my instructions."

"Is she under constant surveillance?"

"That's what I requested in my report. Why do you ask?"

"I'm a very old man, Dave. Death and I have tended to converse in recent times, and believe it or not, I've been learning some new stuff. I wouldn't say I've become like Tiresias, but I have my premonitions. The girl has carried out the mission she set for herself, but she's failed. I'm not sure she'll be capable of forgiving herself."

* * *

Two days after my meeting with Alan Rubashkin, Judge Delucca's secretary called to inform me that Jessica Garcia had committed suicide, taking advantage of an oversight by the officers responsible for her surveillance in the penitentiary.

They were investigating how she had managed to get a rope to hang herself in her cell. The staff and some inmates had been with her a few hours before, and testified that she'd seemed calm to them, without any signs of disturbance.

Some people experience immense relief when they finally decide what they have to do.

FOURTEEN

"I met him when I was twenty-two. He was seven years older than me and that made me feel kind of safe. I hadn't had a boyfriend before him. He was the first man I met, and also the last. In my teens, I didn't get many chances to date guys. I was very shy, my mom had passed on to me part of her terror of what awaited beyond the four walls of our house, and sex was totally alien to me. My body turned strange at puberty. I know that at that age it's something that happens to most people, but it was different in my case. I'd stand in front of the mirror, naked, and I'd spend hours looking at myself, or maybe I should say, looking at that image. I'd raise one arm, then the other, move my head from side to side. The image would repeat my movements. It was fun, and at the same time disturbing. I managed to get that puppet to move as if I were pulling invisible strings. I'd make her raise one leg, then the other, I'd make her dance and shake her head, I could even get her to talk. This last thing was the most amazing. The doll talked, like those automatons invented in the Renaissance that had a dwarf hidden inside. But this doll was much better, because it could really talk. I gave her a name, and although I knew that the image was myself, I couldn't help but feel that that it had a life of its own, separate from me, even though I could get it to obey my orders. I called her Norman."

"Norman? A man's name? Why?"

"I don't know. But that gives you an idea of how lost I felt in those years. Then again, I'm not so sure what I thought back then. I knew I was a woman, and that Norman was a boy's name, but I don't think that deep down I understood what that meant. I find it quite funny to remember, but now that I say it, perhaps the first man I met was Norman. It had never occurred to me! The thing is, from that moment, I had a companion. It was an extraordinary thing, a real miracle. The most important thing is that Norman has been faithful to me so far."

"What do you mean?"

"He's still with me. Even when I'm overcome by that feeling of loneliness that leaves me lying in bed for days, it's always Norman who comes to my rescue. I imagine that sounds weird, but that's the way it is."

"Tell me a little more about Norman. He started off as your image, but some time later he took on an existence of his own. Have I understood that right?"

"Absolutely. He's a friend. Maybe my best friend. I think he's been feeling a little jealous lately because I talk more to you than to him! But Norman is very special. Imagine, we've been together almost all my life. I know that he'll never leave me, nor I him. When I started to go out into the world, at first with great difficulty, Norman was there by my side."

"Does Norman speak?"

"Not precisely. I'm the one who speaks, but somehow he manages to transmit to me something that makes me feel more sure about myself. When Richard left me, when the girls turned against me, Norman was my only comfort. I asked his advice on everything, I told him everything that was going on in my head, and that nearly always helped me. Sometimes I've been so down, not even he's been able to do anything, but I don't blame him. You know how far I can go out of my mind and lose all ability to think straight. Why am I talking about this? Ah, I remember! I'd started to tell you about my story with Richard. We'd often be in the university library at the same time. I told him that they'd given me a year's scholarship in Israel to come to the States. Richard was just finishing his engineering degree. We didn't know each other at all, but one day he asked me if I wanted to go to the cafeteria for a drink, and that was how it all started. It was very complicated at first, because as I said, sex was an uncomfortable area for me. In that sense I have to admit, despite my resentment towards him now, Richard was very patient and understanding. Bear in mind that I had a real dread of my own body, especially anything related to sexuality. You understand me, right? If I tell you that I'd never even … I find this really embarrassing to talk about … touched myself, you'll understand. So if I couldn't do it to myself, the very idea of someone else doing it to me was completely unbearable. I think that poisoned our relationship from the beginning. We could never forgive each other. I'm convinced that Richard was frustrated, I can understand that, and I hated him because I felt forced to do something that revolted me. The only good thing about my present situation is that I've freed myself of that dreadful obligation. Plus, Norman was in the middle, which made me even more uncomfortable. Richard never knew a thing about Norman, or at least I don't think he did. No, I'm sure he didn't. He did his thing, deep down he couldn't give a damn about what was happening to me. He was only interested in Karen. All his attention was on her. When there was nothing else for it but to give in to Richard's demands, I went into a state of panic. Then Norman was there, on the one hand calming me, but on the other hand increasing my shame. The problem wasn't exactly that I couldn't feel anything, in fact I couldn't, but rather the impression that Richard, when he took me, was seizing something inside me. My thoughts, my organs, everything. I'd lose the notion of time and space, something similar to what I've read about amnesia. It seemed that my life, my memories, the ability to recognise and name things, were erased for ever. It's very hard to explain this, because the truth is that later I found out that the experience lasted just a few seconds, but for some reason I felt it took much longer to go away.

"At the start of our relationship, Richard was receptive, but at the same time he couldn't hide how strange he felt about that situation. Over time we grew apart, although we still lived together and got on with each other. After a few years married, I started to feel the need to have children."

"To have children, or to be a mother?" I asked, knowing full well that I was going a little too deep.

Anne was silent, thoughtful. After a minute, she found her answer.

"That's a very good question. It sounds like just a play on words, but I understand perfectly what you're getting at. You're trying to tell me that perhaps it was a question of finding an identity, more than anything."

"That's possible. But how did that come about? Do you remember at what moment in your life that need appeared?"

"Isn't it normal in a marriage?"

"Of course, but that doesn't mean we can't try to reconstruct the moment," I said, trying not to arouse any susceptibility in her about the issue, as motherhood was part of her sacred mythology. I was trying to find out how someone who had such a tormented relationship with her own body could at the same time want to put it through things like gestation and birth. It was clear that Anne was willing to pay any price necessary to become a mother.

"When I made the decision to build my life with Richard here in the States, I carried on with my master's studies and also completed my degree at the conservatoire. Richard had an important position at an insurance company, and I was able to get my first job teaching history of music at a private academy. We lived well, more or less, although rather isolated.

Richard didn't have a very smooth relationship with his family, and not too many friends either. My social life was virtually non-existent, partly because I was a foreigner, but above all because of how reserved I was. In time, I started to realise that nothing much had changed. Living far away from my parents didn't noticeably improve the feeling of oppression that I'd always had. I was neither freer nor more daring. I was still the girl who tried to hide her existence. My mother told me on one occasion that in Germany all the Jews at first tried to use that strategy, to go as unnoticed as possible. But the Nazis wouldn't allow it, and decreed all these laws and regulations so that the Jews could be easily identified. At first, some tried to rebel, but they had no choice but to obey, as the authorities' punishment could lead them to the concentration camps. My poor mother, once she was free and had emigrated to Israel, could never experience again that feeling of being alive, without the need to hide herself away. I was born in the shadow of that shame. I grew up breathing in that fear, contaminated by nocturnal visions of a woman for whom survival meant an infinite torment. Richard promised to be the cure for all that, but after the first years of marriage he started to distance himself, leaving me more and more alone. His excuse was work, that classic alibi of weary husbands. He'd lose patience easily and couldn't stand my depressive crises, which appeared to have gone away for a time, but then came back again with the same frequency and intensity. The pills didn't work too well, and I started to get fat quickly. I felt so wretched, and the worst thing was that I had no one to talk to. My father would often call, anxious to know how I was, but I didn't want to worry him. He had enough on his plate already without adding concern for a daughter who, as well as having left him on his own, couldn't even offer him a reason for happiness. I'd pretend to be in a good mood, I'd tell him that things were good, and tried to divert the conversation towards the subject of my mother. But he's a very special man, and he had a kind of telepathic understanding with me. He could guess everything from the tone of my voice, although at the same time he'd play along with me. I'm sure he knew what was going on, but he respected my privacy. He made me feel like he was close to me, that I could count on him, that I still had the same place in his heart, and that was a comfort to me. But at the same time I could also perceive his deep sadness, his tired breathing, his terrible sacrifice to go on with a life whose only purpose was to look after a woman who inhabited a faraway land from which she would never return. He's a very good man. When he calls me, he asks about his granddaughters. He knows they don't live with me any more, but he acts like he doesn't know. He doesn't ask to speak to them. And it hurts me that my daughters aren't capable of calling him once in a while. I don't get it. It's true that they haven't had much contact with him because of the distance, the fact that my parents couldn't come and visit, and we didn't have the money to go and see them. We couldn't send the girls on their own, either, when they grew up, because of the state my mother was in. The poor things were never normal grandparents. But now Karen is twenty-three and Sophie nineteen, the kind of age when you feel compassion, even for grandparents you've hardly ever spoken to. Plus, my daughters know their story, the tragedy they lived through, but all the same they've washed their hands of them, just as they have of me. At night, when I think about all this, I want to die, or at least sleep for ever. I can't stand it. I can't stand the idea of Richard doing this to me. Do you think my daughters will one day realise the hurt they've caused their mother? Oh, please, don't answer that! Forget it. I'm a dumb woman who asks dumb questions."

"It's not a dumb question at all. But it's very hard to answer. Now it's my turn to ask. We've spoken a lot about your marriage, but I confess that so far I haven't understood why you broke up," I said in my most innocent tone of voice. Of course, it was clear that Anne's husband, unlike her father, couldn't stand her madness. Nor could her daughters, who seized the opportunity to flee from a mother who would turn them into hostages of her own despair. But although this was clear to me, it was fundamental that Anne try to understand some of all that, instead of continuing to cling to her theory of an evil Richard. I had my doubts about whether she could do it. The delirious idea that father and daughter had an incestuous relationship was a very strong construct and hard to tear down. While Anne was capable of sustaining long conversations in which she showed a profound and often serene sense of reflection, her delusion remained intact, stuck to the bottom of her thoughts like barnacles to the hull of a ship.

"Everything snowballed after Karen's crisis, when we had to hospitalise her because of how advanced her anorexia was. I was dead against it, and I took on the medical team and Richard himself, who had taken their side. Richard always took anyone's side but mine. He would judge everything I said and did, and that time was no exception. We had several meetings at the hospital, and they finally succeeded in driving me crazy, to the extent that I had one of my fits of rage and attacked a psychiatrist, a rude woman who was acting smart. I insisted they should leave it to me. Who better than a mother to know what her daughter needs? My girl was going through a bad time, and I wasn't going to allow her to be locked up in that asylum."

"I don't think it was an asylum," I said softly.

"It's the same thing. Asylum, hospital, neither is the right place for a little girl. A daughter should be with her mother, she should be fed and nurtured by her mother, not by nurses who are just doing a job. It's all the same to them if they're dealing with people or farm animals. I was arguing this point when that stupid woman, and forgive me Dr. Palmer, I know that I'm talking about a fellow psychiatrist, but there's a very clear difference between you and that revolting woman, that doctor dared to blame me for what was happening to Karen. She said that I smothered her as a mother, and that Karen's anorexia was a way of rebelling against me. Therefore, the best thing for us was to be separated for a time. When I heard that, I lost control of my senses and grabbed her neck. I was ready to kill her with my own hands. Eventually my husband and a security guard managed to get me off her, but the most terrible thing was that Richard didn't stand up for me. To make matters worse, he agreed with the doctors, and said I'd had one of my fits, as he used to say. He'd say that a lot, 'one of your fits'. He said that I should be grateful they weren't going to sue me. I mean, on top of everything I have to thank these people! Again, to my husband I was the crazy one, the disturbed one, the sick one. That was how he saw me. All our arguments ended the same way, and I started to realise that he was provoking me so that I would end up having one of my 'fits', and that way his theory would be confirmed. So I realised that I was lost, just as my mother had been the day she was taken away with her family. Lost, alone, with no one to defend me. With Karen hospitalised, and Sophie more distanced than ever, I fell into a stupor that left me bedridden for two or three weeks, I can't remember now. I couldn't believe what was happening, but I knew very well what that meant. My parents had experienced it, they'd been through something like this, through the terrifying revelation that the unimaginable can become real. I was in a kind of coma. You must know that state, I think they diagnosed it as catatonia. I was embalmed, floating in space, far from everything, but I still had a minimum current of mental energy that allowed me to think. I was very weak, but even so I didn't stop thinking."

"And what did you think about?"

"It was very strange, Dr. Palmer. I've never told you about it, because it's very hard to explain."

"Would you like to now?"

"I'll try. But first let me correct myself. I said think, but it wasn't exactly that. It wasn't that I thought. The truth is, I heard. I heard a voice that at first sounded very far away, almost inaudible. It went on like that all the time, but I ended up getting used to it, and I started to understand what it was saying. Almost a whisper, a wind carrying sounds that formed words first, then complete sentences, a long monologue that kept me company during those days."

"Do you remember what that voice said?"

"Something, yes. Not all, but perhaps the most important parts."

"Was the voice familiar to you?"

"Of course, Dr. Palmer," Anne replied with a sad, shy smile. "It was my mother's."

FIFTEEN

Don't think I don't understand what's going on any more. My silence doesn't mean I've turned stupid, or that my brain's stopped working. But I'm captive. The others have managed to escape, turned into smoke, but not me. I'm a prisoner. It says so clearly, here on my arm. Look and you'll see a number. One day, everyone will wear a number, not just us. Maybe they'll stamp it in a more sophisticated, painless way, but it will be the same. A number. Everything can become a number. It's very practical, and the Germans have always been practical people. "Über alles", "Above everything", as the anthem goes. One adds or subtracts, multiplies or divides, as necessary. Four very useful operations that can be applied to human beings. The Germans managed to use them very efficiently. They always will, because they are the chosen people, no doubt about it. Who came up with that absurd theory that we Jews were the chosen ones? Maybe it was once true, but we were terribly naïve not to realise that the phrase was incomplete. Chosen for what? Now we know. The true chosen ones, the authentic chosen ones, are the Germans. They didn't wait for God's judgment to proclaim themselves chosen. They did it themselves. Once again, very practical. Chosen to exterminate everyone else. It is written. "Über alles." Two words. Two words are enough. Even one word might be enough. Or none.

Have I told you about Uncle Itzig? He was the elder of my two big brothers. No, I haven't told you much about him. A strong, tall boy. His hands were so big that, despite my father's better efforts, he was incapable of playing the violin. His teacher talked him into trying the cello, and then things changed completely. Itzig had an innate gift. We other siblings had a good ear, we weren't bad at music, but none of us would've amounted to much, if we'd lived. Itzig, on the other hand, was a real artist, and when he was fourteen he joined the orchestra in Chemnitz, conducted by the great Brunstein, who talked to my parents, explained that the boy had an outstanding talent, and that they were to send him to Berlin to pursue his studies. Brunstein offered to put in a good word himself so that Itzig would get a scholarship, but shortly after Brunstein was expelled from his post, in accordance with Reich law, and it all came to nothing. Itzig never played in an orchestra again, until one of the camp officers found out about his talent and named him director of music, and ordered him to put together an orchestra to play by the gas chambers. You know how Germans love music. They're very cultured people, and adore music on all occasions. Their aesthetic sense is so refined that they considered it uncouth not to accompany mass executions with appropriate music. Why not give annihilation that exalted touch? Besides, Uncle Itzig would have the chance to repair the injustice that had been done unto him. He'd been kicked out of the orchestra, but now he was being offered no less than the chance to lead a new one, and on top of that, made up of the musicians of his choosing. The Oberbefehlshaber, or camp commandant, suggested it as a kind of moral reparation, and couldn't understand why Itzig would turn him down. How could that stupid, arrogant Jew have the gall to refuse such an offer? The commandant pulled out all the stops to persuade him, even went so far as to treat Uncle Itzig almost like a normal person. He asked him into his office, offered him a cigarette, and then furiously pounded his majestic desk again and again when Itzig refused.

The orchestra finally gave its inaugural concert. They found a different conductor, and Uncle Itzig was hanged from a cello string. While the musicians played, and the lines of the wretched shuffled into the gas chamber, my brother's body swung gently, swaying to the melody. I know this because one of the violinists survived, and I happened to make his acquaintance in Israel.

No, don't be surprised. At first I couldn't believe what was happening either, and that's considering that, compared with what came later, the beginning was merely a succession of humiliations, abhorrent but nothing fatal. Everything was carefully organised in stages. It's true that at first there were a few amateurish attempts, groups that let them themselves get carried away by their emotions too much. They were so grotesque, even the Germans considered them tasteless. Smashing up shops, beating up pensioners in the streets, breaking windows. It was criticised as unaesthetic, a deplorable spectacle that showed an utter lack of distinction. So the Party quickly changed tack, started using their heads instead of their hearts. Numbers were the most practical thing here. Numbers have no heart. They just do their job, which is to count. This is the principle of efficiency. That's where they started. Counting us. Finding out how many of us there were. Even we didn't know! From that moment on, everything went smoothly, and we found out something very important, perhaps mankind's greatest discovery: everything is possible. Phrases like "That's impossible!", "But that's absurd!", "How are we supposed to think that such a thing ...?", and "You're not expecting me to believe that ...?" were forever excised from the human vocabulary. They are sometimes said, from force of habit, but we now know that they are no more than an echo of our past ignorance. There's one phrase that is even more abominable: "Never again". That one is the height of ignominy.

One needn't be surprised, or think that's all in the past. On the contrary, this has only just begun. It's behind each and every thing that surrounds us. It's concealed in the little details, in the well-being we enjoy, in the prevailing peace, in the messages of forgiveness, in the compensation they send us in every corner of the globe. Our hands are stained, too, because when it comes down to it, we've accepted that money. More numbers. Whereas, Uncle Itzig died pure, pure as he'd always been. His enormous hands, caressing the cello strings until they produced the most beautiful sound the human ear can hear, those hands stayed clean. They never touched what shouldn't be touched.

We must be prepared, because at any given moment we might hear the sound of broken glass again, but then we'll know what's up. That's why we should forget nothing, forgive nothing. It's too late for me, because I couldn't escape. But you've got time. You can still do it. Don't stand for it. Don't let them fool you.

They always insisted on trying to convince me that I managed to survive. That I was one of the few people who didn't die on that march, that I even managed to slip away and take refuge in the forest, where I wandered with a few others for almost a year. Joseph was one of them. We met there, in the depths of that frozen darkness, for it was winter, and we had no shelter and couldn't light a fire, since the surrounding population was willing to collaborate until the dying seconds so that none of us would be left alive. It was odd. They knew that it was all over, in fact news was coming in of the Russians' advance, exterminating every living being they found in their path. Animals they ate. Humans they raped and burned alive, or shot on the spot. The order was to wipe out as many Germans as possible, regardless of age or sex. Revenge came very late, but at least it came. They didn't have time to finish, because it would've taken a few more years. The Russians were never as organised as the Germans, and they did the job in a manner true to themselves, without a great deal of refinement.

Joseph. I was sick. I was consumed by fever and hunger, and he swore he wouldn't let me die. I let him do what he had to do, and to this day I don't know how to repay so much love, but I was already dead, because as I said, I saw more than anyone should ever have to see. There will come a time when human beings will have seen it all, and then there will be no more humanity. It will be something else, another kind of being, hard to classify, no doubt, given that no living being is capable of seeing it all. The fly sees the world it needs to see. The snail perceives only what matters to its survival. A horse can make out only what's part of its surroundings, and is even capable of learning to see some new things, but not many. Man is the only being who has managed to see beyond what matters to him. As long as he hasn't seen it all, he will continue to be a man. Soon, very soon, there will be nothing new left for mankind to see, and then it will die out, and give way to another entity, a being that will need a different name. I am a foretaste of that transformation. But Joseph doesn't understand, and persists in caring for me, in trying to save me, in luring me back to the land of the living. Maybe this is his vocation, maybe he took to heart what our forefathers taught us: "To save one man is to save all mankind." Might we Jews have committed the sin of pride? Because, sincerely, I find that phrase completely idiotic, as idiotic as its opposite: that to kill one man is to kill all mankind. Maybe if we'd accepted that there was no possible salvation for us, things would've been a little better. But Joseph doesn't think of these things, nor did he think of them back then, when that little group of people were holding out, hoping for a miracle. We'd dug a hole in the frozen earth for shelter, covered it with branches, moss, snow. Inside, we gave each other a little warmth, and Joseph would venture out at night like a little animal to search in the moonlight for something for us to eat. Berries, roots, mushrooms, the odd bird that had frozen to death, even a rabbit he once managed to hunt, I don't remember how he did it, and of course we had to eat it raw. I think after that I couldn't eat any more. You know all too well what I'm like with food. If you've ever wondered why I behave so strangely at the table, there's your answer. I'm very sorry that you all had to suffer my quirks, but I haven't been able to get over that, it's etched not just in my brain, but also in my throat, on my tongue, on my lips. Raw flesh has the taste of barbarism, and burned flesh the smell of horror.

They entered the village at night, and flushed us out with dogs and whips. The locals watched from their windows, and some came out into the street so as not to miss the show. You know how in a small town everything can be reason for curiosity. They put us on trucks where we stood, starving, parched, crammed in with our own filth, and travelled through the night to a detention camp. Your grandparents were set apart with other old folk and people who couldn't walk, or had symptoms of disease. An officer took it upon himself to make the selection. It all happened so fast. The machine guns quickly produced a pile of corpses that other soldiers doused in petrol and set alight. The fire rose high into the night, the flames stretching out like arms to touch the sky. Then something terribly strange happened. The world stopped moving. We all stood stock still. The prisoners, the soldiers, the fire, the smoke. We became a photograph. I lost all contact with my body, as if I'd been injected with a powerful anaesthetic that kept me awake but without feeling. The silence was total and all I could do was watch. I saw the faces of soldiers and officers contorted with madness, the mountain of corpses twisted by the flames, the dread reflected in the prisoners' eyes. My parents were being consumed in that slaughter, but I couldn't translate that sight into the language of the senses, simply because my body had disappeared.

And I never could recall at what moment the rest of us were forced to climb aboard the wagons of that train that took us to hell.

What does it mean to die? No one knows for sure. It's an unsolved mystery, perhaps the only one left, perhaps the only one that matters. Humans have cracked all the enigmas, solved all the equations, measured every single thing in the universe. If you really think about it, and none of us ever has, such knowledge serves no purpose whatsoever. And the only mystery that still retains its grandeur is one that has no answer, and it never will. Death. When do we die? Do we die when our heart stops beating, or our lungs resign from their post? Do we die when we lose consciousness, and enter that infinite swoon that doctors call an irreversible coma, about which nothing is known, not even whether the person in the coma suffers, cries inside, or feels the absence? Do we die when the thing that rouses us each morning and gets us going, call it desire, need, duty, inertia, or simply habit, for some reason one day breaks for ever? We don't know. But I am convinced that that night, as the fire roared and the flames towered in the air, I died.

Perhaps death is just that. Standing still, completely still, doomed to watch a great fire that is never quenched.

SIXTEEN

"I'm sorry, Dr. Palmer. I know I shouldn't abuse these calls, but it couldn't wait until tomorrow."

"What's the matter, Anne? Do you know what time it is?"

"No, I don't. I spend the whole night walking the streets. I can't stop. I think I left my watch at home, and my glasses too. I don't know where I am. Please forgive me, but I swear it's an emergency this time. Yes, that's it. An emergency. I feel so stupid, I've lost a shoe somewhere as well. It's unbelievable that this is happening to me at my age. Normal people don't lose their shoes in the street, do they? Something's happened ... I've done something I shouldn't have done. I couldn't help myself. This terrible fear came over me, fear that you wouldn't want to treat me any more. I know I'm a very difficult, bothersome patient, Dr. Palmer, and I try to control myself, but sometimes I can't. I swear that this has been one of those times. ..."

"Calm down, Anne. Everything's all right. And of course I'm going to continue treating you. I don't see any reason why I can't continue therapy with you, unless you've reported me or something like that," I said, trying to lighten her mood with a little comedy.

"God help me! I'm completely crazy, but not that crazy. You see, today I managed to speak to Karen on the phone."

"Karen? Your daughter? But isn't that good news?"

"Yes, but the thing is it didn't go very well. I didn't behave like I should've, and now I really regret it. I screwed it all up, once again. I think Richard's right. I'm a hopeless case. I've messed up my marriage, my daughters reject me. My life makes no sense. I'm a failure, Dr. Palmer. A real failure. I thought at least I was a good mother, but I'm not even that."

"Wait, wait a minute. You have to tell me what happened. All the details. Don't start with the conclusions."

"Well, last week it was my birthday."

"You didn't tell me."

"It's just that since the divorce and all, it's not a good day for me, I prefer to forget it, take it as any other day. But this time I fucked up, I really fucked up. I'm a fuck-up and fucking idiot who just isn't needed. That's it, no one needs me."

"Please, stick to what we're talking about. Start from the beginning. You were saying that last week was your birthday."

"So I had a bad idea, because I knew that Karen and Sophie wouldn't call me, or send me a card, or a text message, nothing."

"A bad idea. What idea?"

"I went to one of those machines they have in the subway, those photo booths, and I had my photo taken. Not the little ones, I chose the biggest size. Then I wrote something on the back."

"Yes?" I said, encouraging her to go on. I could hear she was out of breath, as usual, on the other end of the line, but for some reason she stopped talking. Then I realised that her voice was choked by her sobbing, and that she couldn't go on with the story. "Take it easy, Anne. Calm down. I'm here, on the telephone, sitting at my table where I read and write at night. I'm going to wait until you can go on telling me what happened. We have all night."

"Thank you, Dr. Palmer, it's just that I feel so ashamed. On the back of the photo I wrote something terrible, threatening. 'You'll never see me again.' I put the photo in an envelope and I sent it addressed to my daughters by urgent mail so that it would arrive at Richard's house on the morning of my birthday. When they opened it, they phoned me. They thought I was going to commit suicide, and it's true that what I wrote could make someone think that."

"And what did you want them to think?"

"I don't know, maybe that was what I wanted. I manipulated them, it was a low blow, I admit that, but I didn't know what to do to get to speak to them. It was Karen who called me. I tried to explain what was happening to me, but she didn't want to listen. I asked her to put her sister on. It was no use, Sophie wouldn't come to the phone. So I lost my nerve, flew into a rage, shouted at them, insulted them, and hung up. Now it really is over, I know that for sure. It's all over."

At one in the morning, after a long day's work, it wasn't easy to find the right words to respond to what Anne had told me. Could I really tell her that "to everything there's a solution", or "I'm sure that in a few days things will settle down", or any other idiotic phrase to inspire "positive thoughts" and "self-confidence"? I couldn't let Anne down. I couldn't deny that she was dead right, that life is fucking hard, and that her chances of having a relationship with her daughters, at least in the short term, were practically nil. There was this lethal factor in her that leads so many people to do the thing they most flinch from, to make their most terrifying nightmares reality and confirm their worst expectations. It's a demonic larva that hibernates within us, and which we usually keep dormant thanks to the help of the desire to live, to love, the immemorial Eros that fights to keep us clinging to existence. But life is not the same for everyone, and on some occasions, Eros gets wounded. Then the suicidal tendency takes over the controls and pushes some people towards the abyss. That struggle, whether the happiness preachers like it or not, is as old as time, and the only way to deal with it, which doesn't necessarily mean stop it, is to admit that it's serious.

"I admit that you've really put your foot in it this time, Anne. And if you thought that for that reason I would stop treating you, it's because you know that you've hidden something important from me, something you've done despite our agreement that you wouldn't do anything without talking it over with me first. I'm not going to scold you for that, as I know full well that no one can totally keep that promise, but what happened has made things very difficult for you. Please, don't try to force your daughters to see you, at least for now. From what I can see they would prefer to avoid any kind of meeting. I know it's painful, but it will be much more painful if you keep exposing yourself to rejection. I don't know whether there's a way to reconciliation, but this certainly isn't it. I'll see you tomorrow, Anne."

"Yes, Dr. Palmer. I'll be there, as always."

* * *

How far can our power to cure go? In the years I've spent listening to lives without losing my capacity for amazement, I've continued to ask myself that question. My work is to move in this tight space where therapeutic success lives side by side with failure. And if I ever get something approaching what can be reasonably hoped for, it will depend on that man, or that woman, consenting to a new way of existing, in which pain ceases to be the only foundation that brings meaning to their lives. Human beings cling to their symptoms like castaways to driftwood. But the most surprising thing is that when we try to rescue them, they prefer to grasp on to that float. In fact, they'd drag us along with them if they could, and the boat in which we've come to respond to their cry for help. Deep down in everyone, there is the dark temptation to immerse ourselves in evil, like when we look down from a high balcony and are overcome, for a near-imperceptible amount of time, by the idea of surrendering ourselves to the mysterious call of the void.

* * *

"I think I've caught myself a fine cold, Dr. Palmer. So you'll have to excuse me, because when I sneeze it's very loud. It rained a lot last night, and as you know I spent the night wandering the streets. At some moment my shoe came off, but I was so worked up that I didn't even realise, until after a while I started to notice that people were looking at me weird, and then I realised what was up. You got any Kleenex? I couldn't find any at home. I've been having an awful day. Everything's going wrong, so wrong, you know? I wanted to buy Kleenex at Walgreens, but there was no money on my credit card, I don't know why. I haven't had time to go by the bank and find out. I'm really scared that I might have been fired. I've been on leave for three months, and any minute now I'm going to lose my job. I think that's how they do it. First they cancel your credit card, then they cross you off the list, and ..."

Her sneeze, just as she'd warned, was like an earth tremor. "Excuse me. They cross you off the list and that's that. On the street. My father told me once. They used to do it like that, overnight. You appeared on one list, and you were out of a job. My grandfather, my father's father, was a doctor, like you. An old-school doctor, you know, those who used to do a bit of everything. The whole village liked him. He'd do births, whatever came up. And then they decreed the laws prohibiting Jews from practising their profession, and my grandfather had to stay at home. At first some neighbours would still go to him, but they stopped pretty soon. It's the system, the fucking system. I don't know if my grandfather's credit card was cancelled, maybe there weren't cards back then, it was the only good thing about those days, but he ended up broke. Imagine if the same thing happens to me. What am I going to do? How am I going to ...?"

A second tremor shook my office, and blew a few papers off my desk. In addition to her cold, Anne was in a state of agitation that left her breathless.

"Wait, don't go on like this. Your credit card probably doesn't work because the magnetic strip is damaged, no one's going to fire you from your job, and fortunately the Nuremberg laws no longer apply, not even in Germany. When you leave here, you'll go to the bank and check that everything's in order. They'll probably give you a new card. Let's not waste time on this story. The important thing is what you told me last night."

"What I told you last night. Yes. What I told you last night. Let me think. What did I tell you last night? Ah, now I remember! The shoe. Yes. No. Ah, you mean the photo, right?! Of course, the photo! I told you about what had happened with the photo. I can't understand it. Why did I do that, Dr. Palmer? It was a few days before my birthday, and I knew. I knew, and I wasn't wrong, no. No one would call me. I'm lying, not no one. My father called me, that's right. He never forgets. And he sent me regards from mother. I don't know if my mother remembers my birthday. I haven't spoken to her for a long time. My father is, what's the word? Her spokesperson. That's it. Her spokesperson. He always has been. He wanted us to know that our mother loved us very much, even though she didn't speak. My sister didn't seem to care about that too much. She went her own way when she was very young, went to study in Tel Aviv, and when she was eighteen she left for London. We talk now and again, but not so much. She was here at home once, and I went to London with Richard twice, making the most of some business trips he had to make. But my sister and I don't talk much, although we do get on with each other. I think that she, well, maybe I'm speculating too much, she thinks I'm strange and ... I'm going to sneeze again, Dr. Palmer, hold tight."

I was now prepared, and held on to my desk.

"I don't remember what I was saying."

"Your father called you to wish you a happy birthday."

"Yes. And my sister too, I have to say. She doesn't every year, sometimes she forgets, but this time she remembered. But I knew that my daughters wouldn't, and I was suffering a lot because of it. I don't deserve this, I assure you. I've loved them with all my heart, and Karen should never have done this to me, stopping eating like that. Everyone attacked me, I had no one to fight my corner. My father never knew about that story. He definitely would've fought my corner. He always did. But I didn't want to tell him, the poor man had enough already with his own problems. And then it happened to me. I was the one who stopped eating. But I have to explain the photo. I wanted to receive a gift. It's been many years, since Richard and I split up, since anyone gave me a gift. Well, except Norman. He does give me something at Christmas. Every year. I'll tell you about that some other day. So I went to get my photograph taken. At that moment I had no other intention than that. Get my photo taken. I don't know what got into my head. It was afterwards, when I saw the photo, that it occurred to me to send it to the girls. I didn't mean to frighten them. I wanted them to know that … I'm confused. It was a mistake, a terrible mistake. I shouldn't have written that on the back of the photo. You know what horrible pictures those machines produce, and I was really shocked when I saw myself. "Am I this woman?" I asked myself. "Am I this woman I see in the photograph, an obese woman of indistinguishable hair colour, her face bloated with medication?" I wanted to take another photo, and I went back down to the subway to look for the photo booth, but I must've gone in through a different entrance because I couldn't find it. I asked the people running along the corridors and the platforms, but in this city no one has time to answer that kind of question. I kept the photo I already had."

"And you wrote on the back: 'You'll never see me again.'"

"Oh my God! How do you know?"

"I'm not a mind reader. You told me last night."

"Of course, I told you. It's true."

"'You'll never see me again.' It's a phrase that seems very simple. It's understandable."

"Yes, it's understandable. But I don't know what it's leading to. I think it's trying to make me think about something."

"I mean that although those words seem understandable, I don't understand them entirely. And neither do you. That's what I'm trying to say, Anne. Just that. And now you say that you couldn't believe what you saw in the photo. That often happens. A photograph is ultimately a very strange thing. Especially a photograph of oneself."

I could hear Anne gasping, a sound so familiar to me in the moments when her verbal diarrhoea eased up a little and she started to take my words in, as if she were submitting them to a careful process of analysis. The sneezing stopped, and a long silence fell. Some thick tears came to her eyes, slid down her cheeks, and one of them remained suspended on the tip of her nose, undecided whether to fall.

"You're absolutely right. How strange that was. It could last for hours. Hours standing, locked in my room, looking at myself in the mirror on one of the closet doors. A full-body mirror. 'Can mirrors see?' I'd ask myself. 'Do mirrors look at us?' It was amazing to witness what happened there. As the afternoon passed and the light coming in through the window gradually faded, the image would change. It became more and more distant, until it would disappear completely. Mirrors look at us too, Dr. Palmer. I'm sure of that. I knew it from the first day I discovered what it is with them. They look at us but they can't talk. It's sad. Until after a year, more or less, I managed to get the image to talk. I'd studied it closely all that time. I made it turn its head, move its hands, its arms. No it wasn't just me in the mirror, but also that figure I finally managed to give life to. Then it started to talk. And from the mirror, Norman was born. I think I've already told you about him."

"Yes, and you also said that some day you'd tell me more about Norman."

Anne looked from side to side, then leaned in a little towards me, searching for my complicity.

"Christmas is nearly here, Dr. Palmer. So it would be a good opportunity for us to talk about Norman."

SEVENTEEN

There are certain things that can never be understood. It sometimes happens that something small, infinitely small, manages to break free of the ominous bonds of Fate. Now that everything appears to have passed—although believe me, it's just an illusion, as it's still alive, hidden behind the new decoration they've put up for us—the experts have come out all over the place and started to talk and interpret. I'm not saying that what they propose isn't for a good cause. That's as far as I'll go. Nor am I saying that some time, in the future, maybe in a thousand years, someone will have a bright idea that will enlighten us with the reason for what happened. Personally I don't think so, but I don't want to be too pessimistic either. What I'm sure of is that we were that microscopic particle that the great machinery couldn't vacuum up, and that has no explanation whatsoever.

As you can imagine, not a single day has gone by when I haven't thought about that. I think about it while I'm on the bus to work, when I'm on my way back, when the three of us eat around the table, when I take your mother her meal in her room, when I listen to the radio, and also at night, in the minutes before I fall asleep from exhaustion. I even think about it in my sleep, as I have the impression that my dreams are nothing but that, the continuation of that eternal thought that will only come to an end when my death leaves it homeless.

I suppose others have had the same fate, others who were also tiny particles diverted away from that drain that swallowed everyone, they must think similar things, or perhaps not. I don't know. I've never spoken to anyone about this. Do you remember the Schönenbergs, who lived across the road? Sometimes they'd ask me over for tea and tell rabbi stories. It was a shame your mother wouldn't join me, because Eric Schönenberg made me laugh a lot. He had a special knack for that kind of story. I remember when summer came, and there was nothing else for it but to wear short-sleeved shirts, we would ignore the fact, as if they were birthmarks, that he, his wife, and I wore the address of hell etched on our arms, as we sat in the garden and sipped our cups of tea that scalded our throats. We never mentioned the subject. It was a tacit pact, an oath that sealed our lips. For some reason we believed that silence was the only medicine that could cure us. The idea was as elemental as it was ridiculous, given that we thought everything that we didn't say out loud, but that's how things worked among the little surviving particles. Perhaps because we had the superstitious fear that in having become something so infinitely small, the wind of the words would wipe us out in one puff. The thing is, I thought all the time, and I wondered how we'd managed to make it there, to that village we didn't even know existed, let us no longer say its name. How could we have been hanging over the void a thousand times, about to fall, the finest threads keeping us suspended in the air like a spider's web, while the world around us was a great fire fed by the never-ending supply of bodies that just kept on arriving? I thought about that, about the inexplicable succession of infinite pieces of bad luck that collide into each other, like billiard balls when the player strikes them with such artistry that he makes them move in an unearthly way, closer to magic than physics, and gets them all to go where he wants. I thought about the reason why God, bored of that spectacle that he hadn't bothered to interrupt, from time to time reached down and chose from so many millions a small handful of people to entertain himself with a while. Then he'd make them run one way and another, go through endless challenges, before finally depositing them somewhere safely. For instance, here, in this living room, where your mother and I sit opposite each other, she immersed in her inaccessible muteness, me pondering our unpredictable fortune. Understand me. I don't want to appear ungrateful. Life gave us life, we've even still got almost all our own teeth. Our parents and brothers and sisters didn't have that luck, and that won't cease to obsess me. Why us and not them? Over the years I've gone over every detail, and yet I still can't find an answer. One night, when your mother and I and some other wretched souls were shivering in the hole we'd dug in the woods where we were hiding, I had an idea to go out and crawl through the darkness to see if I could get a bit of food. Imagine. It would've been hilarious, if we hadn't been in the midst of a tragedy. A city man, someone who had lived surrounded by books, converted into a night hunter. What was I hoping for? Hunger drives you nuts, I can't find any other explanation, and so it occurred to me alone, since the other men chose to trick their stomachs by chewing on bitter, rotten roots, to go out on a search mission. I had another reason, as well as my own hunger. I had to find something so that she would stay alive, because she was so weak that she wasn't going to last another day drinking the water that seeped through the walls of that hole and struggling to swallow a few berries, which instead of feeding her gave her diarrhoea, draining away the last of her strength. So, as I was saying, I dragged myself along the frozen ground, barely guiding myself by the dim light of a few stars oblivious to us. After an hour, I dared to stand up and continue on foot. I took the precaution to follow the straightest line I could imagine in the darkness, because the possibility of not finding the way back terrified me. I lost all notion of how long I'd walked, until suddenly I saw something that caught my eye. A house, a kind of tumbledown cabin, but which showed some signs of being inhabited. I carefully drew closer to it, trembling from my head to my toes, as I didn't rightly know what I was doing. Of course I wasn't going to knock on the door, or shout out for them to open up. If there was something we'd learned by then it was that we couldn't expect anybody's sympathy, because everyone wanted our extermination. It didn't have to be a Wehrmacht soldier or a member of the Einsatzgruppe. All the people as a whole participated actively, with that Germanic attention to detail, in the task of wiping us off the face of the earth. Then I found a kind of hut, and entered it slowly. A barely perceptible light filtered through the broken roof, just enough for my eyes to see that there were hens roosting on their perches. I stayed still, not sure what to do in that place that smelled of manure and damp, smells that despite everything were wonderful to me, because I was impregnated with a smell I would never get rid of for the rest of my life, the smell of horror. But my despair wasn't such that I would lose my head and try to catch a chicken, which would instantly kick up a terrible fuss. Instead, I judged it more sensible to turn around and get out of there. But before I did, I saw a basket of eggs in the corner, by some sacks. I crept over, and with all the stealth I could muster in that moment of anxiety, I picked up all the eggs I could carry and left the hut.

There was someone standing outside. At first I couldn't make out who it was. He had a gun. We could hardly see each other, but he knew straight away what kind of being I was. My appearance, resembling more a messenger of death than a human being, left it in no doubt. For a few minutes we stood stock still. My terror was so great that I didn't even realise that I still had those four or five eggs in my hands. And when I was about to surrender, accept that this was where it all ended, in that grotesque scene that amid so much devastation was, at the end of the day, entirely superfluous, something inexplicable happened. The man turned around, returned slowly to his house, opened the door, and closed it behind him without making a sound or uttering one word. I stayed that way for I don't know how long, but I remember it was a long time. I was sure that there was meaning in what had happened, but I couldn't work it out. I couldn't understand what I had to do. In the end, possibly overcome by the exhaustion of standing there, frozen with cramp by the cold and the fear, I made a small movement. I took one step forward, just one, convinced that that man was waiting precisely for that, the slightest movement from me, to take a shot at me. One shot at the target, something I'd witnessed so many times in the Lager, when one of us fell, shot down by a bullet fired as part of the Obersturmbannführer's morning practice. But nothing happened. I took a second step back, and again nothing happened. Then I turned around. One of the eggs slipped from my hand, and on cracking against the ground made a barely audible sound which in my ears echoed as if a grenade had gone off. Once again, I didn't get shot. I moved away little by little, walking slowly, unable to shake off the presentiment of that bullet hitting my back. Even today, listen to this, especially at night, when I get off the bus and walk the streets back home, I have the fleeting sensation that that bullet will finally reach its target. You know why? Because I still don't get what happened. At the last minute, when everything was all set for the grand finale, when there was nothing left to hope for, that man decides to let me live. He doesn't speak, he doesn't ask me anything, he doesn't make me return what I've stolen, when what I was carrying in my hands was worth more than four or five gold bars. I don't know if he did it out of mercy, because he thought I was an apparition, or because he figured it wasn't worth the trouble to waste a bullet on an egg thief, when perhaps he'd need it later, to fight back a greater threat, or kill himself. The thing is I'll never know. As I was saying, it's merely one detail in hundreds that I've gone over and over in my mind. It occurred to me … it occurred to me that that man did one thing and not another. We then have two mysteries. The first is why does A happen and not B. The second is why is it me in this situation, and not someone else. Do you see? That's the secret behind everything that happens. Life comes down to something as elemental as those two mysteries. Nothing else. The rest is decoration, filler. The essence is what I've just told you, and it has no explanation whatsoever.

EIGHTEEN

"Don't you think perhaps that I should see a doctor? I mean, not one like you, but someone who can tell me what it is I've got. You haven't told me yet, and for some years I've suspected it's a disease that no one has been able to detect. I feel terribly weak these days. I can hardly get out of bed, and coming here is an enormous effort for me. I have to take a taxi, and that's something I can't afford. The cheque from the government is hardly enough, and Richard's never helped me. He thinks I'm some kind of actress, or something like that, and the only thing wrong with me is that I don't want to work. That's what he thinks of me. He's told my daughters that, and that's why they think I don't take care of them, when it's they who don't want to see me or take care of me. I must have something. I'm scared to find out, but at the same time the sooner I know the better. Maybe it's a brain tumour. People who have cancer in the brain do weird things, they feel dizzy and weak like I do. Or maybe it's not in my brain, but in my bone marrow. I read something about that on the internet. Plus I have a friend … well, let's say an acquaintance, because I don't think she's my friend any more, like everyone else, and that happened to her.

"That? What is 'that'?"

"The bone marrow thing. And she went through the same as me. She didn't have any strength, and stayed in bed for whole days, barely moving."

"But that doesn't happen to you all the time. There are periods when you come and see me and I can tell you're full of beans."

"You're right. It's the strangest thing. Don't think I haven't thought about it. On many nights I say to myself: 'What you've got can't be bone marrow cancer like …' I can't remember her name any more. Doesn't matter. You said it very clearly. It must be something in my brain."

"I said that very clearly? I hadn't realised."

"Not so much in those words, but you led me to understand that. It's true that often I feel like my batteries have been recharged and I can get out of bed. I do the housework, make lunch, and I have an appetite when I eat. There's no other explanation for that than a brain disorder. Sometimes I've got too much energy, other days it leaks out of me like a punctured tyre. You should refer me to the brain specialists. Maybe this can be cured with an operation. Or I'll die on the operating table, which wouldn't be a bad thing either. I'm dragging such a great fatigue with me, so great that the act of living overwhelms me. I didn't used to be like this. Or did I? Wait, wait a minute. Now I feel a little confused. When did all this start? Can I close my eyes?"

"What's that?"

"Can I close my eyes? It helps me to concentrate."

"Of course. Why didn't you say so before?"

"I don't know."

Anne closed her eyes. Her voice suddenly changed. It turned more serious, more serene. It stopped talking without a pause, breathlessly, and the vertiginous flow of her words began to slow down. I was surprised that she'd never chosen to speak with her eyes closed before.

"I do know. I can do it now because I have more trust."

"In whom?"

"I mean, I don't feel so embarrassed about you looking at me. If I close my eyes, I feel less protected. But at the same time it's easy to get closer to my ideas. That happens to me. I'm terrified of the dark, but it's also in the dark that I think the best. And now I think that my life has had two stages. In both of them the same thing happened to me. For some reason I tend to believe that problems started in the second half, but I have to get it into my head that that isn't entirely true. There's something that hasn't been working right since I was a little girl. Something that possibly happened and went completely unnoticed, because as I've explained, I always knew what my role was in that family. I was expected to make the sacrifice of giving up most things that are indispensable in childhood. You know better than I do that a childhood is not only spoiled by violence, that there is a kind of love that is more lethal than poison, the kind of love that makes us all feel guilty. I was a survivor. My mother practised silence, and very rarely broke her silence. So when a word of hers came out of her mouth, it was like a radioactive leak. What does it mean to be a survivor? Now, after so many years, I'm beginning to realise what it means to live under the weight of a regime whose significance one doesn't understand. There's something very strange that happens with words. I don't know if this happens to everyone, but it happens to me. There are words you end up believing if you hear them enough, and you take them in and use them as if you understand what they mean. But one fine day, I don't know when, something changes completely and the meaning becomes different, strange. From time to time I like to go to the zoo, especially during the week, when there aren't so many people. I like to walk slowly and observe the animals. They're strange, very strange. It's the fact that we're familiarised with images of animals from a young age that makes us perceive them as something we know. But if you stand in front of an elephant, and contemplate it as I do when I go to the zoo, and look at it for half an hour, an hour, maybe more, I couldn't tell you, a long time, then something strange starts to happen, and it's that the animal we think we instantly recognise, so cute, with his long trunk and eyes flooded with sadness, the sadness of feeling so far away, that animal becomes a near incomprehensible thing. You're an investigator of the soul, you must have some theory to explain that. Have you ever done that test? Have you ever done the test of staring at the most ordinary thing in the world, your own hand, a pencil, the face of the woman you love, whatever, but looking at it like I'm telling you now, giving yourself to the possibility that something different will happen? Do the test, Dr. Palmer. It never fails. You'll see what an extraordinary thing it is to discover that we all live in Plato's cave and don't realise it. We only see shadows and we take them as familiar and true, but the clarity of the sun is unnecessary. It's enough to stare, and let yourself be carried away by what happens next, that loosening of ourselves from what we've always thought we understood. The same can happen with words. The idea of being a survivor was something that filled me with secret pride, not only because my mother blessed me with that, but because I thought I glimpsed in my father's eyes a complicity with that term, as if he somehow approved of it, approved of it like something I'd received, a kind of gift that would protect me from who knows what. But one day, I don't remember when, that idea started to sound strange to me. I no longer had such a sure idea that it was a good thing, and I was hit by the opposite idea, the idea that one only survives at the price of another dying in one's place. Don't think that this is an extravagant fantasy."

"I don't," I said. "It's not extravagant, just unfair."

"Exactly. But what happened, I interpret that injustice differently. I didn't consider it as something undeserved directed at me, but rather the opposite. Being a survivor was to be the cause of an injustice, stealing from someone else the possibility of living. How old must I have been when that idea started to filter into my thoughts? Ten? Twelve? Eight? I couldn't say. Nor could I say whether I'd have been capable of putting it into words. I suspect I wouldn't, that they were those kind of thoughts that aren't thoughts as such, shapeless beings with no precise content that act mysteriously, and leave a mark on your past."

"And then what happened? What did that new meaning of survivor lead to?"

"To living more in hiding. Perhaps I can explain it more simply. If until then my name had given me a certain light, now it dragged me into the cone of the shadow that my mother cast. My father's immense effort to try to counteract the atmosphere of death we lived in proved futile. No, it's not that, either. Futile isn't the right word. I think it's fairer to say that my father ended up being defeated. In his own way, he goes on fighting every day, even now, but he doesn't know, or maybe he does know, that my mother gradually consumed the life that was still left. I didn't have my sister's courage. She hadn't received any title, but she was the only survivor, the real one. I can see this now. I don't know how she did it. I don't know why someone can do something that another person cannot. The same conditions, the same circumstances, the same tragedy. One escapes, the other doesn't."

"Your family history is the great metaphor of your life. 'Survive', 'escape', 'live', 'die', it can all be read as if it were the Third Reich," I dared to add. It was barely necessary, because Anne had the extraordinary lucidity to grasp by herself what was at the heart of those terrible words: "… the cone of the shadow that my mother cast". She possessed—and this is where the madness lies—the ability to read messages too well. Not being crazy means precisely not knowing how to decipher them clearly, having doubts, getting tangled up in questions. But Anne never missed a trick, and that was the source of her greatest unhappiness. She didn't miss it even when she raved nonsensically and got caught up in her delusion. Not even in those moments did the truth abandon her.

"The great metaphor of my life. I like that. It shows me in a better light than that horrible photo I sent to my daughters. But you have to help me find another. For many years I convinced myself that being a mother gave me a better name, and that that way I could also pay homage to mine. I know at times I may seem cruel, but I've never stopped loving her, loving even her pain. She was too understandable not to love her. My sister was way more relentless. Not me. Why am I saying this? I think I've lost my thread. No, I've got it. Another name, a better name to call myself. But I'm not so naïve as to think you'll pull something out of your magician's hat. It has to be a brilliant idea, a flash of light. Something that perhaps will never come."

* * *

I've learned, with a great deal of effort, that shutting up at the right time can be better than the imposture of therapeutic optimism. I wasn't going to tell Anne that she was right, that maybe that flash of light would never come. Nor would I have told her the opposite. In this profession, as in the rest of life, silence can be less harmful than words.

NINETEEN

"Would you like a cup of tea? Help yourself, and make me one too. I'll make the most of your visit and not get out of my chair."

"Don't you think it might be time to take someone on to help out a little?"

"I suppose in a few years I won't have any choice, but I'll think about it when I get properly old," Dr. Rubashkin replied with his usual humour.

"That's very sensible of you," I said, following the joke. "No need to make hasty decisions."

"I wasn't wrong about that young lady you spoke to me about the other time. What was her name? Ah, Jessica! Now I remember. Such a shame. Now and again we need cases like these, so as not to forget what the Old Man recommended in writing: don't persist in curing. Neither prophets nor demiurges. The Old Man knew what he was talking about, all right." "The Old Man" was Rubashkin's nickname for Freud.

"I suppose Lacan would've done everything possible," I objected.

"No doubt. He didn't back down from anything. The Old Man was more prudent with that kind of subject. Lacan, on the contrary, challenged everything that was put in his path.

And you aren't much behind, but this time the dice were really loaded. The game was fixed from the start, and you didn't have much chance of winning. Not everyone can be a survivor like this other woman you were telling me about. This one's more resourceful. You know that delusion is the chimney that Anna O spoke of, who of course went down in history with your patient's name, though in fact her name was Bertha. She used to say that Freud cleaned her chimney. What fun times! I imagine the Old Man was well aware of the implication. It wasn't for nothing that he worked out that hysteria always speaks the language of sex. In contrast, crazy people have another system: self-cleaning. That's it. Like those modern ovens. Delusion is the chimney's self-cleaning system. Anne comes with it built-in, but not Jessica. Poor devil, she lived under the martyrdom of a chronic hallucination. Her mother's infinite mourning had become a voice inside her, clamouring in the solitude of the world for the return of her dead son. Anne also appeals for the return of her daughters, but she's managed to fabricate a story, a plot against her, a saga in which she plays the role of the tragic heroine. Rebelling against the injustice of the world keeps her alive, gives meaning to her existence. You must somehow protect her fury. Don't deprive her of that completely, because then she won't have any kind of hope."

"That's what I'm trying to do, but it's complicated. Don't forget she's tied up in a lawsuit, and that muddies the case and complicates my role. I can't move with complete freedom. If she attacks her husband again, the lawyers will make mince-meat out of her. They'll ask for her head. And I'm afraid her daughters will take part in the execution."

"I know, I know. It reminds me in one sense of the Aimée case, the one Lacan used for his doctoral thesis. A paranoid sentiment in search of a limit, and a pass to the act that forces the law to intervene. Your patient puts herself in situations that could land her in court. At the same time, her hatred of her husband has become a very potent driving force, the perfect corollary for her position as victim. The complicated thing in this case is not just the legal question, but that she carries the symbolic weight on her back of those who were real victims. She's managed to interweave her family history and her vision of the world in an ingenious way that deflects any negotiation. You have to respect all her certainties, step around them, even act as a witness to the offences against her, and at the same time prevent her from using them too much to take action."

I smiled.

"I can guess what you're thinking, and you're right. It's a very complex thing. A strategy that sustains a stable, at times absurd balance, which the slightest contingency could bring crashing down. She's one of those people who live right on the edge of the cliff. If you get too close, they might jump or push you. Or try to drag you down with them."

"Why did we choose this?" I asked as I brought the cups of tea over. "I've never been able to find a satisfactory answer to that question. For many years I searched for explanations, some more sophisticated than others, but none really convinced me. Maybe there isn't a reason, just as there isn't for those who decide to take in their hands a sharp object, open up a body they've previously put to sleep, and change a fundamental part, like a heart or liver. It's another form of madness. We don't know how to live life like normal people, and maybe for that reason we set out on unlikely courses of action. We could say that working with radioactive material has altered our brains, although the opposite is always possible, that our madness has led us to this strange profession. I think the second possibility has always been the most likely, don't you think? It's clear that neither of our lives could be used as an example of a normal existence, even assuming that such an abstraction exists."

"Sometimes I've had the sensation of wanting to flee from all that is human, and seek out a life surrounded by animals. Beings who live in a place that belongs to them, who occupy a more or less sensible place in the world, who don't ask themselves questions, or suffer the torments of consciousness."

"That's a common fantasy in people who know the natural world only through poetry and the movies. But even if you join the animals and sympathise with their lives, you'll never become one of them. It's the dream of those of us who've been exiled definitively from paradise, which is non-existent anyway, and to which, for the very same reason, we can't return."

"You're asking some very hard questions today. I suspect that your last answer is that desperate need to assure ourselves a shot at immortality. Deep down, behind the complicated machinery that makes us up, there always hides the same automatic mechanism, repeating a secret order that doesn't reach our ears, and yet goes right through us. And we obey that pulse all the time, that mute pulse that pushes us towards nothing, along a path full of mirages and decoys. It's the madness of man, something we all share, though each in our own way. Our madness consists of dealing with madness, while other people drive buses or become astronauts, gold prospectors, mountain climbers, or descend to the depths of the earth, dragging themselves along like worms through passages they can barely fit through. It's clear that we find something in this that keeps us tied down, a subtle chain, an alienation which we in particular are aware of. We do what we do because we have no choice. But perhaps it would be more prudent and less ambitious to say that this only applies to me. You probably have a more convincing reason to explain yours. I'm a ninety-two-year-old patient. Don't you think it's a little late for me to change my life? But let's leave that aside and get back to where we were. All this cheap philosophy doesn't get us very far, and even so we could go on and on. I'd rather you told me again what she told you about her imaginary friend, that kind of double who's always with her. I've seen some people like that, but on this occasion there's something truly original, an authentic creation. She is perfectly conscious that ... what did you say the creature's name was?"

"Norman."

"That's it, Norman. She's conscious that Norman came out of himself, that she's fabricated him from her own image in the mirror. It's fascinating. This woman is incredible, Dave. She possesses an innate wisdom about what it is to be human, although unfortunately for her she's too close to that wisdom. More than possessing it, it would be right to say that it possesses her, she suffers it. She sees further than normal people manage to glimpse. Norman is a being that she has managed to separate from herself to re-establish human conversation. All the same, from what I've heard he's someone who isn't always available, who doesn't appear every time he's required. She says this quite clearly. There are occasions when her loneliness is so great, her helplessness so real, that even the voice of a phone operator, or even an automatic voice, the kind of thing that drives me mad, can become a source of calm. As you well know, you have taken on a part of that role for her. Her imaginary companion, her double, but not just that. You're also the universal witness, the intermediary between her and the gods, the messenger who must get the forms and complaints to them. This last part is important, I'd say that to her it's your main mission. Someone who will guide the protest to the right addressee, so that justice can be done. That's what it's about all the time: that a just law should finally come and put cruel fate in its place. It's a very logical aspiration for someone inspired by the nobility of the heart. The problem is that things don't work like that, and there is no possible redemption. She continues to believe in God, in one that has to listen to her. A kind of female version of Job. We can't smash that hope. Therefore, we'll have to withstand her fury. To her, you're the visible face of that absurd multinational we call life, where not a single thing works properly, and you can't even phone a complaints department.

"Dead right."

"Who? Her or me?"

"Both, Dr. Rubashkin. Both."

TWENTY

Jack's blue eyes were veiled with age and melancholy. He was one of my favourites. Can an analyst have that kind of preference? Of course he can, but on the condition that those feelings don't contaminate the neutrality with which we must listen to the vicissitudes of the beings who confide in us. I think that throughout my life I've been careful to keep that distance, and that way I could indulge myself and admit where my sympathies lay. Jack was one of those who, under different circumstances, could have been one of my faithful friends.

In his youth he'd been a jazz trumpeter, and for some time he'd managed a certain taste of fame in those underground dives where the most beautiful music in the world feeds its way through the thick tobacco smoke and human steam. Like many others, he entrusted his talent to heroin, and she returned the gesture with ingratitude, pushing him to the brink. So then he became a street musician, a lonely man who in exchange for a few coins reached for a moment the hearts of the sleepy passers-by, hurrying to work in the first light of day. A series of bad moves took him to some rather unfortunate places, he got in with a bad crowd and that complicated things further. When he came to see me, he'd lost his way back, and was at his wits' ends.

"I wanna go back home, Doc. That's all I want. If I could make it home, I'd consider myself happy. Can you help me?"

I remember those were the first words he said to me. Go back home. The problem was there wasn't a home to go back to, there never had been, because Jack was the product of a bad wish. His Aunt Sally was the only person who reluctantly agreed to look after the son of her sister, who brought him into the world at the age of eighteen and then disappeared off the face of it. But Aunt Sally wasn't fit to look after newborns, since she herself was dying of cirrhosis, so she had the good judgment to call social services the day before the undertakers came into her house and took her away.

That's life. Generally, people tend to dream about getting something back that they never even had.

So it wasn't easy to understand Jack and, at least back then, I wasn't all that sure I was going to be able to help him. But I rightly recall I promised him I'd do my best, although I didn't make any guarantees. My honesty may have helped him far more than anything else that happened afterwards in his years of therapy.

"Thanks, Doc," he said. "That's the first time someone's not made me a promise they won't be able to keep."

So it was that, having come in a little late when the problems already covered several pages of his life, Jack nonetheless got off on a good foot, and over the years we managed to get him a little dignity back, a roof to sleep under, and a slightly dented trumpet from which he could still squeeze some beautiful wailing.

That morning, when he sat opposite me, he took a pile of letters out of his backpack.

"What's all this, Jack? Summonses from your creditors?" I asked him in jest. He'd managed to quit heroin and pay off the loan sharks, who had gone so far as to issue death threats.

"You know, Doc. It seems that becoming a normal citizen involves receiving tons of letters every day. I think most is junk. It's all the same to me, I don't open none, not even from the bank."

"You have an account?"

"Sure do! The government puts something in there now and again. That social welfare crap. I don't know too good, but I'm telling you: of all the things I'm incapable of doing, as well as taking out the trash every day like I'm supposed to, I can never get this straight. Opening letters is the pits."

"Really? I don't think you've ever told me this. What's the trouble with opening letters?"

Jack stayed silent, looking at me through the worn silk of his blue eyes. Then he let out a deep sigh, and breathed in as if to start a long submersion.

"The trouble with opening cards, Doc, is that you gotta see them. You gotta look at the envelope, turn it over and see who it's from."

Silence again. "And?"

Jack took another breath, looked around him as if he wanted to be sure we were alone, and continued.

"So it's like this. Thing is, I got no choice but to accept that there's a letter that still ain't reached me. I've been waiting for it for years, you know? Sounds like a lie. I can't believe this is happening to me at my age. But I gotta confess, every time I open that mailbox, there's something inside me that lights up for a second. I guess it's my heart, that would be the most logical thing. It don't last much, no. I couldn't tell you how long, either. A minute? Two? Yeah, more or less that."

"I see," I said with great tact. "Would you like to tell me why?"

"It happened once, Doc, as I guess it happens to most people, but it happens to most people a lot, while it only happened to me once, and never again. I had enough with just once. Her name was Nathalie. She was a university student, and this was so many years ago I don't even remember what she was studying. Literature, maybe, or philosophy. Anyway, don't matter."

Jack paused a moment, and his eyes turned watery, as if the little sea that lay at the bottom had been shaken up a little. His voice changed, that rough voice worn out by the daily rubbing of sadness turned soft and trembled.

"Thing is, the girl worked nights as a waitress to pay for her studies. She served drinks in a bar I used to play in almost every night, back when I still thought I'd make it as a musician, and I could afford a warm bed every night, and go to bed knowing that the next day I'd wake up in my own home. You already know the story. It all went to shit. But then she was different, and when I saw her, life itself seemed so different. Believe it or not, Doc, I once had all my own teeth, I didn't look all that bad, no sir. Sure, I wasn't the typical musician who sleeps every night with a new chick, though I'd seen that in the movies, like everyone. May the Lord strike me down if I lie when I say that that was something else! Although the worst was still to come, it wasn't like I was living in Wonderland. I'd already been fried on both sides a little, but not so much that I didn't realise that someone had put an angel there behind that bar instead of the usual crowd who came in to get drunk, and who I entertained a little with a pianist and a drummer, Le Bon, Johnny Le Bon, a guy who greased the joints in his wrists with cheap whisky. We had a hell of a beat! Shame I never got even one recording of those shows, but I'm telling you, we sounded pretty good.

"So, as I was saying, she appeared. I thought I'd have to get loaded to be able to hit on her, but to my surprise it didn't go down like that. She wasn't the kind of girl who guys get themselves worked up over and come in their pants for, no way. So no one had noticed her. No one, except me. It's real funny, because to this day, every time the damn idea comes to me of opening the mailbox when no more letters will fit in, I wonder what it was that I saw in that girl, a girl with a skinny ass and pretty enough eyes, nothing out of this world, but a girl who blew my mind.

"I couldn't believe that after one week Nathalie and I were sitting in a coffee shop one Saturday afternoon eating ice cream and gazing at each other as if both of us had seen in the other that thing they imagined might exist but never happens, except on TV. We started dating, but soon I realised that I had to go slow with her. None of that sticking your hand up anywhere, oh no! She wasn't any old girl, and I made the effort to shower every day, put on a clean shirt, and brush my teeth, a good habit, yes sir, which unfortunately I lost along the way. By her side, I felt like I could walk for miles without my feet touching the ground. They say that's love, Doc, and I believe it, because that's more or less what happened to me, and I'm glad that at least I had that once in my life, and even though all what happened after hurt a lot, I don't regret it.

"After a month I was offered a gig playing a club in Vegas for a few weeks. That was something else. At last I was being given a real opportunity, because the pay wasn't too bad, and besides the casino gave us a few chips every night to have a little fun. I suppose you can guess what happened. A week later, after I'd lost all my pay, and picked up a few debts in various gambling dens, I had to hot-foot it out of there before they made mincemeat of me. You know how they don't beat around the bush out there. When I got back, that same night I went to the bar. The only thing that could console me was to find her, take shelter in the smell of her hair, and dream again of a different life, dream of having the chance to save myself with her. But Nathalie wasn't behind the bar, serving drinks with those long, soft fingers. When I asked after her, they told me she didn't work there no more, that she'd left. I thought I was going to go crazy, because I had no idea where to find her. We'd meet up in some part of town and leave each other at the same place, but she'd never taken me back to her place, and I sure as hell had never dared show her the hole that I went back to every night. So I had an idea. As I didn't have a car, I asked Le Bon to lend me his, and I drove all over town asking around where they used to rent out rooms to university students. After a few days, someone gave me a tip about a street, Brixton or Braxton, where there were a lot of student rooms. I headed over there, and believe it or not, at the first house I rang the bell and asked if they knew a Nathalie, just Nathalie since I didn't even know her last name, yeah, I said, a girl like this and like that, and the woman, I remember her well, she was a woman with curlers in her hair and a strawberry-coloured bathrobe, don't ask me why the hell I've retained these stupid details, that woman, as I was saying, scratched her chin with her fat hand and shouted out to another woman who was in the living room. When she heard my story she frowned and said the magic words: "I think you mean the girl who lives in twenty-three. Try there." I didn't have time to thank her, I shot off to where she'd said. With my heart about to come out of my mouth, I rang the bell at twenty-three, and there she was. But she didn't look the same. There was something strange in her look, something I couldn't explain or describe, I noticed it straight away. She made an effort to look happy to see me, but I realised that something was up that I wasn't getting. She didn't even ask me in, she said she was tired, and that she'd meet me at the bar the next day, when I finished my show. I went back to my hole and couldn't sleep a wink all night. I felt like I'd been beat up with a baseball bat, and though I'd at least figured out where Nathalie was, something told me things wouldn't work out too good.

"I wasn't wrong. The next night, after the show, I waited for her but she didn't show. Since I wasn't ready to give up, I asked Le Bon for his car again and took off to twenty-three on Brixton or Braxton and pounded on the door until the neighbours poked their heads out of the windows. Someone finally opened the door, a six-foot dude who looked ready to shoot me, but when he saw how desperate I was he calmed down a little, he even asked me in, but he warned me that Nathalie had taken off that morning, taking all her stuff and leaving no trace.

"I never saw her again, and I never again walked with a girl for miles without touching the ground. Just the opposite, and you know all about that part, Doc. I went from flying to crawling, and I kept up that intimate relationship with the floor until I walked into this room."

"Why have you never spoken about this before?"

"Because there are things that hurt, Doc. And you're a good doctor, but in your medicine cabinet you ain't got no anaesthetic, so I had to grit my teeth real good to come in this morning. A few years later, I found out what had happened. While I was away, some drunk guys, you know, did that thing that men, sometimes, when we go crazy, do to some poor girl; damn sure I'd never do that, but I'm a man, and sometimes I'm ashamed to be one, to be part of that half of the human race that ought to have their balls cut off when they're born. And I got something else to say. I know I'm a complete imbecile because after more than forty years, now and again I still think maybe, who knows, life's so strange, maybe, I was saying, one of these days I'll go open the mailbox and there it is, the letter, the letter that deep down I'm still expecting. Maybe the best thing would be if you could help me get that idea out of my head, Doc. But I don't know. I ain't entirely convinced I want to lose that too."

TWENTY-ONE

"I haven't told you about something that's weighing on my conscience. Sometimes I leave here with the impression that I'm not being completely honest. I'm going to say this straight: I lie. I guess we all lie, that we say the kind of lie that's different from falsehood or bad faith. It's the lie that grows on the edges of fear, or cowardice."

I nodded.

"I'm not a good mother. I sometimes think that. When I'm convinced that I was, and that I was horribly betrayed, then I feel strong. That mix of pain and fury runs through my bloodstream, it's a kind of food that keeps me on my feet. But that's not the whole truth. There's more. Some afternoons I'd delay going home after work. When I remember this, it's like a ton of rubble fell on top of me. I can't move, or breathe, because I can't work out why that used to happen to me. It was before everything started to fall apart, before we had to hospitalise Karen. I need to understand what it was with me, why I acted so differently to what I claimed to be. All I know is that I was seized by a vague terror, the feeling that I wasn't going to be able to do my duties properly."

"What duties?"

"The ones I imposed on myself. Being a mother meant far more to me than for other women. Well, that's what I believed, anyway. I don't know what other women think, because I've never had girl friends, the kind you can trust with a secret, or a question. I haven't been able to compare anything of what happened in my life, so I don't have a frame of reference. From the moment I married and left my parents' home, I started to feel my own way through life. Life with my parents was a tragedy in which my role had been assigned. At first I thought that I'd find a different role with Richard, but now I realise that I was lost. No one assigned me a new list of jobs to do, so I had to devise my own to make it look like I knew what I was doing. Do you know what that's like? Living every minute of your life, glancing out of the corner of your eye to see how those around you react to what you do? I'd been programmed for one decisive task, to always do what was expected of me, and I fulfilled that task completely. With my parents I knew clearly what it consisted of, which text I should recite, or on the contrary, which text I should never recite. But when I had my own family, I didn't know what to do, although the axiom of being a good daughter remained active. It was a kind of autopilot that operated in a void, because it couldn't hook on to a concrete idea. My inner voice had lost its complement. Imagine, like sending someone out to buy something, but not telling them what. You get the first part of the message, but you're left without the rest. All the same, you obey. Obey what? Obey the first order, the order that's the basis of everything, even though it's incomplete. Believe me, Dr. Palmer, that's exactly what madness is. Going out to buy something that isn't on the list and trying to guess what it could be."

"I believe you. I've rarely heard anyone put it that simply."

"That was my life. A string of guesses that I had to make without help, guided only by the results. What do they call that in medicine? Evidence-based. In this case the evidence consisted of perceiving that everyone was happy with me, or whether I'd made a mistake. It happened everywhere. At work, in my marriage. With Richard it was pretty clear to me that I was at fault all the time. I've already told you how I felt about sex. It wasn't hard to realise that I wasn't behaving as I should. For some things I got by, imitating what others did, like when you're at a wedding banquet and you look out of the corner of your eye to see which fork you're supposed to use, the smallest one or the one next to it. But the rest was a total mystery. That's why the birth of my children was my salvation. I had finally found something to give meaning to the role I had to play! That took a great weight off, and I remember those were good years, they really were. But it's here that I get mixed up, and I go back to the start. Because I also have to admit what I told you before, that I'd sometimes delay going home on purpose after I left work. The whole day I'd be thinking about going home, seeing my girls again, the happiness of being with them, making their dinner, bathing them, doing my duty as a mother. But sometimes, and don't ask me why because I could never understand it, as home time approached I'd get this horrible restlessness, a sticky anxiety would creep from my stomach to my throat, and my pulse would speed up. All that I'd seen in images of infinite joy moments earlier became something oppressive, and once again I was seized by the terror of playing a part without a script. It was just like going out onto a stage, watched by thousands of eyes ready to judge my performance. I don't understand why that happened to me on some occasions, but when it happened I felt forced to wander the street, not daring to go up to the apartment, smoking one cigarette after another. I even managed to find some kind of calm in bars. Back then I wasn't taking any kind of meds, I lived through all that without that protection, and alcohol helped take the edge off a little. Richard, as usual, was busy with his own stuff, and didn't notice a thing. When I finally got the strength together to go up to the apartment, I don't think he even noticed the time. He didn't notice what kind of a state I was in either, the despair invading me inside. Even in that period I started to sense that there was something strange about Karen's behaviour, because he only had eyes for her, but at first I couldn't work out what was going on exactly. I think I was really naïve, and couldn't imagine that kind of thing happening. But little by little I started to intuit that there was something strange in all that. And you know what I say? That that psychiatrist woman accused me of being directly responsible for Karen's anorexia, but the truth is no one ever took the time to find out what was really going on, deep down."

Anne's tone increased in pitch as it usually did when she opened up the locks of hatred. A torrent of lava began to flow faster and faster. I braced myself for the explosion, but to my surprise she stopped short, as if an inner alarm had warned her that she was about to burst her banks. She returned to her usual tone, that mix of shame and guilt that she also frequently used.

"I worked a lot at night, long nights awake, but always alert to the eye that's always on me, while my thoughts grow deeper and weave and weave and weave ... it's a loom that never ceases to cross the threads over in one direction and another, trying to form a shape, a picture, a scene that'll help me understand what's going on. During those nights I managed to decipher my anxiety, realise why the one thing I was good at, the thing I could recognise myself in, that gave me worth in my own eyes and not just other people's, I mean being a mother, suddenly became an unsustainable thing, as if I were going to fail in that too, as if I couldn't keep my balance walking on the only rope that held me up. I couldn't reach any conclusions, I'd wake up exhausted, with no strength to get out of bed, but I had to do it, I had to meet my obligations because Richard worked very far from the city and would leave before dawn, so I was in charge of waking up the girls, dressing them, fixing their breakfast, and taking them to school. Some days, not many, but it hurts as if it happened all the time, I found it impossible. My attempts to understand my terror did nothing more than confirm it, and the obsession drilled at my head that I'd wind up setting a death trap myself, a nightmare that I'd be trapped in for ever, unable to wake up."

"And was Richard still oblivious to all this?"

"I think so, as he'd come home late at night, and I'd hide what I was going through. But I swear that never happened more than two or three times, or maybe four, I don't remember too well; now that I see it from a certain distance I don't think it was that bad; maybe if I'd been a more communicative woman, more talkative, I'd have found out that other mothers go through the same sometimes, but as I spent my life alone, the feeling grew in me that I was a freak of nature, an aberration who deserved nothing of what she'd been lucky enough to get."

Anne's face was bathed in tears, and sweat was running down her neck. She'd wring her hands, staring at them, as if she wanted to rid herself of something dirty or sticky on her skin, and then she'd look at me. She repeated that same gesture as she carried on talking. In her hands she was looking for something that she needed to remove by any means, and she looked in my face for a sign of compassion. She begged compassion in a special way, without histrionics or words. She did it through her lost gaze, which at times even went through me, trying to reach something beyond, somewhere close to infinity. A very distinct compassion to feeling sorry for someone, which I'd very quickly gotten used to seeing in my work. It was more the need to be forgiven, a need that never found its consolation, the inseparable companion of an original guilt in which she'd lived her whole life, as if the monstrous history that had brought her forth had declared her damned.

"I wonder whether you raised the mission of motherhood to a height that no one could've reached," I said.

"I'm sure I did. It was something that no one would ever be capable of doing, but for the same reason I find myself forced to fulfil it. That might sound absurd, but it isn't."

"I didn't say it was. Nothing in you is absurd," I objected.

"I haven't found any other way to justify my life than doing something beyond my own powers, which means that right from the start I've failed."

As I listened to her, Jessica came to mind. She had also reached the stage of sacrifice in her attempt to do the impossible. In her case it was to return to her mother the son that fate had snatched away, while Anne had set herself a far more difficult mission, as her mother was immersed in an incommensurable grief, a desolation as great as all of mankind's grief. And yet, despite it all, Anne kept on living, using her reserves of strength, while Jessica had succumbed when faced with such a task. She hadn't been able to withstand it, and in the end she gave in. That difference was as great as the universe, and at the same time infinitely imperceptible if one were to try to explain it. One could play with the hypothesis of God, fate, or one singular virtue. The truth is that no matter what name we choose to give it, it's the kind of enigma that doesn't have an answer.

Fortunately, there are still a few things left that we can't explain.

TWENTY-TWO

This is one of those nights, you know. The difference is that now, with you, I can write, instead of running on the wheel of thought all alone, like a little hamster. I was nothing but that before. A little rodent going round on her wheel, believing she's going somewhere, but always stuck in the same place.

Now I'm fully aware that I'm crazy. I can't go on hiding behind Richard's reproaches, or my daughters'. I still need a little more strength to be able to say it to you in person. For now, I'll do it like this. At least I know that I'm saving energy. Nor should I fake anything any more, and nor should you have to tiptoe around that truth that I have no choice but to admit. Deep down, I've always known. Don't we always know the things we should know, even though we whistle and sing trivialities, or let ourselves get swept up in the world's turbulence, or are dazzled by the shine of appearances? We always know the bottom line, because it's there, lying in ambush, biding its time. The truth is patient. It can wait all your life, it's in no hurry. Even if we manage to outwit it until the last minute, it doesn't care, it will still be there, impassive. If it can't have its way with us, it will with those who come after us. You know much better than I that there is something that is inherited, passed down in the soul, not in the genes. The Germans believed in genes. There was a time when they believed in poetry, but then they forgot poetry and worshipped science, which they placed above God. On the other hand, I have very classic tastes, I swim against the tide of the modern world. My madness is not a disease, or if it is, its cause is invisible. It's made up of the magical threads of words that keep echoing in my ears, like the vibration of a string perpetuating in the air.

I hear those words. She talks to me. Always. For as long as I can remember I've heard her within me. It's a murmur, a sob, perhaps, the sound of stones rolling, falling, the whisper of the wind. Her voice. She talks to me, always. She never stops, and I no longer care if I don't understand what she says, because in reality I don't know, I can't make out the words. It's a litany, sounds, a chant, a funeral prayer, a lullaby sung in our people's old tongue, which I can't speak but I listen, and that murmur is like the sound of a factory in the stillness of the night. That's why I'm terrified of the night, because during the day other sounds distract me from that one, a buzzing, a mixture of noises, sometimes barely a whisper and other times the roar of the storm, or the roar of the fire, the shouting, the barking of dogs, it's a recording that goes round in my head. It's her. It's always her.

There was a time when her voice was silenced. When I met Richard and came here with him, I made a home, my daughters were born, and despite all the terrific work that all that life implied, I was reasonably happy. I didn't ask for much, you know, I was used to living with little. I'd been lovingly trained to put off my wishes, and make my presence as light as a feather. What grace! Even my body followed the rules that suited my parents' needs, because I was a very thin girl. I weighed very little, although I had no trouble eating, it was just that my body expressed the smallness to which I'd reduce myself so as not to upset too much the tomb in which our everyday life occurred, with my mother locked in her room, in darkness, incapable of going outside or standing the slightest invasion from outside reality. Look at me now, look at what I've become. An obese woman who leans forward as she walks, as if dragging her own body with a rope. No I really can't hide my existence in the world! I'm too fat to go unnoticed. The body is an amazing thing. It has its own logic. It takes on the shape it requires to adapt to circumstances. It torments me to think about Karen, what she was trying to tell us with her body when she reduced it to a bag of bones on the verge of starvation, and there was nothing else for it but to take her to hospital. Where was I that I didn't see what was coming? Was I locked in myself, although I wanted to convince myself that I was an exemplary mother, devoted to that sublime role alone? The whole world was against me, starting with Richard, who backed up the psychiatrist at the summary trial he put me through. I thought I was going to go crazy, that they would be capable of snatching away my daughters, depriving me of custody, and I reacted badly, and if the hospital security guards hadn't intervened, I'd probably be writing this from a prison cell. What I wouldn't admit back then is that I was wrong, that it had all gone wrong from the start, and that that start went very far back in time, perhaps to the day when my grandfather changed our surname and agreed to Germanise it. You pointed out that my grandfather was just one more victim in that long history of barbarity, and you were right. But that doesn't prevent me from pinpointing that as the moment when the switchman pulled the lever and changed the train's direction, and I don't just say that in a figurative sense, because that was the end, a train stopped in hell. I've been thinking a lot about the question of my surname, and I've made a decision, but I'll explain it to you when I see you. Maybe you'll consider it something that increases the red numbers in my mental count, but with all respect I will say to you that in this case I don't care, in fact, even if you think it's a totally wild scheme, I'm absolutely convinced of what I must do. Don't be offended, Dr. Palmer, it's not something I'm willing to negotiate, but at least you can be absolutely sure that it's not something that will cause public offence. I'm not going to call Richard and leave him those horrible messages at his office, even though he deserves them, nor am I going to call my daughters and reproach them for anything. They flee from their mother's madness just as I tried to escape from the madness that mine suffered. I wish them better luck than mine in that endeavour.

Having said that, where am I going to go? We've come a long way, as they say, we've made it to the moon, if making it to the moon is an advance, I'm not going to discuss that because I'm an ignorant woman, but what I don't understand is why, when there are so many intelligent people in this world, no one's ever been able to write a good book of instructions. The Torah, the Bible, all that is good for nothing, old wives' tales, cheap moralising. I mean something really useful, something I can use to guide me every day and know what I have to do. I don't know why it's taken for granted that we don't know what to do. Maybe some people have a gift for that, but what happens to those of us who don't have that ability? Why has no one taken us into account? Why does the government occupy itself with so many things, building highways, bridges, power stations, and not occupy itself with those of us who just need little roads, paths so we don't get lost in the woods? Is it just me who gets this? I don't think so. I'm sure there are a whole lot of us who are missing those instructions. Why does it happen to us, Dr. Palmer? What are we missing, or what do we have too much of, those of us who are in this crowd of the lost, who've lost their ticket back, who can't find the way out?

Don't worry about replying, we have our session tomorrow and you'll probably see this email before you see me.

TWENTY-THREE

Very gently, she placed a folder on my desk and slid it to me to open. Her face seemed to show signs of a certain satisfaction, even pride. She looked expectant, anxious to see my reaction. I took a look at the papers inside, forms with information and certification. I didn't want to ask her what it all was, because Anne was clearly enjoying the intrigue she'd managed to create. I soon realised that she had applied to revert to the original spelling of her surname. She wanted to be Kurczynski again. It was highly likely that the procedure would be resolved in her favour in a fairly short period of time. Anyone might have thought it was a superficial thing, even extravagant, but it wasn't at all. In fact, I considered it a very important turning point in the work we'd been doing together. Anne had decided to take control of something as delicate and loaded with symbolic value as her surname, which dragged with it the terrible weight of history. Changing it meant carrying out delicate, precise surgery on the fabric it was part of. We couldn't foresee the consequences it would have for her, but I personally suspected that Anne had crossed a major threshold, and righted something that, in her point of view, had been done very badly. All the same, I'd learned not to leap to conclusions. I wasn't even all that sure that Anne's acknowledgement of her madness was anything more than an exercise in rhetoric. I had to check how far this had revealed itself to her, and at the same time not give the game away, maintain a tricky abstinence, and wait for the next episode. Nothing in a human being's life has a given value by itself, but rather it depends on the way the event, the happening, the random magic, or the product of a determined will settles, or not, within a sequence from where its meaning is drawn. With her change of surname, Anne was aiming for a kind of rebirth, a rewriting of her history. There was a chance of an accident in the birth, and that the geographic fault line of her history would be completely broken. Or on the contrary, the little movement of a few letters could manage to better piece together the scattered fragments, and assuage that drifting feeling.

As Anne was waiting for my reaction, I closed the folder and said with a smile that the most important thing was that she had taken a different initiative, that it was a different demand to the ones she usually made.

"This should help mend things, don't you think?" I asked.

"Mend! That's exactly the word I was looking for and couldn't get it to come! Well done. Do you think it'll work?"

"I wouldn't know how to answer that question, Anne."

"You're very honest, Dr. Palmer. Sometimes I'd like it if you fooled me a little, but I've already learned what it means to come here. We have to be willing to do experiments with uncertainty. It's like Russian roulette, only instead of bullets the revolver is loaded with words. It's true that words can sometimes cause greater wounds than bullets, but there's nothing else for it but to play the game."

Anne made very vivid comparisons, images full of lucidity and irony. Like many sad people, sometimes she managed to transform her inner tragedy into a biting comedy into which she'd slip amazing observations. I thought calling psychoanalysis "an experiment in uncertainty" a find worthy of mention in a lecture, or a speech for a congress. I was sure that Dr. Rubashkin would appreciate it.

* * *

"She said that? An experiment in uncertainty?"

"More precisely, she said it in plural: 'Coming here means being willing to do experiments in uncertainty.'"

"But this woman should be a psychoanalyst! She has an innate talent!" Dr. Rubashkin exclaimed. "I tell you, I was about to take a nap, but this has woken me up. You should write it down so you don't forget it."

"I did. I took a few notes, because you don't find something like this every day."

"Far from it. People don't want to know about uncertainties. They have enough with all the uncertainties the world offers every day, especially since someone discovered that sooner or later everything ends up being digested. Today's uncertainty will be tomorrow's custom. I remember my life in Paris, when people fought for what they believed in. Today the strategy of the powers that be has changed. They no longer repress. They simply don't respond. They wait. They know that exhaustion will always be in their favour. Today everyone's too entertained to think about the serious things in life. So many apps to discover on mobile telephones, so little time to waste fighting for human rights. So many world cups, and finals, and competitions of all kinds. That sates most people, and helps them forget. But thank God from time to time we get a case like this. This is when the joy of knowing that we're doing something worthwhile comes back. If it weren't for that, our work would be a sophisticated form of moral masochism. Freud ended up thinking that the practice of analysis was an unhealthy activity for the analyst. But at least sometimes we have our reward."

"I don't want to celebrate just yet. She's still a little green ..."

"I meant the case, not the treatment or the prognosis. In fact, I was referring to the fact that there are still crazies around who haven't succumbed to this modernity. Your patient says she's a survivor. I'm sure she is, and not just with the reasons her parents convinced her with. She's still resisting being killed by the experts! She was very lucky to get you, and that they didn't stick her in the protocol shredder. If it hadn't been for you, her daughters would now be deciding between cremation or burial."

"Maybe. But that's not an idea I like to think about."

"What idea?"

"That I'm her big chance."

"It's the other way round, my dear Dave. It's the other way round completely," said Rubashkin, and I looked at him, not understanding what he meant.

"*She's* your big chance. Now, if you'll just help me out of this chair, I want to read you something I wrote a long time ago, when I foresaw the world that was coming. Or better still, go over to that bookcase."

I did as he said and went over to a beautiful cherrywood bookcase housing a small part of Rubashkin's literary treasure.

"You see those books bound in red? Look for volume eight and bring it over."

Astonished that the elderly man was really capable of locating a written phrase faster than Google, I ran my fingers over the row of books until I found volume eight, and gave it to Rubashkin.

"Let's see. Here it is. I wrote this a few days after visiting the Oracle of Delphi. We'd organised a clinical colloquium there. I don't believe there is a more appropriate place on earth for talking about man. Have you ever been? No? That'll explain why you don't believe in Zeus, and why you don't throw pieces of meat into the fire in his honour, like Robert Graves did at his retreat in Mallorca, dressed in a linen tunic and leather sandals. Listen:

"I heard from the mouths of the inhabitants of Delphi that the gods had left, that they had abandoned the oracle and the temples

surrounding her to their solitude, a solitude that no longer has a cure. With the gods' departure there is something that has been profoundly affected, something without which we human beings are condemned to desolation, something as ancient as the very condition of man, and which is called Truth. With the flight of Apollo, the god of Logos, and of Dionysus, the god of pleasure, the journey began to where we are now, to a world that is on the verge of losing for ever the meaning of the Truth, the Truth as the only antidote we still had against cynicism.

To what is the old gods' exile due? Why has the oracle fallen silent, and why does the holy water no longer flow from the spring? The gods were expelled because they are not scientific, because their truth, the truth they whispered to men through the lips of the Pythia, is a kind of truth that does not fit the demands of scientific method. The gods have not approved the experts' evaluations, and the public powers have deemed it more convenient for the health of the population to trust the management of the oracle to the pharmaceutical companies and psychiatrists' associations, and also to behavioural psychologists and neuropsychologists, and all that new class of priests who, dressed in a false science, claim to assume a knowledge that washes its hands of the Truth.

We, the psychoanalysts, will also be expelled one day. We are so unscientific that we still practise a profession that requires no technical object, and unlike the head of New York Mental Health Services, we think the spirit suffers more than neurotransmitters, and that the spirit is not made up of molecules or proteins, but words.

Just like the old gods, and just like those who worshipped them, we psychoanalysts believe in an order of truth that is invisible to the microscope, weightless to scales, intangible to numbers, experiments, and protocols, and yet a truth so powerful that it can blind anyone who sees it, make he who fears nothing tremble, steal a piece of memory from he who has a healthy brain, and make someone hear voices that no one should ever have to hear. That blindness and trembling, that forgetting and those voices, which affect the spirit of many through words, will cease to torment them through the means of other words. It is a terrible sin of psychoanalysis to dare to make the tradition of Logos stand, the tradition of the ancient gods, in an era when subjectivity is an anachronism that must be eliminated, so that people might become more flexible to social administrators, those responsible for planning future states as spaces in which happiness is administered, in the same way that harvests or fluctuations in the stock exchange are programmed.

"As I was saying, that woman has been lucky to get you and not a serious doctor. But you've been lucky too, because she's going to teach you far more than I ever could."

TWENTY-FOUR

"What a terrible day yesterday was," exclaimed Anne as she collapsed with all her weight onto the chair on the other side of my desk. "The worst. It's the end. I said I was going to end up screwing it up. I couldn't help it, I never could," she said, her voice cracked from the sorrow and the anguish. "I'm a real disaster. Richard told me a few days after his suicide attempt. He blamed me, he kept saying that life by my side was unbearable, that I forced him to live in a chronic state of emergency. He was right, oh yes he was. I understand that in the end he got tired of me. It's terrible for me to accept that, but it's the pure truth. And yesterday I proved it once again."

"What happened? This is all a surprise to me. Also, this about Richard's suicide attempt, I think it's the first time you've brought it up."

"I hadn't told you till now, no. I probably wanted to hide it from you, to avoid the shame I feel for all the damage I've done to others. Sundays are my worst days. I've always been like that. It's like a day that was invented for regret. Just for that. It's the day of punishment for lonely hearts, like mine. Sundays are truly bad. I do everything I can to make them go quickly. On Saturday night I stuff myself with sleeping tablets so that I sleep in. But no matter how hard I try, at about midday I wake up. Then I stay in bed, totally still, with my eyes closed, trying to concentrate on something that relaxes me, see if I can get back to sleep again. I can pass the time a little more like that, but not much, because that trick doesn't bring very good results. I'm assailed by thoughts, like biting teeth attacking from every side. Yesterday I was in that state, when suddenly the phone rang. I didn't have time to pick up, because whoever it was hung up straight away. No one ever calls me, except my father, but never at that time. I sat there watching the damn phone for an hour, as if I could get it to ring again just by staring at it. At the time I made up all kinds of theories about what had happened. It was just two rings, so someone had changed their mind about calling. Everyone changes their mind with me, because I'm sick to the core. It's best that people run away from me if they want to go on living. I give off a kind of lethal radiation. I mean it, Dr. Palmer, it always happens. I have the fatal power of destroying everything that surrounds me. That telephone triggered my desperation, because I started to think something, and when a thought gets going in my head, ah! Then it's all over. All over! It's like a hunting dog that closes its jaws and won't open them unless you shoot it. That's what happened to me. Suddenly, I don't remember how, my ideas all linked together and I realised that it was Karen. It was she who had called me, but someone had intervened and forced her to hang up. Who could it be? No doubt about it, it was Richard. Once again he was poisoning my daughter's mind. I convinced myself that Karen was in danger, that she needed a mother, and that son of a bitch was holding her against her will.

"So I couldn't take it any more and I called. And do you know what happened? Karen answered. I hadn't heard her voice for almost a year, and when I heard her on the other end of the line I felt like I was about to faint. 'Is that you, Karen? Is that you, daughter?' All I got by way of reply was the sound of her breathing. 'Please, Karen, it's your mother. Please don't hang up, I'm begging on my knees, don't hang up, don't let me die like this!' Then I lost control and started crying, bawling my eyes out. I couldn't stop, I couldn't get my words together. I wanted to calm down, say something, attempt a conversation, but I couldn't stop crying. The strangest thing is that Karen stayed on the line, I could hear her breathing, but she didn't say a word. I couldn't tell you how long that went on, maybe a few minutes, maybe hours. I don't know. Eventually I passed out, and when I came to, I had the phone in my hand, but the call had ended. I tried calling again, but Karen wouldn't pick up any more. I kept calling all afternoon, but it was futile. I must have frightened her with my screaming, or perhaps she felt such repugnance that the only news she wants to hear from me is when I die. She'll have that soon, that's a fact. Richard couldn't do it, he tried it but he got it wrong, and maybe he didn't have the courage. I don't either, but there are many ways to die. It doesn't have to be suicide.

"I got dressed as quickly as I could. I went out, stopped a taxi and gave Richard's address. When I got there, I sat in the bar across the road and watched the door to the building. This time I wasn't going to repeat the previous number. That's why I was sure to take with me a good dose of tranquillisers. In these cases, I swallow one after another until they eventually have an effect and I can get serene. Just to be sure, I backed up these preventative measures with a double whisky, so that a few hours later my head was slumped on the table of the bar. Night had fallen, and the bartender told me they were closing. I stood up as best I could, because I could hardly keep my balance, but I managed to pay and get outside. I sat on the sidewalk, like on that other occasion, but I was very discreet. I realised that it had all been a waste of time, that Karen had had time to leave the building and come back several times while her mother slept, sprawled out at a table in a bar, with her head full of pills and alcohol. I only prayed to heaven that she hadn't seen me, because I couldn't have given her a sight more … shameful, more ignoble. I walked home, with considerable difficulty, because in my hurry I hadn't brought enough money with me. It took me ages to get home: I got lost several times, I went round in circles, not daring to ask anyone where I was. I must've looked like a bum, if deep down I'm not really one, because people passed by me as if I wasn't there. On top of that I'm too voluminous. I take up so much space that I don't fit anywhere. I'm doing this all wrong, Dr. Palmer, so wrong. I'm your worst patient, I have no doubt about it. You're wasting your time, and there are a lot of people who deserve to have you looking after them. People worth fighting for."

I had exactly a fraction of a second to stop her. If I let her go on, then what Anne was saying would become true, and there would be no way to prevent complete destruction.

A fraction of a second for the coin to come down heads or tails.

"Are you wearing both your shoes?" I asked her with forced curiosity, even peering over my desk, trying to look at her feet.

Perplexed, Anne looked at me and didn't know what to say. "Excuse me? What's wrong with my shoes?"

"I was asking you if you are wearing both of them, or just the one."

Anne drew her chair back a little and bowed her head to get a look at her feet.

"Well … I'm wearing both. Why do you want to know that?"

"Don't you remember what happened that last time, when you lost a shoe and walked in the rain for hours?"

She was silent a few seconds, her mouth half open, looking at me as if I was a Martian.

"Now that you mention it, I think you're right. I don't remember too well when that happened, but it was like that."

"I'll tell you: it was your birthday, when you sent that photo, where you'd written on the back something, shall we say, rather worrying."

"Yes, I remember it well now. That night I was wandering around and I lost a shoe. I'm sorry, Dr. Palmer, but I don't see how this matters right now."

"It matters a great deal more than you can imagine!" I exclaimed, faking an emphasis charged with enthusiasm.

"Oh! Really? And do you think you could explain it to me?" she asked in an authentically curious tone, which contrasted with the pathetic tone that had seized her just a few minutes earlier.

"Of course. The difference, Anne, the difference! That can be found in even the most trivial detail. Even more than that, it is in the apparently insignificant detail that we often find what really matters," I added (and it was true). "You've been feeling defeated because you think you've gone back to wandering about, that what happened is a carbon copy of the previous time. But here we have the proof. It couldn't be more objective. Your disorientation didn't reach the limit this time. You were able to control yourself at the last minute. And keep both your shoes, which is like saying 'keep your head'."

Even I didn't believe what I'd just come out with, but it had clearly had an effect, as Anne was so astonished that she wouldn't stop looking alternatively from her feet to my face. She was completely confused, but with that I'd managed to push her back from the slope on which she'd been about to release the brakes. Taking advantage of how extraordinarily easy it was to influence her, I had no choice but to use an almost childish trick, like when you stop a baby crying by distracting its attention with some absurd decoy. The main thing was that it had worked, I'd managed to stop one of those states in which Anne was dragged under by the ferocity she aimed at herself. Could it be that the procedure she'd started to change her surname wasn't mending her the way we'd hoped? Was this the first sign that, on the contrary, that act had set off a catastrophic chain reaction? Any answer was premature, as I started to harbour doubts about Anne's prognosis. Defeating therapeutic optimism had been a fundamental part of my training, and to top it all I had to make an immense effort to achieve something that most people, both professionals and patients, considered an aberration. Our time was marked by a delirious worship of a passion to cure everything, and my position was an anachronism against which more and more objections were raised in the name of scientific modernity and the advances of historic and social progress. For millennia, the death of a loved one or a similar loss was followed by an obligatory mourning process. Everywhere in the world human beings invented ceremonies and rituals so that mourning would have its place and role in the transient time of existence. Disobeying those rituals was a serious affront to memory and honour. Now that the definition and keeping of the universal model of happiness has been delegated to science, any manifestation of sadness is immediately diagnosed as a pathological symptom. Medicine and psychology have started a crusade against sadness, in the same way that very soon we will see, as in previous centuries, indigence and poverty decreed as punishable misdemeanours. If Anne constituted a "resistant" case, there would be no lack of people proposing surgery in some part of her brain. At the bottom of this eagerness to cure, which can at times reach a bloody limit, is the real purpose of eliminating all those subjects who do not adapt to the model of good citizens. As for me, defending Anne included the possibility of admitting the failure of therapy. But if she was incurable, if her pain wouldn't admit any possible negotiation, I at least had to find the way to show it, and that moment had yet to come.

TWENTY-FIVE

I am five years old. It's the last day of classes at kindergarten. Everything is ready for the end of year party. I'm wearing a very pretty dress, because I'm going to act in the play. I have an important role, and the teachers think I play it very well. We've been rehearsing for months, and I know my lines. I'm a little nervous. I'm the leading actress, and there's one moment when I'll be alone on the stage, reciting out loud a poem that, according to what the teachers said, is by a very famous poet who died a long time ago. And I'm going to have to recite it in front of all the parents and teachers, and the other children too. There's going to be a very big party, a lot of people are coming. That's what I've been told. The hall is decorated with garlands and flowers. In the room next door the children in the orchestra are practising. I can hear the conductor's voice explaining how they have to play. I think we all have a little stage fright. My teacher tells me again that everything's going to go fine, and that I shouldn't worry, but I can't help it. My belly's starting to ache. It's like little needles. I try to hold on and don't say a word.

The play is starting soon. Now everyone is running here and there. The teachers are a little nervous too, although they're trying not to let it show. A girl has fallen over and is crying. The needles in my tummy are pricking me harder, but I'm not going to say a word. If I say anything, they might take me out of the play.

Daddy promised he'd come and see me and that he'd get here early so he could get a front row seat. Mommy, on the other hand, won't be coming. She's very strange, and is afraid to leave the house. Daddy told me that mommy is very proud of me, and that when the party's over and we go home, she'll be waiting to give me a kiss and congratulate me. I would've liked her to be here too, but I'm used to not being able to ask her to do things like that. Mommy only likes staying home. Actually she likes staying in her bedroom. She spends most of her time there. She lies there in bed, not sleeping but thinking. It's true, because although my sister and I aren't supposed to go in when she's in bed, sometimes I take a peek and I see that she's awake. Daddy explained to us that she's thinking about our grandparents and aunts and uncles who died. They were killed. We don't quite understand why they were killed, and daddy said that one day, when we're older, we'll understand. That we shouldn't think about it for now. It's hard not to think about it because mommy thinks about it all the time. We can't talk a lot or make a noise when she's in her bedroom. Daddy told us that mommy can't stand loud noises. She doesn't like dogs either, and when the neighbour's dog barks, she covers her ears so she can't hear it. I like dogs, but I know we'll never have one.

The teacher told me not to go over what I have to recite any more, but I ignore him and say it to myself all the time. I want to get it right, because daddy will be watching me and mommy will congratulate me when I get home. Otherwise, she's bound to get very sad, even sadder. I'd love it if she'd smile some time, but daddy explained that she can't, and that one day we'll understand. From what I can tell, in a while there will be a load of things that we'll understand, although I'm used to it already. My sister gets really upset by what's happening at home, and sometimes she argues with daddy, and kicks up a fuss. My sister says she hates our mother, but I don't. I don't hate her. I feel really sorry for her, because she doesn't like going outside, and because she doesn't like dogs. I think she could have a lot of fun with a dog, it could keep her company while daddy's at work and we're at school. Maybe mommy just feels very lonely, and that's why she's sad, although daddy says that isn't the reason.

It looks like the play is going to start very soon, and they're letting in the parents and the older students to take their seats. I can see my daddy! He's waving at me, a big smile on his face, and he runs to sit in the front row. The needles are really pricking me now, and I really need to pee, but I can't now.

The school principal has taken to the stage to welcome everyone, and tell them what's going to happen at the party. First the orchestra will play some songs, then the choir will sing too. Then it will be our turn, those of us in the play. I keep going over in my head the words to the poem, it isn't very long, but I don't want to forget a thing. Plus I have to say other things in the play, as I'm the most important actress, but it's the poem I'm most worried about, because it was written by someone who's now dead and I have to get it right.

The principal has finished explaining what we're going to do, and everyone's applauding happily. Daddy can't see me now because I'm to the side of the stage waiting for the orchestra to perform, but I can see him. Daddy is usually sad too, though never as sad as mommy. Today, though, he has a very happy face. I'm sure it's because I'm going to act in the play. What a pity he came on his own.

The orchestra plays very well, although one of the boys in the choir at the end wouldn't go out on stage. I don't know why, but he started crying at the last minute. I'm not going to cry. There's just one more song to go before the play begins.

It's now our turn. The principal has just said the name of the play, and the lights have dimmed a little, because we have to make it look like it's night time in a village street. My boyfriend is going to come on a horse, and I wait for him in the square. As I do, I have to recite the poem, which is a very beautiful poem. I'm calm because I know it very well, but I need to pee more and more and the needles keep pricking my tummy. I'll close my eyes as I say the poem, because that's what the teacher taught me to do. That's how I have to do it. Standing, with my eyes closed. It's better like that. I'd rather not see everyone looking at me. If I think about that, I'll get embarrassed. I even feel a little embarrassed to know that daddy's there, so close that I could almost touch him if I reached out to him, but I have to act as if there were no one in front of me. That's what the teacher told us, and we understand.

I'm doing it very well. So well that I can't help but open my eyes to see the people's faces. Then something strange happens, because I could swear that I just saw my mommy at the entrance to the assembly hall, half-hidden behind the door. Am I dreaming? Maybe I just imagined it, it must be someone else's mother. But no, now I get a good look and I realise it's her. It's her! She's come to see me! But why didn't she sit down like the other parents? How I'd like to wave to her, but I know that I can't now, that I have to concentrate on my role! What's going on? Mommy! Why have you turned around? Aren't you going to stay? Won't you wait until it's over? You have to clap! Please, don't go! Wait a while!

I'm starting to feel dizzy. I can't go on saying the poem because everything is spinning. I feel like the hall is spinning faster and faster and that I'm going to fall over. I'm going to fall over, and to make matters worse I'm peeing my pants, I can't hold it in any longer. Sorry daddy! Forgive me! I memorised it so well, I swear, but … but …

Now I'm in the nurse's office in the school. I've woken up on a bed, and I see daddy smiling. He strokes my head, and whispers in my ear that nothing's wrong, that I'm fine. I fainted, but I'm not sick and we'll go home in a short while. I want to ask him what happened, where's mommy, but I don't have the strength. My voice won't come out. I also want to ask him what happened to the play. How it all ended. Did they go on without me? So everything I practised was for nothing?

We're back home. Mommy's in the bedroom. Daddy puts a finger to his lips, and tiptoes to the kitchen to make me a cup of tea, but I don't feel like drinking anything. Daddy says that later I'll understand what happened. I don't think I'll understand anything.

I think I'm just going to hate her for the rest of my life.

TWENTY-SIX

For her, no one had the right to be alive. After all that had happened, it was forbidden to enjoy the slightest thing that life had to offer. Her conviction was unfair, but at the same time, logical. No one could imagine what they'd been through. Not even my sister and I, who were born and bred under the same roof, could ever come close to understanding the full extent of what had happened. Entire nations became bloodthirsty assassins, and a large part of the rest of mankind collaborated. The only proportionate punishment would've been to wipe out the human race. Man reached the pinnacle of his ill-fated glory, and from then on the whole planet should have exploded into pieces, so that the universe would never again have to contain such a creature. If God had been anything more than a product of human fantasy, he would've sent a new flood, but this time without giving us a second chance. If I think about it like that, with the perception that reflection allows, my mother was right. Don't think I'm just a being driven by wild impulses. I'm also capable of thinking, and when I think from this point of view, I think my mother was overwhelmed by her strict sense of dignity. But the problem is that she wasn't a pure philosophical argument. She was flesh and bone, a human being, one more victim among millions, and we had to sip the bitter milk of her tragedy every day. The shadows of so many deaths lived within her that they couldn't all fit in the house. It was a home where there was no room for the living, as we were invaded by the spirit of those who had been wiped out by the fire.

I've already mentioned that she hardly ever talked to my sister and me. She was a sacred being, and my father officiated as priest of that mysterious, sickly deity. We'd address to him any messages we had for her, and it was he who interpreted her designs. Over the years I grew up and understood that our mother was no more than a defenceless, moribund creature, but by then the disease had been lodged in my mind for many years, a larva awaiting the right moment to grow and come out into the light.

I haven't been to Israel these last years. It may be that I'll never see her again, she's already very elderly. It's funny, but in contrast to my mother, I can't conceive of my father dying too. That idea is unthinkable to me, I feel like he's always going to be there, that I'll always get phone calls from him, that I'll be able to count on him for the rest of my life. I've been a bad daughter, Dr. Palmer. I used meeting Richard to get away. I left them completely alone. But I got my just deserts. My daughters have abandoned me too, and now I know what that's like, I can feel in my own flesh the pain that I myself have caused. It's too coherent a history, a mortal circle too perfect to be undone.

When I speak to my father, I find it impossible to ask about her. My sister has washed her hands of them completely, but I just can't. He's never reproached me for a thing, and he's even had the delicacy not to intrude in my life. He limits himself to listening to all that I tell him, but never tries to dig any deeper. I've no doubt that he knows perfectly well what's going on, because he reads my thoughts, he can perceive every timbre in my words and work out things I don't so much as hint at. What will become of him? Who will look after him in his last days, when death, which incomprehensively let him off a thousand and one times, decides that his end has finally come, as even survivors have to die some time? These questions torment me too. It's ironic that not only my madness causes me pain. When sanity takes over my thoughts for a moment, I can hardly say that things improve much. So, what is there left for me? I understand very well that deep down I'm torturing you. You must be very well trained to put up with patients like me, people who don't provide a single way out. But I imagine that despite that, you'll still feel at times sick and tired of so much complaining and negativity. I once heard a man who lived on the seashore saying how many times he'd saved the lives of bathers who were about to drown. He said that some people, when they were rescued, would cling to him with such desperation that he had to knock them out with a punch to prevent them both from drowning. Now I understand very well what that man was doing. I am also one of those desperate people who perhaps doesn't want to be saved, and drags down those who come to my rescue.

* * *

"Lacan learned many things from the great masters of psychiatry, and he maintained them to his dying day. One particular thing was the idea that there is no greater lucidity than that which springs from madness. This woman is capable of creating amazing constructions, with a rigour that is impossible to knock down. I have seldom heard someone explain so simply the human drama of lives turning around a vicious circle. Guilt doesn't give them the right to heal, their deep destructiveness is directed as much at themselves as at their therapists, hatred makes them prey to their own existence and the existence of others, and it proves practically impossible to dislodge them from that hell. She has created her own concentration camp. Her parents fled after incredible events, but she's still a prisoner."

"That's the way it is, Dr. Rubashkin. Sometimes I'm about to throw in the towel, and think I'm going to let her go."

"You can do so, of course. But don't forget that she is certainly following the fundamental principle of analytical therapy, turning you into the depository of evil. Her comparison is spot on. She wants to free herself from herself, and for that she can turn to suicide or crime. The latter is incompatible with her ethics, and as she said, there are different ways to commit suicide. One of those is to abandon anyone who might help her get out of her hell. But come on, Dave! I'm not saying anything that you don't already well know!"

"Yes, but talking to you about all this gives me a fresh perspective. Anne is a castaway clinging to a few remnants. It's a matter of getting her to stay afloat and those remnants holding out until she reaches the shore. Except that she is intuitive enough to realise that reaching land is also something that terrifies her. She's never been comfortable anywhere."

"Except for the first stage of motherhood, that idyll that lasted just a few years. We mustn't forget that. Maybe that's the key!"

* * *

Now that the years have passed, and Dr. Rubashin is part of my life's happiest memories, I wonder whether those words were said by chance or were simply premonitory.

I'll never know.

TWENTY-SEVEN

That morning it was absolute chaos at the service. I'd barely gotten out of my car when Miles Donaldson, the morning guard, came up to me in the parking lot to give me the news. During the night shift, a patient who had been discharged ten days earlier showed up in a fit of rage, knifing the duty nurse Maria Lafuente and Dr. Melissa Timbaldi, a twenty-nine-year-old psychiatrist in the second year of her residency. Maria was in a coma and in a very serious condition at Brigham and Women's Hospital. Dr. Timbaldi died instantly from a laceration to her throat. The assailant, a twenty-four-year-old white male, had been admitted to the acute unit a few months before for a delirious episode, accompanied by very intense hallucinations. Diagnosed with paranoid schizophrenia, in his two months at the centre he showed himself to be docile and cooperative. A few days after his first shock pharmacological dose, he joined the group psychotherapy programme, psychopharmacological treatment, and occupation therapy activities. Once a week he had a one-to-one interview with one of the psychiatrists on the team, to talk about his problems and discuss the state of his recovery. At the end of the first month, the whole team believed that Harold Yardcore had made notable progress, and that he was stable. His delusion had ceased, his hallucinatory experiences had dissipated, and he participated actively in group therapy and the rest of the programme prescribed for him. Furthermore, Harold got on as well with the other patients as with the medical and nursing staff. He was attentive to the other people in the ward, and in group therapy he not only talked about his personal issues, but also took an interest in other patients' stories, giving his opinion, and encouraging those who were depressed or demoralised.

The police managed to detain Harold a few hours later. He was wandering the city, in a confused state, and didn't put up the slightest resistance. In the first interviews he couldn't remember a thing, and the blood and urine tests did not suggest that he was under the influence of any toxic substance. It was without doubt an acute attack, pretty inexplicable, as according to his parents' testimony he hadn't stopped taking his medication at any time, and he had been calm and in a good mood since his return home.

The previous day we had had a team meeting in which we discussed the case of a patient under Dr. Timbaldi's care, and I still had her face etched in my mind, a charming girl, who expressed herself very confidently, and showed very sharp clinical intuition. She was going to get married the following year, and when she broke the news, those men on the staff who were single let out a sigh at the thought that they were too late.

When I got to reception, there was a real brouhaha of police, journalists, and cameramen running one way and another. Outpatient treatment had been cancelled, and the police had cordoned off with yellow tape the little break room where the tragedy had occurred. From what I could find out, Harold Yardcore had shown up at the hospital at about 3am. The guard at the entrance recognised him, and Harold greeted him very politely, without showing any signs of being upset. He asked to be allowed in to speak to someone in emergencies, and when the guard asked him to take a seat in the waiting room, he ran off towards the break room, which he knew well from his stay in the hospital, and without saying a word leapt at nurse Lafuente and Dr. Timbaldi, who had no time to react. On hearing the screams, the guard took out his gun and opened fire on Harold, but he missed. Harold ran down the hospital's central corridor, and took off like a cyclone via the rear emergency exit. The guard was terribly upset, and kept blaming himself for what had happened, even though everyone, from the medical staff to the police inspectors and the district attorney, tried to calm him down. They eventually had to administer him a sedative, as he grew more anxious as time passed.

Although the secretaries had managed to contact many patients to cancel that day's appointments, over the course of the morning some of those showed up who it had not been possible to contact. At about 12, while I was standing with a group of colleagues commenting on what had happened, and trying to contact someone from Brigham to find out the latest on the condition of nurse Lafuente, I heard shouting at the hospital entrance. I went over to see what was going on, and there was Anne, who had come for her appointment, and was struggling with the police officers stationed at the door. I'd completely forgotten about her, and I went over to calm her down and explain what had happened.

"I'm sorry, Anne, the secretaries tried to let everyone know this morning."

"Dr. Palmer! Blessed be the Lord! Yes, of course they let me know!"

"So why have you come?"

"Why have I come? This morning I heard the news on the television. You know how I have it on all the time, day and night. At first I couldn't believe my ears, and then when I got the call from this girl, I can't remember her name, the receptionist, who always speaks to me so sweetly: hey honey, I said, is it true what I just heard on the TV? What an awful thing! And she said yes, it's terrible Mrs. Kurczynski, we're all in shock here.

And I said to her, is Dr. Palmer all right? And she told me that you were fine, thank God, but I had to see for myself, so I came here, and these numbskulls wouldn't let me in. You can't imagine how desperate I've been all this time. Thank goodness I've seen you! How could such a dreadful thing happen? And that poor doctor, so young! I don't remember the nurse, but as soon as I saw the photo of the psychiatrist on the television I said to myself: I know her! I've said hi to her a thousand times! It's terrible, Dr. Palmer. Do you think something like that could happen to me?"

"Calm down, Anne. I suppose they've already given you a new appointment with me. I'm sorry I can't see you today. What do you mean by 'something like that'?"

"I mean, that guy, he had an illness like mine. And I've said it many times that I've had ugly thoughts, and once I pushed my mother-in-law when I bumped into her in the supermarket. Imagine, they sell knives in the supermarket. They're within everyone's reach. They shouldn't allow that. Could I be capable of doing a thing like that?"

I was about to reply that we're all potentially capable of doing a thing like that, but I stopped myself.

"Of course not, Anne. You have your temper, but you would be incapable of harming anyone. I'm absolutely sure of that. Now, go home and try to forget this business. And please, don't argue with the police. They're only doing their job."

"Don't worry, Dr. Palmer, I'll be going now. I'm very relieved to hear what you just told me, and also that you're all right. I don't want to think what could have happened if you'd been on duty instead of the doctor!"

Nurse Lafuente passed away two days later from a massive internal haemorrhage. We were terribly upset, and the investigation went on without turning up any clue as to the motive. The defendant remained in isolation at Bridgewater State Hospital, a specialist centre for inmates with psychiatric disorders. The district attorney and the inspectors spoke to all the professionals at our hospital involved in Harold Yardcore's treatment, and the judge requested a copy of his medical chart.

Some colleagues suggested the possibility of an erotomaniac delusion, although the patient hadn't shown any sign of that. On the contrary, it did not appear that sex or his love life in general played an important role in his life, as tends to occur with certain psychotics. I personally didn't have a hypothesis, as the monitoring and control of that case was the responsibility of a clinical meeting held in the inpatient unit itself, and I was entirely unaware of the details.

All this had shaken up our lives very seriously, as well as the lives of some of the patients, particularly those who'd been in treatment for a fairly long time, and for whom the service was a place of safety and support. Most of them had very intense emotional bonds with their therapists and with the support staff. As was to be expected, Anne was one of those most affected, given that her style was to feel an automatic empathy for any dramatic or mournful situation. Furthermore, she was still obsessed with the fear that her own madness might lead her to commit a criminal act, and that concern required various sessions which she spent confessing a list of people she hated with all her might. Her mother-in-law took pride of place, probably because she offered her the chance to offload onto her part of her hatred towards her own mother, which she found impossible to acknowledge, and of course her ex-husband Richard, who she held responsible for most of her misfortune.

She would develop incredibly twisted arguments to "forgive" her daughters for the scorn they supposedly showed her, although at the same time she still spat out all kinds of poisoned reproaches at them.

"Is it only parents who have obligations to their children? Do children not have any obligation to their parents?" was one of her favourite and most repeated questions.

"Ever since I was little I was brought up to look after my mother, to make sure I didn't do a thing that could upset her! Are my daughters incapable of bearing their mother's problems? Is this how they pay me for all the sacrifices I made for them? Explain one thing, Dr. Palmer, why has life consistently dealt me such a bad hand?"

Injustice was one of the themes that occupied her therapy the most. She didn't mean anecdotal injustice, the kind that most of us mortals put up with in small daily doses. For her it was something cosmic, the undeniable existence of an original evil of which she was the target, a conviction that made the real basis of her family's tragedy unassailable. I'd learned the importance of respecting that idea, of not attempting under any circumstances to contradict her, but rather I had to encourage her to attempt to live *in spite of* the terrible injustice she was caught up in. That strategy used to perk her up, because she considered it a show of solidarity from me, which allowed me to remain on the list of people who had a beneficial influence on her. There was always a latent possibility of an unfortunate action of mine sending me automatically to the persecutors' side. Anne listened to my words in a special way, she was capable of perceiving in them the most unexpected connotations, and her ability for deduction, while on occasions delirious, followed an amazingly solid line of logic. Everything that made her vulnerable, at the mercy of life's inclemency, was also what gave her an exquisite sensitivity to think about many things, and express a philosophy that surprised me with its tremendous humanity.

* * *

I couldn't get what had happened to Harold Yardcore out of my head. I was used to believing that people's actions always obeyed a reason that might remain hidden, but which nonetheless existed somewhere. The fact that we couldn't find it didn't mean that things had happened for supernatural or inexplicable reasons. Therefore, there must have been some cause that explained why that man showed up unexpectedly at the hospital and started a bloodbath. Was he looking for any of those women in particular? What would have happened if other members of staff had been present instead of those who were there at that time? From what I could see, no answer could be found to these questions. The summary proceedings were held under rigorous secrecy, but after a few days I thought that someone might be able to help me.

* * *

Delucca ordered a light salad and a glass of Chardonnay. I chose a chicken thigh and a beer, a rather unsuitable combination from the point of view of gastronomic rules, but I generally ignored them. I wasn't much of a gourmet.

"I've been asking around a little, as far as I could. Judge Robinson is a good friend, but naturally he doesn't like people poking around in his affairs. I haven't been able to find out much. This Yardcore has no priors of any kind. Not even a parking ticket. He's an IT technician, with an average academic record. His neighbours describe him as a reserved person, who's never given them any trouble. The police checked his computers, there isn't so much as a trace of strange mail, visits to hardcore pornography sites, things like that. His crises have always been depressive, and on one occasion, when he was in his teens, he had a pretty serious suicide attempt when he swallowed cleaning products. You know better than I do that that method is favoured by a few nuts. He didn't show any signs of aggressive behaviour to his parents or fellow students either.

"He did odd jobs, and none of his employers had any complaints or noticed anything strange, save his extremely shy personality. You know how these things work. You catch a serial killer, a psychopath, or a cannibal, and people will always say that he was a charming person and they never suspected a thing, so we're not going to get anything down that route. Sorry, but that's all I've been able to get. And one more thing: not a single piece of information on his sex life or love life. He's a kind of asexual being, according to this clinical chart, though I guess you already know that."

"Could I interview him?"

"I doubt it. I don't think Robinson would authorise it. He's got his own forensic team, besides Yardcore's lawyers wouldn't allow it."

"I wouldn't do it with a view to contributing anything to the summary proceedings, it'd be just for my own interest. I could say I'm a journalist. After all, the media manage to get into the trials, no matter how secret they are."

"The media's a different story. Don't try to compete with their power. Besides, Yardcore's incommunicado now, so not even his podiatrist can visit him."

"I understand."

* * *

A week later I managed to pull some other strings and found myself sitting opposite Harold Yardcore in a room in the Bridgewater Hospital. I imagined he'd be taller, well-built, but the man I saw across the table was short, very slim, with the skin on his face stretched over his cheekbones. He looked anorexic, although he wasn't, and it was hard to believe that such ferocity could have been unleashed in this sad-faced, fragile individual. His profile was closer to that of a typical, shy, hard-working student than a barbaric murderer, although my impressions were completely out of place, as Harold had committed a very serious crime without being a criminal in the strictest sense, and besides, a homicidal act requiring considerable energy can flare up in the most insignificant and apparently harmless individual. Despite it all, I was still surprised by Harold's ingenuous, absorbed expression. He still wasn't fully aware of what had happened and the situation he was in.

He'd already undergone numerous rounds of questioning, so I decided to try a different tack.

"Are they treating you well, Harold?"

"Oh, yes, Doctor. I can't complain. The food isn't at all bad, and I can watch TV. They told me I might be able to have my computer in a few days. That would come in real handy."

"What do you usually use it for?"

"I like video games, some TV shows, and also to talk to Jimmy. But I can still speak to him without the computer. It's not essential."

This last part particularly resonated in me, but I thought it prudent not to approach that subject immediately.

"I like some shows too. But at night I tend to be too tired, and I fall asleep half way through," I said. "What are your favourites?"

"Depends. I really like criminal investigation shows, but I'm also hooked on one about the Civil War. I haven't been able to see it here, but I'll catch up when they bring me my computer."

"What do you do for a living, Harold?"

"Actually I do a bit of everything to get by, Doctor. I'm an IT analyst, but if necessary I can also do carpentry work, plumbing, I know a little about car engines, stuff like that. My family hasn't got a lot of dough, you know? So I try to earn my money. My dad's retired, and my mom's a housewife. We don't really have a lot coming in. So I have to get out of here as soon as possible, to look for work. My parents need the money."

"You'll have to be patient, Harold. This is going to take some time. Do you remember why you're here?"

"To be honest, I don't really understand, I got discharged a month ago, and I had to come in for a review. But this isn't the hospital I was at, and no one's explained why I have to stay here a few days. I feel pretty good, I haven't had any more complications."

"What kind of complications did you have?"

"Well, you know, you don't come into this kind of place for fun. I had trouble sleeping. I found it hard to get to sleep, and it got worse and worse, until I went a whole week without sleeping. That got me real worried, so my mom took me to the other hospital."

"Why weren't you sleeping? Was there anything troubling you in particular?"

Harold looked doubtful for a few seconds, as if he didn't know or wasn't willing to answer.

"Can I trust you?"

"Of course."

"It's a long story."

"If you're willing to tell it, don't worry about me. I've got all afternoon."

TWENTY-EIGHT

Harold Yardcore turned out to be a real box of surprises. During his stay at our hospital, he'd fooled everyone, maintaining remarkable control of his delirious ideas.

"It all started more or less a year ago, when this Led Zeppelin song got into my head. You ever heard of Led Zeppelin?"

"Of course. I'm the same generation, they're one of my favourites."

"So you know the song 'Stairway to Heaven'?"

"Sure. Who doesn't?"

"OK. The thing is a year ago I was working for a cleaning company, and there was a woman there, a cleaner, called Mary Queen."

"That's a strange name."

"I thought so too. I guessed it wasn't her real name, because it sounded funny, right? So, one day it just so happened that we both ended up in a house we'd been sent to clean up after building work. We didn't know each other at all. She was wearing earphones, and spent all the time listening to music while she was cleaning. Sometimes she'd sing along, and then she goes and asks me if I like this song by Led Zeppelin. Truth is, I hadn't heard much of the band and I didn't know the song, so she gave me the earphones so I could listen. It was strange, because the minute I started to listen to the song, it was at the part that goes 'It's just a spring clean for Mary Queen', and I thought that was strange at first. That night, when I got home, I looked for the song and paid attention to the lyrics. I realised that I'd gotten it wrong, that the line really said 'It's just a spring clean for the May Queen'. It was all really weird and kind of a coincidence, because it was spring, and that woman had an almost identical name. Then I found out something really important that gave me the key. The secret to the song is in the line that goes 'There's a sign on the wall, but she wants to be sure, you know sometimes words have two meanings'. I realised I'd just received a fundamental sign, and that I had to analyse all the lyrics really carefully, concentrating on that thing about two meanings. From then on I spent day and night listening to the song, taking apart the meaning of the lyrics. That took up nearly all my time, but it was time well spent, as little by little the pieces of the jigsaw fell into place. The most defining moment was one night when I realised that 'Then the piper will lead us to reason' showed me that I was right. I was the piper who was to lead everyone to reason. Do you remember how the song starts?"

"I think so. 'There's a lady who's sure all that glitters is gold.'"

"Exactly. And don't you think that's a totally clear message?"

"Maybe, but I have to admit I can't quite grasp it. Perhaps you could help me to understand it."

"It's referring to women. To throw you off, the lyrics talk about a lady, but it's actually referring to all women. They think all that glitters is gold. My mother does too."

"Really?"

"Straight up. That's why I'm the piper who must lead them to reason. I started with Mary Queen, given that from what I could tell she was completely lost. All she did was clean, and didn't stop laughing and listening to music. She didn't seem to understand what was going on."

"What was going on?"

"It wasn't something that could be explained in words. It could only be felt."

"Could you feel it?"

"That's right. I felt it. I felt that we should prepare to go up to heaven, and that I should take on the role of leading all women. I couldn't do anything for Mary Queen, as after a few days she quit her job and I never heard from her again. I was real upset for a few weeks, because I couldn't get it out of my head that she used to repeat out loud 'This is real shiny,' or 'I'm going to get the shine out of this.' I got more and more worried, I tried to contact her, but I couldn't. The people at the cleaning company wouldn't give me her telephone number or email, they gave me all that privacy crap, but the real reason was that because it was a cleaning company, they have an interest in women believing that all that glitters is gold. That's why I decided to quit the job. I wouldn't be in any shape to carry out that mission if I didn't concentrate on my duty. I was lucky to get to the core of the matter, to pay attention properly to the fact that words have a double meaning. That opened up the way for me."

"And what happened after you quit your job?"

"I decided that I had to get to work, and lead all other women to heaven. Upstairs."

"You set yourself a titanic job! *All* women?"

"That's a very good question. That's what I believed at first, so then I started having trouble sleeping. As you just said, I felt overwhelmed by the burden of a mission that was way too much for me. Taking care of all women was impossible. Plus, at the time I wasn't too clear on how I should proceed to lead them to heaven. I realised that being a piper was a formula that needed a translation. First the story of the Pied Piper of Hamlin came to mind, but it couldn't be that. I've never played the pipes, I've only seen them in a couple of movies, so there had to be a hidden meaning. I also kept coming up against the problem of how I was going to get together all the women and take them up the stairway. On top of all that, I had no idea where that staircase might be. Do you realise the kind of trouble I was in? I went back over the song a thousand times, I searched in every corner of the lyrics, applying the double meaning rule. I paid special attention to that part that goes 'Yes there are two roads you can go by, but in the long run, there's still time to change the road you're on.' That was a real relief. On the one hand, there were two roads, plus I had time. On the other hand, the song very clearly said 'And as we wind on down the road, our shadows taller than our souls, there walks a lady we all know, who shines bright light.' I knew then that I had to find that lady. She was every woman rolled into one. The Lady Who Shines Bright Light. And I also understood where the road was. By then, I was in a terrible state, because I had to find the Lady Who Shines Bright Light. I stopped sleeping completely, and spent my time walking all over the city trying to find the Lady. It was a terrible time, because I couldn't see clearly. The song was in my head day and night, and Jimmy started to talk to me."

"Jimmy?"

"Sure, Doctor! The voice of Jimmy Page."

"You heard Jimmy Page's voice?"

"Yes."

"This is remarkable what you're telling me. And what did Page's voice say?"

"At first I couldn't understand him too well. At times it was a whisper, other times he repeated lyrics from the song. He was trying to tell me something, or maybe just trying to test me, he wanted to see if I was ready. I clearly wasn't. My strength was running out, and it was then that my mother decided to send me to the hospital. There, in the emergency room, I was seen by Dr. Timbaldi, who later took care of my case.

"Were you able to tell Dr. Timbaldi what was happening to you?"

"Not really."

"No? You couldn't tell her at any time. You couldn't tell any of the people who treated you?"

"That was totally out of the question. It was a very delicate matter, I had received a mission that demanded every part of me, but fundamentally it had to remain absolutely secret. I couldn't trust anybody. Even at the hospital, I couldn't stop thinking about how to get in touch with the Lady. I was very cooperative, so that no one would suspect that I was the piper, the man who was to lead the Lady to heaven. I made them believe that I was taking my meds, but I'd put them to the side of my tongue, and then spit them out. I had to remain pure, with my soul and body free of contamination. At the same time, I was in a state of alert, waiting for a sign. So that was how it finally happened."

"What happened?"

"I found the Lady. I had her right in front of me, I saw her every day, but it took me a few weeks to figure it out."

"The Lady was Dr. Timbaldi?"

"That's right. Life can be strange, Doctor. I'd been looking for the Lady all over, and I found her in the place where I never would have imagined."

"And you didn't even explain then to the psychiatrist all this that you're telling me?"

"Of course not! Dr. Timbaldi was completely oblivious to what was going on. Besides, the song made it very clear: 'Your head is buzzing and it won't go, because you don't know, the piper's calling you to join him, dear lady can you hear the wind blow, and if you don't know, the staircase lies on the whispering wind?' She couldn't hear the whispering wind! She didn't know that the piper was calling her! It wasn't her fault, it was just that destiny had decided it that way. I was aware that I couldn't hope for anything else, so it never occurred to me to convince her. If I'd tried, she would probably have thought that I was totally crazy. No one was going to believe me. I was completely alone, and only trusted in what Jimmy told me. He kept repeating

'Stairway to heaven', and I could only hear those words, and the guitar. The guitar played all the time. The guitar was the instrument that helped me concentrate on what I had to do.

"But you know what the system's like. They discharged me. I didn't want to leave, I was doing fine there, because I was getting my strength back, and because I felt confident. I tried to convince them to admit me again, but the system's really fucked, Doc. It's a bureaucracy, it works like a big factory. The product has to be out on the street as soon as possible. And that's how it went down. I was forced to go home, when I'd already decided to take action. I'd finally found the Lady, and no one could stop me from carrying out my mission. I'm the piper, I had to lead her to heaven, but those jerks all agreed to cut me off. I have to say I wasn't surprised at it all either, because I was in that hospital about two months, and that gave me time to get to the bottom of all of them. At first it was just a suspicion, but then I had no doubt that they knew what I'd come to do. First they tried to take away my music. One of the nurses, who pretended to be on my side, gave me a CD of Led Zeppelin songs, clearly to confuse me. I had to concentrate on 'Stairway to Heaven' alone, and in fact it was the only song I devoted myself to, with all my energy. I took the CD and made her think I'd listened to it. But I'm not stupid, I knew what they were trying to do. When I got home I felt very nervous, because I had to prepare my plan to lead away the Lady. Two months is a long time, and I made sure I found out how it all worked, the times, the guards, everyone's shifts."

"Why did you kill them?"

"I haven't killed anyone, Doctor. I have only done my duty. Nurse Lafuente shouldn't have got in my way. She wasn't the chosen one. I didn't intend that, I can assure you. I'm calm now. I'm confident I'll be sent home soon. You know what this rotten system is like, Doctor. They send you home as fast as they can, because the factory has to keep on producing, it can't stop. Life's a bitch, but you gotta put up with it, Doc!"

TWENTY-NINE

"I've been very upset these last days. I still can't believe what happened in this hospital. I think about the psychiatrist, such a young girl, and the other woman, nurse Lafuente. I think I saw her here sometimes. The doctor I don't remember."

"Dr. Timbaldi worked in the inpatients unit. She didn't generally spend much time in our area."

"That must be why. I don't forget a face easily, and when I saw the photos they showed on TV, it didn't ring any bells at all. But I thought I did recognise the nurse. Poor women! Honestly, Dr. Palmer, I don't understand why there isn't more security in hospitals. They should put more police in public places."

"There was a guard on duty that night, Anne. But the man didn't imagine that such a tragedy was going to happen."

"My father said the same. No one imagined it could happen. The Jews were convinced that everything would settle down. My father told me a few years ago that his neighbours had decided to leave, and in fact they did so before the war started. There was still time then, because the Nazis were still allowing people to leave. The Eisenbergs tried to convince my grandparents, but they wouldn't listen. They couldn't accept it. We human beings are like that, and you know better than anybody. I'm not going to explain it to you. When we finally open our eyes, it's usually too late. That's what happened to me with Richard. I was blind. I should've broken up with him when I realised what kind of a person he was, instead of waiting for him to kick me out and then go and poison my daughters against me. This week I was thinking about what I told you when I saw you at the hospital door, when the police wouldn't let me in. Are crazy people like me dangerous? Imagine if I could do something like that! The mind is a strange thing. I keep remembering the afternoon when I ran into my ex-mother-in-law in the supermarket and shoved into her with my shopping trolley. I was completely out of myself: that could've ended very badly. I think about it and it makes me shiver."

"Being dangerous doesn't depend on being crazy or sane. Human beings can be dangerous regardless of their diagnosis."

"So what does it depend on?"

"It's not easy to answer that, Anne. You yourself know very well what your parents lived through. I think it would be preposterous to think that all those Germans were crazy. But the society of that time came to be far more dangerous than the man who killed Dr. Timbaldi and nurse Lafuente."

"You're absolutely right. I should wipe that idea from my mind. But sometimes I've had real terrible thoughts. I've read about it, and I think that deep down it's all about desires."

"We all have desires that we find hard to admit. But desiring isn't the same as acting."

"Yes, I do bear in mind what you've taught me. It really helps me a lot. But when I'm anxious, like I am now, I wonder if the barrier that separates desires from actions will stand up to it. Because there are also cases where the barrier can't take it, am I right? Even river dams can burst. Why shouldn't that barrier that's supposedly inside us collapse too? You just said so yourself. How did the barrier that was inside the Germans collapse? Is it not that desires can push with such force that they end up carrying everything away?"

* * *

The difficulty of working with patients like Anne is that their reasoning often follows such an extreme logic that they are capable of winning any argument. Ordinary people don't usually use such rigour, they contradict themselves all the time, they say things and then take them back. Anne could branch out the thread of her argument, sail along various channels, move away from the main course and go into apparently unrelated issues, but at no time did she really lose control of the helm, even when her impulses cast her adrift. She was always capable of finding the missing meaning again. On top of that, she paid complete attention to my words, she x-rayed them, she captured straight away the modulations, the tones, and—far more so than Harold Yardcore—she was capable of perceiving not only double meanings, but triple and quadruple meanings, too. Sometimes, I felt the temptation to respond to her objections with an "OK, you win". If I said nothing, it was, among other reasons, because Anne would've considered anything I said a criticism, and turned my comment into an argument to feed her terrible moral conscience.

* * *

"Christmas is upon us, Dr. Palmer. Do you like Christmas?"

"Yes, it's pleasant. Do you have any plans?"

"Of course. Every year, since Richard and I split up, or should I say, since that bastard decided he'd had enough of his responsibilities as a husband and father, Norman and I have been going to the Hotel Eliot on Christmas Eve, and we have dinner in the room."

At first I thought I'd misheard.

"The Eliot? Did you say you spend Christmas Eve at the Eliot ... with Norman?"

"That's right. We have this custom. Just like me, Norman loves classic hotels and the dinner there is wonderful. We get a waiter just for the two of us. It's the only luxury I allow myself, and I save up for it all year."

"Sounds great! And what does Norman do while you have dinner?"

"I can see you haven't quite understood," she replied, letting out a laugh. "It's a dinner for two. Norman eats too! He's been my greatest companion in life, as well as you, so there's no way I could allow him to watch me having dinner and deprive him of his chair and his plate at the table."

"You mean you order a dinner for two?"

"That's right. And with an excellent wine. Not the most expensive, but an acceptable one. I don't understand wine a whole lot, but there's a chef on the TV who recommends them, and I've got them jotted down on a piece of paper."

* * *

I couldn't resist a smile, which Anne fortunately interpreted as approval from me. Her money troubles were one of the many issues we covered in therapy. She had an unstoppable tendency to spend excessively, way beyond her means, so that most of the time she was in trouble with banks and credit card companies. At the start of our sessions she also owed money to a lot of people, who had stopped trusting her and wouldn't lend her another cent. Her parents lived on a tight budget, but all the same her father would send her something now and again. It was very hard to understand how Anne spent her money, because at first sight she didn't appear to fritter it on clothes or expensive items in general. She hardly left her house because of her sick leave, she didn't eat out, although she did allow herself the luxury of taking a taxi to come to her sessions with me because, as she explained, she found public transport oppressive. She suffered a great deal when she was surrounded by people, and avoided crowds and closed spaces.

When she started therapy, she was in a very chaotic situation that required a certain amount of direct intervention from me, something I rarely do and which I reserve for emergency situations. Anne had started renovating her house, and was arguing every day with various contractors and companies. I couldn't understand what all that fuss was about, until I realised that she resolved a problem or an incident in the building work by, absurdly, hiring another company to add to the previous ones, so that at the end of so many weeks her house looked like a building site for a skyscraper, and she was constantly handing out money to architects, machinists, technicians, and assistants. In turn, that money came from a desperate juggling of credit cards. From what I could see, she had dozens of them, making the most of the banks' apparent generosity, especially towards people like Anne, who were willing to bog themselves down in interest rates that increased by the hour. It was necessary that I take action in this matter, and help her very emphatically to put a stop to this unbridled spending. However, in time I learned that Anne could only partially take in any kind of regulation, and that it was futile to expect her to adapt her life to a relatively moderate balance. Excess was part of who she was, it was the most authentic manifestation of her being, something she tended to account for as a reactive behaviour to the life of restrictions she had had as a girl. Although the cause was rather more to do with her difficulty in containing impulses that dragged her here and there, leading her crashing into the walls, I didn't object to her theories, as they had the advantage of giving meaning to her that she found understandable, and that allowed her to justify some of her actions without feeling entirely guilty.

The Eliot was one of the best hotels in town, and I couldn't imagine what a room with dinner included could cost on

24 December. And of course, the whole story aroused a curiosity in me that I had to cut off at the root. Even so, it was hard for me not to keep imagining what the hotel staff must think, especially the waiter responsible for serving her in her room.

Fortunately for Anne, we were in America, the place where money can buy it all, and also cover it all up.

Even perplexity.

THIRTY

"Jews? German Jews? Are you sure? Where did they come from?"

"We found them not far from our position, Captain. In the woods, about ten kilometres away. They appear to have escaped from a camp near the Polish border."

"How many'"

"A group of eight."

"Men, women?"

"There are three women and five men, all in very bad shape. They've not eaten for a long time."

"And what do they want us to do, comrade Zaitsev?"

"They want nothing, Captain. We found them half dead, and we brought them here to the camp."

"You brought them here to the camp? Do you not think, comrade Zaitsev, that we already have enough problems without having to worry about our enemies' health?"

"In this case I don't think they're enemies. They're Jews, you know."

"You said they were German, right? So, above all, that's what they are. Besides, how can you be sure what they say is true? They could be spies, or resistance soldiers."

"You should see them for yourself, Captain Semionov."

"Now listen to me, comrade Zaitsev. I intend to cross the river and reach the second front in three days, no more, no less. Get rid of those people right now and concentrate on what we came here to do. Understood?"

"Yes, Captain. Understood."

"You don't know how happy that makes me," grunted comrade Semionov.

"Thank you, sir."

* * *

Sergeant Zaitsev slipped through the cold of night. He was on guard, and heading for the tent where he had accommodated the group of men and women who were resting under a roof for the first time in months, having survived by sheltering in holes they had dug in the frozen ground and covered with branches and leaves. Sergeant Zaitsev was an ordinary man, He wasn't a career soldier, he just followed orders, and his only goal at that time was to destroy as many Germans as possible, wipe out everything that crossed his path. But to him the Jews were different, even those who spoke German. It's not that he had any special feelings towards them, but he didn't associate them with the bloody Germans. What he didn't know was how to be rid of these people himself. Perhaps the simplest thing would be to tell them to leave, although he wasn't sure if that was what Captain Semionov had meant. What did "Get rid of those people" mean? Sergeant Zaitsev had seen and done some awful things since the day he was drafted, so many things that he had completely lost any moral scruples. He'd brought those Jews to the camp and had picked them up for the simple reason that they were there, in his way. He would have done the same with anyone else, because it was his way of understanding his obligations as a soldier. It wasn't a personal initiative. Therefore, he could interpret comrade Semionov's orders any way he chose, he just didn't know which interpretation was best. For a moment he thought to go back to the captain's tent to ask him for clarification, but he ruled out this idea straight away. The comrade wasn't in the mood for that. Besides, he'd been rather concerned about

Captain Semionov's comment. He hadn't asked those people many questions, mainly because he barely knew a few words of German, a language he found as repugnant as the people who spoke it. But the refugees, on seeing the Russian soldiers' uniforms, put their hands up and with what strength they had cried out "Juden!, Juden!" and that he understood. Nor did he need much explanation to see that they were dying of starvation and thirst. He'd given an order for them to be fed very little, because he knew that otherwise they could die straight away. Sergeant Zaitsev had experience in these matters, on some occasions he'd even had his fun with some German soldiers who hadn't eaten for weeks, feeding them until they burst.

Now, smoking a cigarette, sitting on a box of ammunition, breathing out the smoke as he looked at the starry sky, he remembered his wife, who he hadn't heard from in months, and wondered how his eldest son was, and his daughter, and his mother too, who lived in the countryside, so far away that not even the Germans had managed to make it there. He also thought of putting an end right now to this hassle of the eight Jews, who were a burden and a waste of food, but he decided the most sensible thing would be to pass the buck on to someone else, so when his shift ended, shortly before dawn, he ordered a couple of soldiers to load the Jews onto a lorry leaving that morning for the south, where Commander Novikov's camp was. He'd know what to do with them.

Comrade Novikov looked at the handwritten, stamped paper, itemising the provisions, munitions and the list of eight Jews who had been added to the cargo. He called one of his soldiers, who spoke German more or less well enough to act as interpreter, and one by one interrogated the men and women, who could barely utter a word due to their physical weakness and terror. One of the women remained in silence, and it was impossible to get her to answer the questions. It was perfectly clear to Commander Novikov that these were neither members of the German resistance nor spies but, unlike Sergeant Zaitsev, he felt a profound dislike for these skeletal people who, from what he could tell, did nothing but look pathetic and complain. What interested him was to find out whether the detainees had any useful information about enemy positions, but he soon realised he was wasting his time. Commander Novikov had been in Stalingrad, and there was nothing now that could move him, especially having seen how some of his compatriots had had to feed on corpses to stay alive. Why should he be moved by a handful of Jews, German Jews to boot, and who therefore spoke that revolting, barbaric tongue? He gave no more thought to the matter, and had them transferred to a prison camp 300 miles east. They'd know what to do with them there. He, in turn, was not prepared to spend another minute on the issue.

That same morning, the eight Jews, your mother and I among them, were transferred to some place in Romania and shut away in a camp with all kinds of prisoners. After all we'd been through, it felt almost grotesque to find ourselves in that place, mixed in with our own assassins, although by then our assassins had wasted away as much as us, in fact some had even lost the power of speech, or otherwise talked to themselves and shouted out in the night. Then the Russians would drag them, kicking and striking them with rifle butts to the yard, where they would put an end to the racket with a shot to the head, or hang them from a post put there for that purpose. They'd laugh uproariously, pointing at the bodies hanging from the ropes, calling them "Wurst, Wurst!", "Sausage, sausage!" We reached the conclusion that the whole of Europe had become a vast, savage territory, and that it had probably always been that way.

We stayed there for a year. We didn't even know that the war was over. That sewer remained out of time, with the difference that most of the German prisoners and allies of the Reich had been all but eliminated or transferred to other camps, and only we Jews were left. We were still a problem, even for the communists, who had inherited us in the middle of a disaster of immeasurable proportions. Years later, when we got to know the magnitude of the deaths and losses, we found it inconceivable that two insignificant beings like us could have survived so much destruction. I try, in vain, to reconstruct the interminable succession of random events that collided incomprehensibly, like billiard balls on an enormous table in flames, and cast us out here, I can't explain it, to this strange part of the world, surrounded by people who recognise us as their own. But our life no longer exists, it's just a painful memory, an increasingly faded photograph, a history covered with faces that disappeared, leaving holes everywhere. In our hearts, in our bodies, in the air that we breathe. The air that, despite everything, we have to thank.

THIRTY-ONE

The receptionist at the Hotel Eliot smiled and shook Anne's hand. All the staff knew her very well, and although they were accustomed to certain guests' extravagances, Anne was a special case who didn't go unnoticed. She would stay just one night, but the taxi driver would remove enough luggage from the boot for a month. With the same dignity that he would show if they were authentic Hermès or Louis Vuitton cases, he loaded her motley old bags onto the luggage trolley, reinforced with string and duct tape, more befitting the luggage of a tramp than someone about to stay at one of Boston's most legendary hotels. After a few words about how quickly the year had passed and other similar commonplaces, the receptionist handed her a card to open the door to the room she had booked. On seeing the look on Anne's face, he clicked his tongue, put his hand to his head, and hurried to prepare another copy, muttering something about being absent-minded. With the two cards in one hand, her mobile phone and a handful of grubby, crumpled papers in the other, her glasses hanging from a little cord, her handbag crossed over her shoulder, and dragging her feet as was her custom, Anne let the porter lead her to the fifth floor, where a luxuriously prepared room awaited the guest, or rather, the guests, as the porter wished them both, in plural, a pleasant stay, and held out a hand to receive a ten dollar bill.

* * *

"You know something, Norman? This is the best day of the year. I know I always say the same thing, but it's true. I don't care too much about Christmas, as you know. It's a holiday I started celebrating when I got married and came to live here. Yes, I know, I know. I've told you hundreds of times, but let me tell you one more time, don't be mean. When I was a little girl, living in Israel with my parents, we had some friends who celebrated Christmas, even though they were as Jewish as the rest of us. Of course I understand, Norman, you've got it all stored there in your memory, but don't deny me the pleasure of wallowing in my reminiscences. They'd invite us over every year, but because of my mother's condition we could never go. Do you remember Mr. Ehrenfeld? Adorable Mr. Ehrenfeld used to send us a very pretty card covered in silver glitter with a picture of Santa Claus and his sledge in the snow. Can you imagine? On the back, and in a trembling hand that still retained some elegance, Mr. Ehrenfeld would address himself to my parents very solemnly, in the German style of the time, sending season's greetings and an invitation to dinner. A few days before Christmas Eve, the Ehrenfelds would let you and me into their home so we could look at the tree adorned with decorations, and when Christmas was over they'd have us round so we could help them take down the tree and put away the garlands and baubles, which were made with a glass so light I was afraid to touch them. We'd put them all away in wooden boxes that Mrs. Ehrenfeld would then fill with straw, and then she'd give me a package of marzipan, wrapped in white silk paper, which mom of course refused to try and looked at with distrust. Those people didn't have any children, and they liked it when I spent time with them. My sister on the other hand never wanted to go, even though the Ehrenfelds would've been delighted, I'm sure.

Just like mom and dad, Mr. Ehrenfeld had a number tattooed on his arm, but that was so common in nearly all the adults we knew that my sister and I only understood its meaning some years later, when we learned at school about what had happened. People didn't used to talk about that at home, much less in front of the children. Poor Mr. Ehrenfeld, who had miraculously managed to survive so much, died when he slipped in the street, near to where he lived, in the silliest way you can imagine, in that faraway land where he thought he was finally safe. You see how strange everything is, Norman? As I always say, it's more proof that God's only mission is to laugh at us. But let's not talk about that. Today I'm happy, because tonight is ours, because I have you, because we're here inside, in this pretty room, I feel like nothing can go wrong, and that all the ugly things in my life have been left out on the street, at least for one day. What are you going to wear to dinner tonight? That dark suit I like so much? At least indulge me that pleasure. You wouldn't put it on last year, you said you wanted a change, but none of them suit you as well as the dark one. When you wear it, you remind me of the Kaprinskys' son, little Fishke. He was such a beautiful boy! He had a head of hair like yours, full of golden curls. He looked like a prince. Imagine how charming he was, that even my mother would sometimes let him come to our house, when she couldn't stand to have any visitors, she even smiled at him and sometimes called him over to caress his hair, while she mumbled something we couldn't make out. Dad explained to us once that Fishke bore a great resemblance to my uncle Effrain, my mother's youngest brother, the baby of the family, the one the Germans killed the night they entered the town, throwing him out of the window. The day Fishke turned thirteen and had his bar mitzvah, his parents bought him a dark suit. I remember he looked very smart, so much so that for the first and the last time I felt like I was in love. No, you have no reason whatsoever to be jealous, Norman. You're so funny! This was different, I was a child, when I still believed that one day mom would get better. I really believed it! My sister Norah made fun of me, and said I was an idiot, that mom was crazy and would never get better. Norah could be very cruel when she wanted to be, even without really trying. Maybe because of that she managed to save herself, because from a very young age she realised that she had to escape. We've spent our lives running away. What was I saying? Oh, yes! Tonight you have to do as I say and put on your dark suit. I think the bow tie will suit you very well. What do you want me to wear? I thought I might surprise you! I'm going to wear a new dress. I'm sure you'll love it. Yes, I know you think I look good in anything. Oh, Norman, you're the sweetest, most generous person I've ever known! I'm so lucky to have you, otherwise tonight would be the saddest of the year, instead of being my day of happiness! I've ordered your favourite dish, as usual. I, on the other hand, will be having something different this year. No, I'm not going to tell you! But I'll let you try it. You know what I'd most like us to do until dinnertime? Lie down together here, on the bed, and hug and keep each other warm. I won't ask for anything more. You see how easy I am to please! That's it, this bed is wonderful, I'm a princess, a princess for a day, like in the fairy tales, and tonight my prince will accompany me to the banquet at the palace!"

* * *

The hotel manager had given all the necessary instructions to the waiter. Mr. Hamilton knew how to give his guests the right treatment, and felt a particular liking for Ms. Kurczynski. She had told him her life's story, given how easy she found it to open up to anyone who showed the slightest willingness to listen, and Mr. Hamilton was as attentive and professional as a psychiatrist. If Ms. Kurczynski wished to have dinner for two even though there was no one else with her, the Hotel Eliot would grant that wish, just as it would for the French ambassador or an emir from the orient. He would personally see to it that everything was carried off to perfection.

So in the afternoon he checked all the details, ensured that the table in the room was properly set for two, and that the chef had prepared the trolley with the food that Ms. Kurczynski had ordered, just as she liked it. Finally, shortly before dinner, Mr. Hamilton had said goodbye to those employees who were working that night, wished them a Merry Christmas, and left for home, happy in the knowledge that everything was perfectly organised and in good hands. Once home, and making the most of the fact that he lived alone, he took a double dose of his favourite sleeping pill and slept through the whole of Christmas, which he hated with all his soul.

At 8pm, the waiter knocked at the door to the room. He had to do this several times, because Ms. Kurczynski had fallen fast asleep. When she opened the door, her face was bloated from the pills, her hair a mess, and she stood there staring at the waiter and the food cart, not knowing where she was. Then she suddenly reacted and straightened her hair, trying to fix her appearance.

"Oh, I'm so sorry! Come in, come in, please. I fell asleep, and I haven't even had time to get changed. How could you let me sleep so long, Norman? I told you I just wanted a little nap. The problem is it's too comfortable here. I can never rest at home like I do in this room."

The waiter pushed the cart over to the table.

"Shall I serve you now, sir, madam? If you prefer, I can come back a little later. I came at the time you asked."

Anne was in the bathroom, looking at herself in the mirror, which returned a shabby, untidy image. She hurried with the hair brush.

"I'll be right with you, hold on a minute, I'm coming! You can start serving in the meantime," she shouted from the bathroom as she painted her lips and perfumed herself with the cologne she'd found by the washbasin.

Finally, her head clearer, she came out and let the waiter pull back her seat so that she could sit. He was an older man, who knew his work well, and was able to make the service an exquisite ceremony. Anne was thrilled, following all his movements as if she were a little girl, and throwing complicit glances at the empty chair at the other end of the table.

"You see this, Norman? This is what I call life's true pleasure. Happiness may only be possible once a year, one night, but that's why we must make the most of it. Let's toast to us! Merry Christmas!"

Anne raised her glass and clinked it gently with Norman's, which the waiter had also filled. The sound of the crystal was like a musical note that remained in the air a second, and then Anne started to eat, at first letting herself go in a voracious frenzy, but then controlling herself a little by conversing with Norman.

"Let's eat slowly and enjoy the moment. This cream of vegetable is exquisite, don't you think? I know you men are all carnivores, that you don't know how to order anything but steak. You come from the caves. But you won't deny me that this tastes glorious. You see? You have to vary your diet. That's what I always used to say to Karen, who'd only eat sausages and vanilla ice cream. Why just sausages and vanilla ice cream? Ah! Who knows? What's that? I set a bad example? I don't know what you're trying to say. All right, though I don't think it's funny. It's true that I do go crazy over a tub of vanilla ice cream. What do you want me to do? Yes, yes, it's also true that I can finish off a two-pound tub while I'm watching TV. I give up, you're right, I won't argue. It's my fault. You happy now? That's clearly how things work. Karen goes from eating all kinds of crap to eating nothing at all, but poor little thing, she's not to blame at all! It's her witch of a mother, of course! That psychiatrist said so, and apparently you share her opinion.

What do you mean you didn't say that? I'm sorry, I think you *did* say that. Oh no? You didn't say that? Are you completely sure you didn't mean to say that? Then I'm very sorry, honey, I'm very sensitive with this whole business, so let's just drop it. I don't want a misunderstanding to spoil our evening. Is everything to your liking? That's the good thing about coming to these places. There's real class here. And this charming man, a true professional. What's your name?"

"Frank, madam."

The waiter, who was standing to one side, straight as a soldier in the imperial Russian guard, and with a smile that seemed moulded in wax, nodded slightly, thanking her for the compliment. As it was his first time serving this curious number, a colleague had brought him up to speed on what to expect, so that he wouldn't find it too hard to maintain a serene look on his face. Besides, he'd been brought up by his grandfather, who would spend the whole day talking to his orthopaedic leg, so the situation wasn't completely alien to him.

"You know, when I was a girl I used to dream of this. Yes, believe it or not. I used to dream that you and I would one day spend Christmas together in a place like this. And that dream has come true, Norman. Did you used to imagine it too? It's wonderful how we always agree on everything. It's true that I gave you life, you must never forget that, but we're very fortunate that we get on so well with each other. Richard was a real jerk. I could never have spent a night like this with him. He was always worried about money, he couldn't spend it on anything, and he nagged me day and night about controlling my spending. It's true that I'm a little absent-minded about that, but you should see him, he behaved like a real miser. He used to say that I used to spend like there was no tomorrow! If we can't treat ourselves to something like this, what's life for? Besides, it's once a year. You haven't seen my new dress! Because you didn't wake me when you were supposed to,

I didn't have time to change. Don't look at me! Tomorrow, before we leave here, I'll put it on. On the other hand, you look magnificent in that dark suit. I told you that colour suits you. You're as handsome as Fishke! All right, I won't say another word. I don't want to make you angry. You know something? You didn't used to be this jealous. But tell me, honey, what do you have to worry about? I only have you, and no one else. You're the only person who's never left me, Norman, and nor have I left you. Remember when we were kids and we swore we'd always have each other? You remember that, Norman? I preserve that moment in my memory as if I were living it now. We were under the bed one night when mom had had one of her nightmares, and was sleepwalking around the house, letting out bloodcurdling screams, while dad followed her closely, making sure she didn't trip over anything. The doctors had told dad not to try to wake her, because it could be very traumatic, and to just stay by her side to stop her hurting herself. I got under the bed, as mom's screams terrified me, and so did the things she said. She'd see the dead, the piles of burning corpses, the flames roaring, and the smoke going up to the sky. Mom saw all that in her dreams, but the worst thing is that she had really seen it before. The nightmare drove her back to that same horror nearly every night. She'd wander about the house, with her hands on her head, and her screams would set our hair on end. You'd whisper in my ear and try to calm me down, in fact you were the only one who could do that, and then we promised each other we'd always be together. And we kept our promise, Norman. Here we are, after all these years. Things haven't gone well for me, but it would have been far worse without you. Maybe one day I'll be more entertaining company, but I really don't know if I'll make it. Oh, that's very kind of you to say so! No, it's not true. I did nothing special for you. I would've liked to, but you know that life has cost me dear. I'm not well, Norman, I doubt that I ever will be, that's why you have to be patient with me. Yes, sure you are, but sometimes I'm afraid you'll get tired of me. You've put up with so much, although it's also true that I don't ask you for much. I've never asked for much. I just want you to hold me tonight, Norman, don't leave my side, and when the morning comes we'll look at the city lights and the sky together. It's very cold outside, but here we're just right, my darling. It makes me want to never leave, ever. What a pity we can't stay here like this for ever, in this room, you and I alone, watching life go by!"

"Shall I pour a little more wine?" asked Frank, considering it an excellent opportunity to refill their glasses.

"Yes, of course! This wine is exquisite, don't you think, Norman? You can't deny I chose well. My mother would never understand any of this, and I think my father only once bought a bottle of wine, when Richard came over for the first time. You remember that? I was terribly nervous, because I was afraid that mom would have one of her fits and lock herself in her room. Richard had been warned about what went on at home, but all the same I couldn't relax. I'm sure you remember very well what happened. In the end, mom excused herself, saying she had one of her headaches, said goodbye to Richard, and went to her bedroom. But at least she was calm. I don't think she was at all pleased that Richard wasn't Jewish, although she never said a word about it. Well, to tell the truth the poor thing never said a word about anything! Dad didn't care, he even showed a certain liking for Richard, though I suppose he would've preferred a Jewish son-in-law. You see, Jewish, Catholic, whatever, the truth is that marriage was a failure, dear Norman. That's that. And you know what the worst thing was, Frank?"

Frank stood stock still, thinking it was a mistake, but Anne asked again.

"What do you think the worst part was, Frank?"

"I don't know, Ms. Kurczynski. I couldn't tell you."

"The worst thing of all is that the same thing would've happened to me with any man, don't you think?"

"Excuse me, but you must understand that I'm in no position to offer an opinion on that matter, Ms. Kurczynski. I don't even know what happened."

"Oh, Frank, if I could tell you everything that happened! Although we'd need time for that. Why don't you sit and eat with us. I think there's enough for three. What do you say, Norman? Don't you think it would be stupendous if Frank joined us tonight? It's Christmas! You see? I knew Norman would love the idea. Please, Frank, pull up that chair and sit yourself down. There are more plates and clean cutlery on the cart. Come on, make yourself comfy."

Frank hesitated a moment, but couldn't find an excuse to refuse her, at least not one that Ms. Kurczynski wouldn't take badly. Besides, Frank was used to weird guests and unusual requests, so he decided to take his seat.

"Pour yourself a glass too, Frank, and let's toast to the three of us. That's it! Merry Christmas! Are you married, Frank?"

"Yes, Ms. Kurczynski."

"Please, call me Anne."

"As you wish, Ms. … I mean, Anne."

"That's better. So you're married."

"That's right … Anne."

Frank felt uncomfortable, but did his best to hide it.

"All good at home?"

Frank cleared his throat and noticed that his face was getting hot and taking on a reddish tone.

"I would say so. Of course, you'd have to ask my wife as well!" he added, trying to come across as friendly and relaxed.

Anne sat there looking at him in silence, as if her mind had suddenly gone very far away.

"Sure, you're right. We'd have to hear her opinion, but at least you seem satisfied."

"No doubt about it," said Frank in a convincing tone.

"Hey, you're real lucky. I couldn't say the same for me. Well, right now I couldn't say a thing because I'm divorced, but even when I was married I don't think things went too well. Don't think that I'm one of those typical women who devote all their time to running their ex down, oh no! I've never wasted my time on that kind of talk. But Norman here is my witness. He knows my life better than anybody. Ask him, you'll see I'm not lying."

"I don't doubt it, Ms. ... Anne, I don't doubt it," replied Frank, a slight hint of fright now noticeable in his voice.

"Go on, ask Norman," Anne insisted, pouring more wine into her glass, and discreetly swallowing one of her pills. "I have no secrets from him, and besides, he wouldn't let me lie. Ask him, Frank, then you'll know I'm not exaggerating."

"I never thought you were, Anne. I'm sure that you're an absolutely straight-up woman, and I'm terribly sorry that your marriage didn't work out. Have you ever thought about remarrying?"

"Did you hear that? Did you hear that, Norman? Frank's got a sense of humour! Oh, yes! You're a hell of a guy, Frank. I guess a lot of people have told you, but I want to tell you as well. There's more: you've got a big heart, I can feel that. I can tell. I can always tell when someone has a heart of gold, and I felt it as soon as you stepped into this room. Right, Norman? I bet you felt it too, huh? Norman and I have been together for ever, Frank, and that's why our perceptions are identical."

Frank nodded, smiled timidly, and immersed himself in his dish of cream of vegetable.

"It would be the last thing I would do in my life, Frank. I assure you. I'd rather die than see myself sharing my life with a man. I've had enough already. No offence."

"None taken," said Frank, after wiping his lips with the napkin. "I understand you very well. Sometimes we have bad experiences," he added, and went back to concentrating on his cream of vegetable.

"Norman is the only person I need by my side. Don't I say that all the time, honey? Dad took care of me too, poor thing.

And he still does! But he lives very far away, and we see each other very little, although he calls me almost every week. I don't know where he gets the time to think about his daughter, with all the work he has looking after my mother."

Frank adapted the look on his face to Anne's conversation, as he sipped his soup and glanced at the bread basket.

"He must be a good father, and a great husband, then. Would you mind passing me the bread?"

"Here you are. He certainly is. He always has been. Sometimes I wonder what kind of life he's led. The second half didn't make up too much for the first. And the same thing happened to me. I've had a very bad life, Frank. As a little girl I hid in the shadows, and when I grew up and tried to form my own family, it was a real disaster. My own fault, I'm sure. But I couldn't do it right. You know something, Frank? There are people who are a mistake, an error in the calculations of the universe. From time to time, and excuse me for putting it like this, because personally I don't believe in God, nature produces a flaw, it gets the ingredients mixed up, or just doesn't pay proper attention and allows a flawed creature to come into this world. Something like that happened in my case. That's why I'm condemned to dragging around my own burden."

"I thought things had only gone badly in your marriage," Frank took the liberty of saying. He was more relaxed, and started to tuck into the turkey pie. "Fantastic. Despite all that you've told me, at least you have excellent judgment when it comes to choosing food, yes ma'am. Anyway, that boyfriend you're always talking about sounds like a good guy, right?"

"You mean Norman?"

"That's the one."

"You hear that, Norman. Frank's so sweet! No, Norman's just a good friend, the only friend I've ever had in life."

"Ah, I didn't get that part. Sure, but that's a wonderful thing, madam, I mean, Anne. At the end of the day a friend can be better than a relative, a brother, or even a partner. That's what my father always used to say, may he rest in peace. You see? I haven't had that luck. I can't complain about my wife, but as for a friend, a real friend, that's something I've never had. You pay a lot for this meal? I'm thinking of doing something like this next year, 'course I'd have to find another hotel, at least, if I'm still working here. But I wouldn't mind. As I was saying, my father thought that friendship was the most important thing."

"I completely agree with your father, Frank. I bet I would've hit it off with him, for sure. But you know something? I've never even been able to trust anyone at work. Everyone goes their own way, and if they have to step on your head to make it, they won't hesitate for a second."

"Absolutely. You wouldn't believe the things that go on in this hotel. You know, some of the kitchen staff steal food and accuse us waiters. That's life, Anne. It's just as well that Mr. Hamilton, the manager, has known me since I started here, as a porter, and he knows I could never take so much as a piece of bread. Speaking of which, is there any bread left? Sorry, but eating without bread is like sleeping without a pillow."

"That's very good!" replied Anne with a loud laugh. "Didn't I tell you, Norman? Wasn't it a magnificent idea to invite Frank to our table? Now we're a little less lonely. We're very grateful to you, Frank."

"Oh, not at all! I'm the one who should be thanking you two for being so kind to me. Imagine, it's tough working on Christmas Eve, being away from home, without my family. You guys have made me feel like I was in my own home. I'm speechless. What do you say we move on to dessert? I must congratulate you again, Anne. You've made a perfect choice. The hotel's cranberry pie is the best. They make it right here, in the kitchens."

"Will there be enough?"

"Yeah, don't worry. If we run short, I'll go and get some more myself. But the portions are very generous, so we should have more than enough."

Anne had had quite a lot to drink, and was euphoric.

"Listen to me both of you! I want to make a toast. To friendship, and to our new friend Frank. May this marvellous dinner be repeated next Christmas. I think it's one of the best we've ever had, right Norman? There you go. Norman is happy that the three of us are here. Is there any wine left? Then fill those glasses, Frank! To the brim! Tomorrow it'll all be over. Let's make tonight last as long as possible. Tomorrow, when we leave this refuge, the same fucking world will still be out there. You know, I'd love it if tonight never ended. A toast, a toast!"

Anne, raised her glass, clinked it with Frank's, stood up, and bowed to where Norman was sitting. Then she staggered over to the sofa, and fell like a tree that had just been chopped down. A light sob began to come from her throat, it turned into a faltering cry, and finally she fell asleep.

Frank crammed down the last mouthful of cranberry pie, put everything on his cart, and headed for the door.

Before leaving, he went back on himself and covered Anne with a blanket.

"Sleep tight, Ms. Kurczynski. It's been a great night for all of us."

THIRTY-TWO

"I'm not having a good day today, Dr. Palmer."

I looked at her questioningly.

"I always get this way after Christmas. It's like a big hangover after the holidays. I open my eyes to reality and a deep sadness overcomes me. I know it's all just been an illusion, but I can't help it, and deep down I think I was happy for a while, and that happiness has evaporated in the blink of an eye. Everything I have before me is always the same. The endless nights, the fits of hatred, my own melancholy. I have to hurry home like in the fairy tale, because after midnight I'll turn back into Cinderella. It's true that I've made great progress with you, Dr. Palmer, but there's still no point to my life. I'm still not in any shape to work, although I'd like to go back. I can't stay off any longer, wallowing in my ideas. I need something to snap me out of it, some useful activity I can put my mind to. I'm a good teacher, as I said, better than you can imagine. I am."

"Have I ever doubted that?"

"No, of course not, Dr. Palmer. If there's one person in the world who believes in me, it's you. And Norman, of course."

"Of course," I nodded. "We can't leave Norman out of this. It would be unfair of us."

"That's right. The thing is that at the same time I'm terrified about going back to work. I'm full of doubts, because sometimes I think my mental capacity has deteriorated, that what I had wasn't just a simple breakdown. I've had too many not to realise that I'm sick. There are days when I'm more optimistic, and I convince myself I'll get better. But when I feel like this, like this week, I see a very black future, and I'm afraid of not knowing what to do with my life any more. I'm lost without my daughters, so much so that I've started to fantasise about adopting a child, but I know they won't let me at my age. What kind of people make the laws? Am I so old that I can't give a child love, look after him as if I were his real mother? Have mothers been given expiration dates, as if we were yogurts?"

Anne stopped suddenly.

"Don't worry, Dr. Palmer. I'm not at the stage I was at when you first met me, when just talking about these things set me off on an uncontrollable rage. I haven't had a fight with anyone for years, or raised my voice! I suppose that's what adapting to social life is. But I'll tell you one thing: there's another side to this. I've often wondered whether in turning off my hatred, some part of my energy will also run out, that cable that keeps me connected to life. There are people who have been saved by love alone, the love they've received, or the love they're able to give. That's my father. Love saved him, his unconditional love. I know you shrinks suspect everything, and you're probably right to. Perhaps a deep hatred lurks behind so much love, and what we see is no more than a mask, a disguise, an imposture. I'm not saying it isn't. But it's all the same to me. Real or fake, my father saved me thanks to his unbreakable capacity for loving. He forgave everything. First of all he forgave his family's murderers, or at least decided not to waste time feeding a grudge that was of no use to him. My father needed all his energy for one specific goal, which was to save my mother. He'd saved her when they were fugitives and she'd given up, because she no longer had the strength to live. He looked for food for her, made her drink the water from the dew and the puddles, carried her weight over miles, warmed her with what little heat came from his own body. Then, when they made it to Israel, he had to start the second phase. My mother was already safe from a physical point of view, but he had to rescue her from a second death. The first was brief compared to the second, which still hasn't ended. And my father has coped with it. In contrast, we others are made differently, my dear doctor. We stay on our feet thanks to the strength we get from hatred, which really isn't hatred towards anyone in particular, no. It's hatred of everything, of existence itself, hatred of all the forces that conspire every day to destroy us little by little. Hatred keeps people like me alive, it's like air, or oxygen. Contaminated oxygen, of course, oxygen full of all kinds of toxic substances, which at the same time slowly poisons us. A very strange mixture but one that can't easily be altered, at least without running the risk of being unable to breathe."

I let Anne talk without interrupting her for an instant, as I said to myself: "You have to remember this. You have to be able to write it down some time, because you won't have many chances to hear truth like this. Let yourself be taught, Dave. Don't miss a word of what you're hearing."

"Of course, it's hardly a matter of doing nothing," Anne went on. "Hatred brings many complications, and it definitely takes more than it gives. That's why I need to support myself with something. Things are unlikely to change too much in the time I have left to live. I say this, and I recognise that it's a very big step, because I've tried to stop thinking about suicide. It will be fate, or nature, or whatever, that puts an end to my existence, not me. And I owe that to you, Dr. Palmer. But now we have to start a new phase, and for that I need a ladder. A ladder to climb up a tree, and look around from up there, and see if I can find a place where I can prepare myself. Does the Foreign Legion still exist? There was a time when all those who were lost joined it, those who had lost their way, or were seeking exile to get away from something that had broken them inside. Of course, they wouldn't take women! It was the convent for them. But there are no convents for Jewish women, and even if there were, it wouldn't change my life very much. I'm shut in enough as it is. I just want to be able to go back to work, and find something in my free time so that life isn't something that happens sandwiched between my bed and the ceiling. I'm not asking to be happy, because I've never believed that was possible, but it would be good not to have to wait until next Christmas to feel there's at least one day in the year worth getting up for. For many years my main occupation has been to wish the night comes soon, and when it finally does, then I have to find the way to make it pass as quickly as possible, because if it traps me it does with me as it pleases. For someone like me, time is a flow that can't be measured, and that's why my ideas ooze hatred, because they're like an anchor that stops the current from dragging me away. I didn't like Richard's mother from the first day I met her. Well, I think we can say the feeling was mutual. We never had a good connection. Truth is, I never understood what happened between us. Maybe I expected her to behave like a mother, and give me the attention that mine couldn't give me. But she always kept her distance, and didn't even show much interest in her granddaughters. She has one daughter rather older than Richard, who never married or had children. So Karen and Sophie are her only grandchildren, and she's never taken an interest in them. But I even managed to tolerate that. I managed to make it so it didn't matter to me. My daughters filled my life so much that I could do without pretty much anything else. But when Richard left, and shortly after he wiped them out of my life, I was left completely empty. That woman lived near our house, and we'd sometimes see each other in the street. We'd both try to avoid making eye contact, though we both knew full well that we were both there, almost brushing past each other. Then an unbridled hatred took control of me, a really criminal desire, something I'd never felt for anyone else, not even Richard. The thing is after those fits of hatred, when I imagined all sorts of atrocities, I experienced a kind of relief. That wild, ruthless anger had the curious ability to rescue me, get me out of the intense darkness I found myself in, and bring me back to the surface. It was a strange catharsis, for which I had to find a suitable victim, someone who would allow me to unleash all the fury that had built up in me since I came into this world. Hatred is a kind of antidote against sadness. I'm carrying the grief of countless unavenged deaths, Dr. Palmer. And I assure you that I don't want to be cured of that.

THIRTY-THREE

Rubashkin listened to me as he always did, with his head to one side, his eyes closed, completely still, the living image of a sphinx in deep concentration. When I'd finished, he remained in the same pose for several minutes, and then opened his eyes as if he were emerging from a trance.

"Remarkable. Someone who managed to mislead a whole psychiatry service. A real tragedy, but it could've been worse. Imagine if that guy had showed up in the middle of the day, with the hospital full of people, with an automatic weapon instead of a knife. To make matters worse, this kind of thing only gives more fuel to the fire of the old myth about the danger of madness. An isolated case revives the age-old prejudice against crazy people. Meanwhile, the master criminals sit comfortably in their government offices, ordering the deaths of thousands of people, safe from any kind of accountability. Harold Yardcore will pay with a life sentence, no question about that, but most murderers die in their beds. As you can see, I'm too old and I've just given you a speech worthy of a TV preacher! Pay no attention to me. The question is, Jimmy Page and Robert Plant could never have imagined that so many years after they plagiarised that song, a schizophrenic would use it for his messianic delusion. You have to admit it's a good, tempting title, 'Stairway to Heaven.'"

"Did you say plagiarised?"

"Sure, didn't you know? Led Zeppelin had a special predilection for other people's music. In fact, they stole that song from a group called Spirit. It was composed by a kid who was playing with Hendrix when he was fifteen."

"Wow! I had no idea of your erudition in the subject of rock music. You never cease to amaze me."

"Well, I was young myself once! And Led Zeppelin was one of my favourite bands. Did you know Page's guitar solo in 'Bye, Bye, Blackbird', sung by Joe Cocker, is considered one of the most unforgettable solos in rock history?"

"Yes, that I knew. In fact, I listen to that song a lot, just to hear that incredible solo again. No one's beaten that."

"This conversation's taking an interesting direction. We're drifting away a little from the clinical side, though personally I couldn't care less."

"Me neither. What do you say we continue this in a bar I know downtown? There's a Chicago band on tonight who are pretty good."

"That sounds like an excellent idea! I think the last time I did something like that, the Twin Towers were still standing. All signs pointed to my falling before them, but I'm still here. It's amazing. Give me two minutes while I get my coat and change these sneakers for something smarter."

* * *

The band turned out to be even better than I imagined. It was two in the morning, and there we were, Dr. Rubashkin and I, enjoying the music and a couple of beers. I couldn't have imagined a situation like that when I started my analysis with him in my youth. I owed many things to him, and that night I felt particularly happy that we were together in that marvellous joint.

"This was one of the things I missed when I lived in Paris. This kind of joint. There were some pretty good jazz dives over there, but the French never did rock too well. You ever dream of being a musician?" he asked me in the interval. "Professional, I mean."

"There was a time when I imagined I'd be a famous writer, but not exactly a rock star."

"Well I did. And I can assure you I had what it took."

"Did you sing?"

"I played the guitar, and wrote a few songs. But then psychoanalysis swept all that away. A real shame. Freud knew that the practice of our trade is something that kills all creativity. It can help some people develop their talent, but I don't think that happens to us psychoanalysts ourselves. It's a coin toss. Save some exceptions, we're banned from art. We have only the consolation of being able to enjoy what others do."

"Kristeva made it as a writer."

"Kristeva was a very poetic essayist. Her writing is something of great beauty, but in my opinion a writer is more than that. However, I can admit her onto the list of exceptions I was referring to. But you'll agree that there are no psychoanalysts who are also professional musicians, for instance."

"But doesn't the same thing happen with any profession? I don't know any lawyers or physicists who lead double lives as artists. On the other hand, I know some people who gave up successful careers to devote themselves to music."

"I agree. But there's a curious difference. We do something that we can rarely separate ourselves from. Psychoanalysis is like a snake bite. Once the venom reaches your heart, you're gone. It's not just simply practising the profession. It's something that gets into your bones, and then you can't give it up. No one retires from this trade, Dave, no one who's really been hooked by it. You can see my own example, at this absurd age. I still see some patients, I supervise cases, I write essays, and from time to time I accept an invitation to give a lecture. I don't paint watercolours, I don't have an allotment, although I can bend down a little, believe it or not."

I looked at Rubashkin, I looked at his bony hands, the skin speckled by time, his peregrine falcon eyes, his few white hairs, and I admired for the thousandth time the vigour of his intelligence, that profound humanity that had turned him into a wise man. And above all, the precise, perfect irony with which he dissected life's every muscle.

THIRTY-FOUR

"I'm sorry I'm late, Dr. Palmer. I don't know what happened today, because I left early enough, but I went the wrong way. You know that lately I've been taking the subway, because thanks to you I'm getting over my fear of crowded places, but I'm so absorbed in my thoughts and today I missed my stop. I'm very sorry, I really am, because I'm usually so punctual."

So punctual that in general I'd see her in the waiting room an hour before her appointment, listening to music on her earphones and writing non-stop in her notebook. I once asked her about that, and she told me she kept an exact and meticulous account of every one of her sessions, with various reflections, dream notes, memories, and plans for the following day. I looked at my watch, and I saw that she was only three or four minutes late.

"Well, personally I consider that a sign of improvement."

"Really? You guessed it!"

"What have I guessed?"

Anne remained quiet and thoughtful.

"We'll talk about that another day."

"As you wish. You're very mysterious this morning!"

She smiled and rolled her eyes comically.

"I've had, how can I put this? An inspiration."

"I can see that. We can talk about that if you like."

"It's something that I'm still working on, but I can tell you that it's the best thing that's happened to me in the last few years. You won't believe it!"

"I'll be very patient, and try to bear the intrigue you're bringing into my office today," I said, laughing.

"Oh, Dr. Palmer! I spent the whole weekend thinking all the time. But this time, instead of the ideas bursting in my head like popcorn in the pan, it was an oasis of wonderful images! I'm so excited, I haven't slept for three nights!"

Although I managed not to let it show, I felt an alarm go off inside. I knew that Anne could go into manic phases, and that what started off as a happy mood, an optimistic temperament, an easy sociability open to anyone in the street, a crazy use of money, it ended up being corrupted into an unstoppable furore, requiring an increase in sessions and more medication. Nonetheless, I decided that I had to tread very cautiously. In those states, Anne was extraordinarily sensitive to anything that could be interpreted as disagreement, so I had to walk on tiptoe and try not to rush things, or press her to talk about something she wasn't ready to talk about.

* * *

I didn't even have to wait until the next session. That night, at home, as I was checking my email, the mystery was revealed to me.

Dear Dr. Palmer,

I'm very sorry about how I behaved this morning. It was a little childish of me to keep you on tenterhooks, but the reason is that I was terribly afraid that you would object to what I was going to tell you. I know you never work like that with me, but I couldn't help but feel it. I swear that when I left your office I felt a little ashamed about how I'd spoken to you, so I decided to write you this afternoon, so that the same thing wouldn't happen at our next appointment.

Last Friday, well after midnight, I was channel hopping when I suddenly saw a documentary that pricked my curiosity. It was about life in Japan. You know that people live very strangely there. I've never been, but I've read things, and seen a lot of reports. They're fairly solitary people, and they have some rather special inventions to combat the isolation many of them live in. There are cat bars, where those who need to stroke a living being can go. I hate cats, no way I'd go to a place like that. Then they showed some dolls that are women, they make them real size. It's amazing how lifelike they get them to look. The documentary said it's not just the appearance, but they're also made with a material that reminds you of a real human when you touch it. I thought it was a bit revolting to imagine that men can do that with a doll, but I'm not completely surprised, as they tend to have fairly repugnant habits. But then they showed something else that grabbed my attention. There's a company that manufactures babies for women who can't have one, or don't have the time to look after a real one. The film said the doll behaves like a real human baby. You have to bathe it, feed it, change its diapers … It cries, laughs, moves its arms and legs, and goes to the bathroom. You can't imagine the things these people can do with technology. They say that when women take them for a walk down the street, it's hard to tell that they're dolls. So I noted down the name of the company that makes them.

You'll probably think I've gone crazy, but I assure you that I have a hunch, a kind of good feeling. Nothing like this has ever happened to me. Besides, it's done now. I've contacted the company. They asked me if I wanted it to have someone's face in particular, and that I'd have to send them photographs for that. I didn't know they could make a doll to measure, and the question took me by surprise. They also offered to send me a catalogue, but I said no. Then, logically, they asked me if I wanted a girl or a boy. So I told them that they could decide. I don't want to know until it arrives. I don't want this baby to look like anybody.

I want it to be mine, and for no one to ever take it away from me.

Anne

When Anne said, "Nothing like this has happened to me before," that meant two things. Firstly, that it had happened to her dozens of times. Secondly, that she was making it understood that nothing in the world would make her change her mind. So I reread the email carefully, wondering what to make of it all. I smiled, imagining that a modern version of the angel Gabriel was now appearing on television. Might this be a delayed effect of the change Anne had made to the spelling of her surname? Could it be that in touching a sensitive nerve in her ancestry, she had set off a chain reaction that could give her a foothold on life, based on her unshakeable certainty that she was a "professional" mother? Whatever it was, I had to admit that it was like nothing I'd ever seen in all my years of clinical practice. If there was one thing that being a psychoanalyst allowed me, it was precisely to be able to focus on Anne's unusual decision without thinking that she had completely lost her mind. I remembered when a few years before I'd defended a schizophrenic woman's right to try to have a child with her husband, despite furious objections from my fellow psychiatrists and psychologists, who demanded that I call for legal intervention to get the woman declared unfit. My total refusal led to a terrible argument that left me isolated in the hospital, an isolation I've never entirely left behind. Time proved me right, as the patient had a child, and with the help of analysis, medication, and her husband's infinite faith in her, she was able to take responsibility as a mother and give the child a love not much more sickly than the average "normal" mother.

All the same, I had a real challenge before me, something unprecedented, something that was only possible in a world where the difference between delusion and reality was shown to be completely useless, if indeed it was ever worth much. Anne might be more or less crazy, but now her madness would find the support of a system that could satisfy her most extravagant desires by merely entering the magic number on her credit card.

* * *

"A while ago I told you I needed a ladder to climb up a tree, and look around from there to find an answer. Do you remember? Well that's exactly what's happened. It may seem a coincidence, but it wasn't at all. You know I don't believe in coincidences. Instead, I think I've been alert, awake, I've been able to respond to my instinct. Despite what the experts say, we mothers don't have an expiry date. No way! You can't imagine the wonderful things they're capable of making at that company. It's incredible. Hundreds of models in an internet catalogue, hoping to find a home, and on the other side of the screen, thousands of women looking for someone to devote ourselves to completely. I've spoken to them, and they say that in no time at all you completely forget it's a doll. Every day they get hundreds of letters from grateful women, and in fact I entered a forum where women from all over the world share their experiences. I could be part of that forum too, and I'll have heaps of people to talk to! Just you see, Dr. Palmer, this is going to bring a surprising twist to my life, exactly what I needed."

"And when will you get the ..." I couldn't help a certain hesitation in my question.

"The baby? In nine months, of course! You should speak to them, you'll see that they've thought about everything. Their philosophy is that the process should reproduce reality as faithfully as possible. Meanwhile, the future mommy, meaning me, has time to get everything ready, and most importantly prepare herself. I've already been through that, this isn't my first time, but although I have my two daughters this is different, in a way, because I feel different. It's something I'm going to fight for like never before. I won't have to depend on anyone, and I'm going to bring up my child as if it were my best work of art. There will be no mistakes this time, or anyone to argue with, either. I feel like for the first time in my life I'm going to undertake something completely on my own. And I'm going to show what I'm made of, I'm going to show I'm capable of creating something good. I feel very happy, Dr. Palmer. It's a feeling I'd forgotten, or to be honest, one that I don't remember ever having so intensely. I think it might be about time I went back to work."

THIRTY-FIVE

Anne went back to her school a few weeks later, after completing the necessary papers. At first she found it hard to adapt to the course and pick up relationships with the other teachers, but soon she was managing to cope with it all. I realised from her comments that her colleagues held her in high esteem, unlike what she had told me, and welcomed her back affectionately. They held a surprise welcome back party and the school principal called her into his office to offer her his full support and help. Anne was very moved, and in her sessions she kept talking about the strange feeling of noticing that some people liked her. She started to discover that in the dark hostility that had always surrounded her there nonetheless existed a little passage that led to another world, a world where she could be.

"A world where I can let myself be," she said, more precisely. "This is all very weird, Dr. Palmer. It reminds me of what happens to an insect on the glass of a window."

"Explain that, please."

"When I was a girl, I'd feel a mix of horror and fascination when I watched the confusion of a fly, a bee, or any another flying bug that tried to go through the glass of a window, trapped by an invisible obstacle that it couldn't perceive or understand.

I tried to imagine what that poor bug might be thinking, having the place where it wanted to go in its sights, but prevented from getting there by a mysterious force. I'd spend a long time watching its futile efforts, its poignant insistence on getting through that barrier by repeating the same movement, incapable of changing, of making that little shift that would've been enough to discover that a couple of inches to one side or the other was the exit. So I'd try to help them, try to guide them to freedom with a cloth. That gave me an enormous sense of satisfaction, because deep down I must have been that insect, that bug impotently banging its head against an incomprehensible wall, crashing into the same place, incapable of changing that pointless mechanical movement. That's been my life until now, Dr. Palmer. A butterfly trapped in front of an invisible wall that holds it back as if it were cement, and desperation means you can't attempt anything else but keep on banging, banging, crashing into it a thousand and one times until the pain and the futility of the effort no longer matter, a butterfly falling, defeated, that's given up and lost the hope to keep on flying. That's been me, Dr. Palmer, and that's the little summary portrait of my life. Here I've been able to recall that memory, see myself in it, and I think that now I have the strength to take flight again."

* * *

In the months that followed, Anne spent most of her time in her sessions talking about her baby. Anyone who heard her could have sworn this was a woman commenting on how she was getting through a real pregnancy, since she experienced the whole process with the same vigorous and often anguished intensity with which she felt life. Anne had somewhere in her soul a kind of switch that connected her to the world, but without any kind of protection, so she'd crash into reality like the butterfly she identified with, and then everything hurt even more. The pain turned into hatred, because that was the only way she had found to guide herself through the confused mass of thoughts and delirious ideas. When that became unbearable, the switch would disconnect itself. She didn't just distance herself, she really cut herself off from the world around her, went into a kind of emotional coma, a kind of corpse-like levity that kept her suspended in the middle of nothing, anaesthetised, neither dead nor alive. And despite her serious illness, she was a survivor. That word her father had named her was always the log she clung on to so as not to go under in the inner torrent that dragged her down. Perhaps her father saw something premonitory in her, or perhaps he himself unwittingly gave her a way to survive. In any case, Anne was right. She was a survivor, and she had given me the privilege of being able to help her recover her strength.

* * *

I didn't become a surgeon, as my father had hoped. I became a doctor, but I ended up spending my time at the counter of this lost property office, where people come in the belief that they will find what is theirs here. It's a very special office, because although what they're looking for isn't here, in the process of looking for it they find something else they didn't even know existed.

And the most extraordinary thing is, that changes their lives.

* * *

"I talked to my father yesterday. He phoned me, like every Sunday. He seemed sad and tired. He's very old now, and this terrible fear has gotten into me that he could die. It has to happen sooner or later, but I don't think I'll ever be prepared. What hurts the most is that we hardly talk about my mother. He knows I'd rather avoid the subject, but then when we hang up I feel terribly regretful, because I have no right to act like that. I should love my mother, I should have been able to give her something in return for everything that was taken away from her. I feel like my selfishness is so absolute that I abhor myself. How could I have abandoned her like this? How can I have the nerve to reproach my own daughters, when I myself have committed an unforgivable sin against my poor mother? How could I have added more cruelty to what she's already been though in her lifetime? You should judge me, Dr. Palmer. You should judge me as harshly as you can, because there are sins that are unjustifiable and I've committed the worst one. I'm not a good example to anyone. Now I want to raise a new child, and I wonder if I have the morals to do so. I always thought of myself as a mother who was absolutely devoted to her duty, but I never questioned the kind of daughter I've been. The worst thing is it's too late now."

"Why are you so sure of that? That could just be an excuse so as not to make the effort to try something."

"But what could I do? We've grown so far apart that I don't even know how to speak to her any more! Does she think about me? I'm not even sure that she remembers me, or wants to see me."

"You have to choose between guilt and risk. I don't see many other options."

"Guilt or risk, guilt or risk. That's very direct, Doctor."

"You asked me what you could do. I answered the question."

"Yes, of course. Guilt or risk," she repeated to herself, almost in a whisper, as if she were carefully checking the meaning of the words.

* * *

When she came to her next session, I noticed immediately that something important had happened. She walked slowly into my office, and sat slowly in the chair, unlike the impetuous way she usually handled her body. Her head was bowed and I could only hear her breathing. After a few minutes, she looked up at me.

"You were right, Dr. Palmer. Guilt or risk. It was a premonition. My father called me this morning. My mother's been taken to hospital. She had a stroke. I'm leaving for Tel Aviv tonight. I should have organised this reunion a long time ago. Now it really is too late, but I still have to go, at least to be with my father. My baby won't be here for a few weeks yet. They gave me the time off at work, no problem. I can't say anything else today, Dr. Palmer. Everything else is unnecessary."

"It is, Anne. I wish you a good journey. I hope you make it in time to say goodbye to your mother."

* * *

Anne made it in time, and her mother died three days later. She'd gone into an irreversible coma, but at least Anne could stroke her face, look into those eyes that had seen the end of humanity, witnessed all hope flounder for the last time. Anne's father had managed to reconcile himself with life, but her mother decided she would never give it another chance, because that meant forgiving, exculpating human beings, and she wasn't willing to do that. She added more sacrifice to her pain, but maintained with absolute resolve her will to never forgive or forget a thing. Her position might have been questionable, there was even the possibility of wondering whether that was the sign that she had lost her mind. But since everyone else had lost theirs, any diagnosis would have been invalid from the outset.

THIRTY-SIX

"What will you do now?"

"I don't know. It's too early to say. Nothing special, I suppose."

"You could come back with me. You know I'm on my own, and we could keep each other company."

"Thank you, Anne. I'm sure we'd get on well together. But I'm far too old to move house, move to another country. I don't speak English, and there's no time to learn. I'd be a burden to you, and to be honest, I owe myself to this place where at least I've been allowed to live in peace. Besides, now that your mother's gone, I have to look after her memory, and I couldn't do that better anywhere else in the world but here. I stole her from death, I swore I'd care for her until her last breath, and now it's up to me to guard her memory. Don't believe I did all that because I'm a good person. I am, but that's not the point. The most important thing is that doing that allowed me to live too. I still want to live a little more, despite everything, and I know that to do so I must respect all the promises I made."

"I feel like I've behaved terribly. I let so much time go by, and there's nothing more painful than feeling that you can't go back."

"Oh, believe me, there are plenty of things more painful than that! And that's coming from someone who's known all kinds of pain. I could've made a living talking and writing about that unfortunate wisdom, but I preferred to keep quiet and hide it in silence. I always believed that you and your sister weren't born in the best of conditions, so to speak. I have nothing to reproach you for, nor you me. Maybe if I'd talked more, if I'd explained more things to you, your life would've been better. But I did what I believed I had to do, although now too I think that may have been a mistake. I can admit it, but it's too late now. As late as it is for you, or maybe we should leave out that way of thinking and accept it all. When you accept it all, there comes a moment when you find a certain calm. I think I've reached that place. I'm at peace, and I want you to be too. I've spent most of my life running away. You grew up thinking that your mother was a sick person and I was a strong man, the backbone of this humble home where at least we managed to find shelter. But it wasn't exactly like that. I wasn't as strong as I made you, your mother, and your sister believe. What I did was to set myself a goal, and I clung to that so as to carry on, and not sink. I chose not to question anything for the rest of my life, and that's why now, without your mother, I have to reinvent myself. That's why I decided to continue my role, and continue to keep your mother alive in my memory. Does that seem to you a less serious illness than hers? They say that when you lose a loved one, there's a mourning period, but that sooner or later you have to get back on your feet and accept your loss. I don't know what they say about people who lose everything in one go. What I did was madness too, the madness of not dying."

"But that was admirable madness."

"Listen, Anne. There aren't many admirable things left in this life. At least, that's the way I see it. Sometimes I'm still surprised when rain falls, and the drops make a noise on the window. Or when the neighbour's cat watches me from the window, with his wise look. I can even admire the colour of the sky when night starts to fall. But not much more than that. If you think about it, I've given you examples where I can trust in the innocence of things. The innocence of the rain, of the cat, of the colour of the sky. There aren't many other things that inspire me with innocence, and therefore admiration, so I'm nothing that you can admire, although nor do I deserve disapproval. Maybe your mother was far more admirable than me, deep down, because her rejection of her life was her way of getting revenge."

"But we had to pay that price too, and we weren't guilty."

"You're right, honey. Many times I wondered why we brought you two into a world your mother wouldn't forgive, a world which I was barely part of. I had nothing, no friends, no hobbies, only a job to put food on the table and a family to feel responsible for. Perhaps we didn't need to become something more than the two of us, a couple of poor cast-offs dispossessed of even their teeth. I remember one of the first things they gave us when we got here were false teeth. Our mouths were empty, not just our stomachs and our pockets! I still had most of my own teeth, but I had to use all my patience to persuade your mother to wear her dentures, because she refused to replace any of the teeth she'd lost. That's how stubborn she was. But let me tell you one thing: she was right. She knew that time would gradually erase the memories, the imprint, that even the tattoos on our arms would become part of the furniture, and that with the striped material the Germans used to dress the camp prisoners, trousers and shirts would be manufactured, designed by major brands. I was fully aware that life would mend itself, following that age-old force, that immemorial principle that cannot stop. She was opposed to that. She opposed it with all her strength. She demanded that life stop for ever, and since she knew no one would listen to her, she decided to go on strike by herself. She didn't want anyone to feel authorised to carry on, to turn the page. What did the world care what one poor woman did, if it was capable of ignoring what happened to millions of people? But your mom didn't care about that. She didn't frame the success of her revenge in the number of souls she was able to convince, but in the fact that she wouldn't back down on her promise. And it's true what you said: you two, and certainly I as well, also paid the price. But for her, there were no exceptions."

* * *

"That was all, Dr. Palmer. But I think this trip has changed something in me. I've opened up a little hole and the hatred is slowly seeping out of it, like the air in a burst tyre. There'll be a little left, that's for sure, but I'll be able to get by with it much better than before."

"I think so too. Your father painted you a portrait of your mother that puts certain things in perspective. And that's changed you as well."

"And it's only four weeks until my baby arrives! I'm so excited. I've gone over each and every one of the details, and I don't think I'm going to forget anything. I'll mail you some photos of how I've decorated the baby's room. I'm going to start afresh, Dr. Palmer, and I hope I do a little better this time. Do you think I'll do better?"

"Does anyone else know about the baby?" I asked so as not to answer her.

"Not yet."

"What about your daughters? What will you do about them? I mean if you're going to tell them about the baby."

"I haven't decided yet. I'm not sure if I should. They're convinced that I'm mentally ill, and they want nothing to do with me. The baby thing will only make them think worse of me. Besides, there's Richard. He'd use this to destroy me, take away my house, or find a way to ruin my job. I can't tell anyone."

"I understand. So you'll keep it secret, for now at least."

"For now at least."

A secret only I knew about, which would make this child the delirious product of the relationship Anne had with me. Of course, there was no way I was going to tell her this interpretation, but there was no doubt that that was what it was.

THIRTY-SEVEN

Rubashkin listened to my whole story without saying a word, his eyes quite wide open this time, as well as his mouth. He didn't seem to believe what I was telling him. As for me, I felt uncomfortable with what I first interpreted as a disapproving look.

"Amazing," he finally said. "Amazing. I've been sitting here for sixty years and few times have I heard anything like it. I told you, Dave, I told you and I swore it to you. That woman is something else, and she is giving us a clinical masterclass."

"But this solution … I don't know. It's something that I can't rightly place."

"Rightly? Did you say rightly? My dear Dave, I don't think that adverb does the moving image of Mrs. Kurczynski justice. There is nothing right in this story, nothing was right and therefore that's a criterion we should throw in the trash right away. Ah! I think I hear the voices of our ecclesiastic orthodox colleagues!" he exclaimed, standing up and rubbing his hands as he paced around the room. "I'm sure that Monseigneur Atkinson considers that she's acting out, because the castration complex wasn't detected in time, to which Bishop McLean will add with a great exaggerated display of feeling that these things happen when the ego isn't properly reinforced. It's just as well you and I are old enough not to waste time on that kind of crap. We're facing something huge here, Dave, something that doesn't come up every day. We don't know how it will end, but I have the impression that this lady knows very well what she's doing. You must follow the process closely, don't interfere in any way, or encourage her delusions either. Let's see how this evolves, what happens when she gets this doll, or baby, as she calls it. That's modernity, Dave. These things will be completely normal before long, but the thing is that Mrs. Kurczynski has gotten in there a few hours ahead of us, and left our clinic a few steps behind. But don't you worry. We'll quickly make up the distance, we'll catch up with her, because she's the one showing the way, and that's how it should be. That was how Freud intended it, and that marvellous free spirit, the beautiful Lou Andreas Salomé, understood it as well, destroying geniuses in her path when she wrote that essay titled 'The Patient is Always Right'. Isn't that extraordinary? But of course the patient is always right! Come on, Anne, let's get going! We're eager to see find out what happens next! Wait a moment, Dave. What about the name? The name! What will she call it? Has she chosen one? That's very important, as we know. It's the most powerful sign. The name!"

* * *

Three weeks before the "baby's arrival" (by this stage even I was thinking in these terms) Anne signed up for an antenatal course. Taking advantage of how uninhibited she could be in many situations, she'd managed to convince the instructor that she was going to adopt a baby, and that she was very curious to know what it felt like when one was going to be a mother for the first time. Whether the instructor considered this an acceptable explanation, or whether it was enough that she paid the signing-on fee, the point is she put up no objections. I was probably unable to hide something in the look on my face or the tone of my voice, because she immediately rushed to explain that she wasn't as crazy as she looked, and that her participation in the course was a way of "soaking up" her role as mother to a baby.

"I'm a veteran mother, Dr. Palmer. At my age, I'm closer to being a grandmother. But I'm finding this course very useful in preparing me for my new duties. Besides, I'm making friends. At the end of the class, a group of young women and I go to a café to chat about our lives. Anyway, you know that in America no one pokes their nose into other people's lives. None of them ask awkward questions."

The way she explained it, Anne's idea didn't seem so crazy. She needed to "introduce herself" on the scene, live the whole experience in a way that having a "baby" would give her full dignity. Somewhere in her mind she knew all that could dangerously fall apart into ridicule, or even something sinister. The synthetic baby could replace a real baby, or end up being a corpse in her arms, and it was impossible to predict what would happen. The promise of happiness ran the risk of turning into a catastrophe with no rescue possible. On thinking of the word "risk", I remembered I'd used it myself when I told her, "You have to choose between guilt or risk." I said it in the context of Anne's doubts about travelling to see her mother, but I also wondered whether I might have made a mistake in suggesting something to her that could drive her to the brink.

Nonetheless, as she herself had said, what's done was done. I had no other choice but to follow Rubashkin's advice: follow the process discreetly, and be alert to where it might take her.

* * *

Shanice Tide had sent me a letter and a funny photograph of her dressed in a yellow jumpsuit next to the infamous statue that had led her to my office. She wanted to let me know that she was calm and happy with her work, and that for the last few months she'd been living with a woman who she was rather in love with. She thanked me for the help I'd given her, even sent regards to "that bastard judge Delucca", to whom she no longer bore a grudge. I was just putting the letter back in the envelope when the service secretary knocked on my door to tell me that Anne has shown up unexpected. She didn't give me any time to be worried, because behind her, not waiting so much as a second, there she was sticking her head through the door, smiling, with her face excited and sweaty.

"Sorry, Dr. Palmer, for bringing my appointment forward, but it's just that today they cancelled the class because of a power cut and I said to myself, 'Why not make the most of the morning and pay the doctor a visit?' Last night I couldn't sleep so much as an hour thinking about the names."

"The names?"

"Right, the names of the boy or the girl!"

"Ah, of course!"

"As I told you, I won't know the gender until the day it arrives. So I have to think of a boy's name and a girl's name."

"And have you decided already?"

"I think so, that's why I was impatient and wanted to see you before the day I was supposed to come. May I sit down a few minutes?"

I checked my diary, and although I had several patients with appointments and not a single gap free, I decided that Anne's visit was more important, and that the others would have to wait a little.

"Go ahead. Tell me what you're thinking."

"This name business is really strange, Dr. Palmer. If I'm honest, I no longer remember how my daughters' names came about. Last night I felt like I was sticking a ladle in the pot of memories, and stirring all the contents real slow. From the bottom, some really old things started to come up that must have been down there for decades. Did I ever tell you about Rivka? Rivka Schultz? I don't think I did. She was the best teacher I had at school. She had an amazing past, which she never told us, and that I found out about many years later. She was

German, from a village on the border with Poland. In 1939, when she was five, she was one of the passengers who boarded the *Saint Louis,* a ship carrying almost a thousand Jewish refugees to Cuba, where they imagined they would be granted asylum, and planned to get from there to the USA. It was a tragedy, because when they got to Cuba they weren't allowed to disembark, then the captain headed for Florida, where they wouldn't let the refugees enter either, and as a last resort he tried the Canadian government, but they also refused. Eventually the ship had to return to Antwerp. All those poor people spread out over Europe, and most of them eventually died in the concentration camps. Rivka was one of the survivors. Some Dutch peasants hid her in a farm and looked after her, until after the war she met an American soldier, married him, and moved to the same America that years before had stopped her from entering. She had a great sense of humour, and when they asked her about her life, she said she'd taken a little longer than expected in making it to the United States because the ship's captain had decided they'd take a trip around the world first.

"When I arrived in the USA and started my scholarship studies, Rivka was one of my teachers. One morning, when we got to the university, we heard that she'd died. No one gave us an explanation, but eventually we found out she'd committed suicide. I've always wondered why she did that. I guess like so many other people, she succumbed to the pain of her own history, which wouldn't stop attacking her for one minute of her life. You know, many survivors ended up killing themselves many years later, when no one imagined they would. In Rivka's case, it was even harder to imagine, because she was such a cheerful person. I could never understand why cheerful people sometimes commit suicide. Maybe cheerfulness is just a disguise for some people, a mask that doesn't show the true face beneath. Maybe under her mask, poor Rivka's face was the same as all those wretched people, starving and parched, forced to enter the mouth of the monster that fed on human flesh and breathed fire. I felt a special affection towards her, because she'd realised that something wasn't right in me, and tried to help me without asking too many questions. I owe her a lot.

"I also remembered Isaiah Szklarz, who used to sit next to me. Isaiah was the son of a family who had escaped from the Lotz ghetto. His father was a doctor, and his mother played violin in the Tel Aviv National Orchestra. Isaiah was born almost blind, but he had incredible willpower to learn, so much so that he was first in the class every year. When I was fifteen he wanted to go out with me, and he asked me out one afternoon when we were leaving school. I turned him down, because the idea of being with a boy made me very afraid, but he thought it was because of his blindness. I didn't know what to do to make him understand what it was with me, and from that day on he never spoke to me. Many years later, when I was married, I went back to Israel to visit my parents. One morning I saw Isaiah Szklarz walking down the street with a white cane, holding hands with a boy who appeared to be his son. I got up the courage and went up to him, calling him by his name. But when I told him who I was, he shook his head and carried on walking. He said, 'I'm sorry, I don't remember you.' I knew he was lying, that it was impossible that he could have forgotten me, but then I realised that one person, for whatever reason, could be dead to another. They could be erased, wiped from the memory, crossed out. Isaiah had removed me from his life, the way you get rid of things that just take up space and get in the way for no reason. Of course, I didn't press him. Somewhere I would have continued to exist to blind Isaiah, as he did to me, but the memory of that afternoon after school must have been too painful for him, and he preferred to act like I'd vanished for ever.

"I think I can guess what you're thinking, Dr. Palmer. Isaiah and Rivka are both innocent names, but in the story of my life they're tainted by sad stories. I'm not saying they aren't. But I thought that using them for something beautiful would be a way to give them back their innocence. They were two very good people, and I'll settle for that."

"Isaiah or Rivka. We'll find out very soon!"

THIRTY-EIGHT

Isaiah arrived quite punctually, only a day later than the date given on the delivery order. I'd had a look at the manufacturer's web page, which detailed all its products. As well as the babies, which could be ordered with the appearance of all the stages of growth, from a newborn to a one year old, an immense range of complementary articles were also on offer. Beds, changing mats, diapers, bottles, pacifiers, clothes, bathtubs. In short, all the paraphernalia that consumer society has come up with so that children represent a major sales target. The doll possessed a number of very sophisticated mechanisms, imitating different kinds of cries, gurgles, laughs, and baby noises. In addition, the face could also take on a wide variety of looks. It could frown when angry or in pain, turn red in a tantrum, cry tears, cough, sneeze. It had a series of programs that allowed you to feed it regularly every certain number of hours, or at random, so that the baby would cry to be fed. It could also be programmed to wake up a number of times at night, as tends to happen in the first months of a child's life, or sleep for several hours at a stretch without troubling you. It was fed with a bottle filled with a synthetic imitation milk (recommended by the manufacturer), or real milk, in which case the internal circuits joining the mouth to the anus had to be cleaned once a week. Shortly after each meal, the baby did its business, and so the diaper had to be changed. The program was truly sophisticated, because it had been conceived so that the doll recreated, as realistically as possible, every typical situation involved in raising a baby. It could have colic, diarrhoea, fever, constipation, wind, colds, flu, and the company provided all kinds of "medicinal" articles, including an online chat service with a "paediatrician", whom the mother could consult on any question or problem related to bringing up a baby.

There was a whole other sector dedicated to toys, lullaby players, strollers, swings, baby chairs and tables, and a wide variety of jars containing a synthetic paste that the baby could be fed after six or seven months, along with the bottle.

As I imagined, over the nine months of her "pregnancy", Anne had devoted herself to filling her house with most of the products that the company offered consumers. As she had explained to me, the child would have no other family but her, he would not even have godparents or friends, so she was obliged to be his only provider. She was completely determined to give the baby all the comforts and whims that took their fancy. Logically, I held back from giving my opinion about this at all times. Besides, this kind of baby allowed for all kinds of overprotection. Maternal madness did not imply any risk (aside from ending up in the junk room or in the garbage pail), so Anne could overfeed it, hold it in her arms day and night, and spoil it every way she pleased. However, every one of her decisions had its consequences, as the inventors of the product had thought of everything. If the baby grew accustomed to being picked up every time it cried, the program would set that response, so that as the weeks passed the child would become progressively "tyrannical" and "spoilt". Designed for a variety of users, the doll could behave in different ways, leading to its developing a kind of "personality profile".

"I'd forgotten how a child can change your life, Dr. Palmer! Ever since Isaiah has been with me, the house has been turned upside down. I can't cope with all the work involved. He wakes up very early, and starts the day with a tremendous appetite. But he's a very good boy, I assure you. The thing is at my age all these jobs are a bit much for me, but I'm happy."

"Yes?"

"Absolutely. I knew that this would give some direction back to my life, and I wasn't wrong. Besides, now when I come home from work, it isn't solitude awaiting me, but Isaiah. I don't need to call the operator any more just to hear a voice on the recorded message, and feel that there's someone on the other end. I have him, and Norman too, of course, who's taken to the boy very happily, although if I'm honest, Dr. Palmer, I get the impression that Norman's a little jealous. Lately he doesn't come round so much, and although he seems happy with Isaiah's arrival, I think he feels like he's been replaced a little."

"In a way, that's quite logical. Norman is no longer as necessary to you as before. And you will probably have to get used to a new relationship with him. But as the weeks pass, I'm sure that everything will fall into place."

"I think so too. Besides, I've explained to Norman that this is a different kind of love. The point is that the poor thing realises that I've changed so much, and he's a little confused! But I try to calm him down. He has to understand that there are three of us now, and that if everything carries on like this, at Christmas the three of us will go and spend the night at the Eliot. That would be wonderful!"

"Of course."

"I'm trying to get organised as best I can. I get up very early, feed the boy, change him, leave him to sleep in the crib, go to work. In the afternoon I give him his bottle, change him again, and we go for an hour's walk in the park. When we get back, he plays in his crib with his toys while I prepare my classes and get dinner ready. Last of all I bathe him, give him his last feed, and put him back to bed. Last night he woke up a couple of times, so I'm exhausted today! But it's wonderful not being able to sleep for that reason. I've spent years of sleepless nights besieged by voices, thoughts, waves of broken words, and my body shattered or floating in a limbo of stupor. What a blessing to be woken by a baby crying! I've spent a lot of money on all this, so now I can't afford to hire help to do the cleaning. All the dirty laundry and dishes are piling up, and I don't have time to sweep up a little around the house. Some days I forget to take out the trash, but all that doesn't really matter. Of course, I'm in no position to have anyone round for dinner! The house looks like a squat, but Isaiah is fine; I can tell he's a happy boy, and his mother is bursting with joy. Every day I say to myself 'Anne Kurczynski, you are the luckiest woman in the world. Now you really deserve the title of survivor. You've earned it.' Don't you think I've earned it, Dr. Palmer?"

"No doubt about it."

"I owe a lot to you. Actually, I owe you almost everything."

"No, Anne. I only accompanied you, followed you along the route you drew out with great effort. The merit is yours. There are many kinds of people. Some turn tail as soon as they come up against trouble, but you decided to forge ahead. That's why I think you're something more than a survivor."

* * *

Over the months that followed, and as expected, Anne spent the sessions talking about Isaiah. As was also expected, the idyll of the first weeks gave way to moments of anxiety or anger, feelings that threatened to overwhelm her. However, at no time did she express a desire to get rid of the doll, or to store it in a drawer, both feasible options in this case, unlike with a real child, who tends to have to be kept until he comes of age. To her, the baby was as legitimate as a flesh and blood child, and she took on its care and upbringing with the same commitment she had shown her two daughters, and probably the same sickly anxiety.

One day she arrived for her session looking utterly out of it, as if she were about to explode.

"Children are diabolical beings, Dr. Palmer! You give your life for them, and they pay you back with contempt. Isaiah has decided to declare war on me. Now he doesn't want his bottle, he spits it out, cries constantly. I hold him in my arms, I sing to him, but he's like a little devil. He wouldn't even do as Norman tells him, and he's totally used to him and talks to him every day."

"Norman talks every day? I don't think I understand. With whom?"

"Norman talks to Isaiah too. It's an amazing thing. The boy already understands everything he's told."

"After just a month? That's remarkable."

"I know it sounds weird, but that's the way it is. Isaiah is a prodigy. The thing is that he devotes all his intelligence to ruining my day, and my night too, if he can."

"Do you really think that?"

Then she sat in silence a while, thinking, breathing quickly through her half-open mouth, her head facing the top of my desk.

"I don't know, children are very mysterious," she went on in a calmer tone.

"That is very true."

"Is it true that your teacher Lacan believed that we women are crocodiles? I read that somewhere."

"I've never heard that."

It was true. Lacan had said that, but I lied to her. Trying to explain the meaning and the context of that statement could lead to undesirable complications.

"Like many famous people, a lot of things are attributed to him, but who knows?" I added, acting oblivious.

"And didn't he say something about the fact that children can be vampires? Or even worse: a child who doesn't yet speak is a terribly dark and troubling thing. You have to guess what he wants; it's like trying to decipher the meaning of a remote, unknown language. Sometimes I look at Isaiah and I wonder what he's thinking, I see he's watching me but I have no way of knowing what's going on in his head. I try, but I can't do it. What is it that a child hides at the back of his mind? Is there any way of knowing? It gets me worked up sometimes."

As was her wont, Anne was able to put her finger on some sensitive and real point. No doubt, a baby is an enigmatic and unknown being. His apparent ingenuousness or innocence conceals an unknown side, one that exists in any human being, but redoubled by the absence of words. Most people are relatively blind to perceiving that in a child, which is a great advantage. When the opposite happens, when the case arises of someone, for example the mother, being capable of seeing it too clearly, the baby can cease to be an adorable creature, deserving of love and care, to become something incomprehensible and disturbing. Being crazy doesn't mean imagining non-existent things, but feeling too intensely something that most people don't even notice.

Just as had happened with her daughter Karen, Anne took it very badly when her baby's behaviour prevented her from playing her mother role according to the model of perfection and wisdom that she believed she possessed. She didn't have the ability to adapt to circumstances, but demanded that reality adapt to her prior definition, and when reality refused, the reaction could be rage.

At one session she returned to the burden of the baby's behaviour and I exclaimed, almost shouting, "If you want this to work, it's you who has to adapt to Isaiah, not the other way round!" I had never raised my voice like that, but I risked that intervention to put the brakes on the threat of a cycle I knew very well: first the uncontrollable torrent of rage and despair, then the fall into a state of general paralysis, before veering to sadness and self-loathing.

It worked. For a few minutes, she just sat there, totally still, not taking her eyes off me, stupefied. Then she stood up very slowly, nodded her head without adding a single word, and left with her unstable gait, muttering something inaudible but which seemed to me to be a show of agreement.

From that day, Anne went through a change. She started to dedicate herself more to her work, and the issue of Isaiah took second billing. She'd mention him now and again, giving the understanding that life with him had taken on a routine, amenable pace. But now the emphasis was on her work, her relationship with her colleagues, and the satisfaction she received from teaching. The baby was a source of company that brought her pleasure and entertainment, but was not the centre of her life. My intervention had allowed her to tone down the role of motherhood, distance her a little from the dramatic and obsessive meaning that had always contaminated her. Undoubtedly, it continued to be a fundamental support, but was no longer exclusively so. She improved her performance at work and her relationship with her colleagues, and discovered that she could find other family figures in her students to occupy herself with. She became very enthusiastic about this. Suddenly her life spread out, and as the population of people who made up her everyday life increased, Anne managed to take a little distance from herself, that is, from the person who for years had been her worst nightmare. Of course, I knew that these achievements were partial, and there was no guarantee that they would last, but at least they kept the eternal ghosts that had always haunted her at bay. After a few months, the stability of her condition made me think that it wouldn't be long before we put an end to our meetings.

Of course, that was something that I would leave up to her.

THIRTY-NINE

Dr. Alan Rubashkin was buried in the Jewish cemetery on Baker Street, at a simple ceremony attended by his family, friends, and a large part of the psychoanalytical community of Massachusetts. After a long and indefatigable commitment to his profession, Rubashkin left behind the memory of an exceptional man, gifted with an exquisite human sensitivity, a profound knowledge of clinical practice, but above all the inexhaustible capacity to keep curiosity alive, his rejection of any form of stagnant or conventional wisdom, his willingness to allow himself to be taught by experience, instead of trying to adapt it to established knowledge. Those of us who had the fortune to receive his teaching learned a lesson that would stay with us for the rest of our lives: never take anything for granted, distrust our prejudices, always walk one step behind the patient, don't give in to the temptation of converting the patient into ourselves, respect madness, respect it to the point of recognising, even in the most extravagant and broken-down madness, a source of wisdom that it is always worthwhile allowing yourself to be educated by. Even those who had mocked Rubashkin, considering him an old anachronism divulging doctrines that had supposedly been superseded by modern protocols, were present that cold, bitter morning, because deep down they knew that with him died one more member of that rare and dying breed known as ethical man, a man with certain attributes, a man who had made it his principle to take existence seriously.

As the ceremony went on, and various people said a few words of farewell, my mind started to project an endless stream of memories. Rubashkin hadn't just taught me my trade like one passes on objective knowledge. Over my years of analysis with him, he'd witnessed and accompanied a long and often painful process in which I'd had to stare some none too pleasant truths in the face, but which were essential to tackle in order to shake off that immense burden of meanings and interpretations we are wrapped up in. In the end, and aside from all real or imaginary events we went through, the secret lies in the way we tell ourselves a story. More than telling it, we live it, and in doing so we take on a role that we cling to with all our strength, even if it's a bad role, a leading role or a supporting role, but a bad role, because we act it out repeating a text whose author we don't know, and who we are incapable of questioning. A role that generally sends us head first into sacrifice, unhappiness, unbridled and limitless ambition, cruelty towards ourselves and those around us, a role that torments love, degrades beauty, and makes us secret accomplices to the misfortunes of fate. I owed Alan Rubashkin for having liberated me from a considerable portion of that burden, and for having learned to live decently with the remains that never dissolve in the potion of the cure.

* * *

As I'd foreseen, Anne arrived that day and announced that she'd thought about ending our meetings.

"This isn't goodbye for ever, Dr. Palmer, at least I hope you won't take it that way! I'm only daring to take this step because I'm convinced that you'll take me back whenever I need you. But now I feel that I can go on by myself, that I've learned something, and I leave here a different woman. Of course, the old Anne is still there, sitting in a corner. I'm not going to kick her out of my life. Not only because it would be impossible, but because deep down I don't want to. I'm still her too, and given that I've understood the price of denying the truth, I think I have to accept her presence. We've known each other all our lives, and it would be ungrateful and arrogant of me to make her feel like I've forgotten her. I trust that our life as neighbours will be better than our life as Siamese twins."

* * *

Anne left through the same door she'd come in through the first time, only now she did so with a slower walk, leaving in my ears a calm and well-argued farewell. From my office window I saw her cross the hospital garden, her feet flattened with the weight of her fat, tired, body, her eternal bags full of mysterious objects, moving like an old ship that laboriously moves away from the shore and heads for the sea.

A few years later, as I was taking an evening walk along the Charles River, I happened to bump into her. She was sitting on a wooden bench, looking at the sunset, and when she saw me she gave me an immense smile. I had to help her up, because she insisted at all cost on doing so to greet me, and it filled me with happiness to know that she was still calm and relatively happy with her life. We went our separate ways after a few minutes, and I hadn't gone more than a few steps when I heard her voice.

"Dr. Palmer!"

"Yes?" I asked, turning around.

"I've still got my baby!" she exclaimed, and then she waved at me again, and immersed herself in the contemplation of the silver sparkles moving on the water. At her feet rested the usual bags, her travel companions, the same ones that she would invariably bring to every consultation.

As usual, I was wondering what she carried in them just as my telephone rang. It was Judge Delucca's secretary to inform me of an urgent matter. Actually, I couldn't get used to the fact that the girl was no longer Judge Delucca's secretary, but Benjamin Isaiah Casttan's. Delucca had been enjoying his retirement for some time, and young Benjamin, an African American who had been a psychoanalysis patient of mine for a few years, now occupied his position. We got on really very well, and he called me often to ask about cases in which he suspected a "mental element", as he liked to put it. Once, at one of those dreadful art exhibitions that I tend to avoid by all means possible, a woman who wouldn't stop talking to me asked me, "Do blacks do psychoanalysis?" as she chewed on a greasy canapé.

"Of course," I replied. "Especially the men. They get a terrible complex when it's shorter than seven inches." It was a bit of an overreaction, but at least I managed to get away from both that lady and the exhibition.

I soon realised that I had a full day ahead of me. Deborah Chester sent me a text message. She was no longer at the hospital, but from time to time she'd send me her news.

"I'm passing through town. I wouldn't mind if I was asked out for dinner."

I looked at the time. If I organised myself right, I'd probably have time to get to Casttan's office and then swing by mine. I hadn't dined in company for some years, and therefore had to prepare myself calmly. Language, death, and sex. I had plenty of words, and the Grande Dame let me know from time to time that we were friends. But as for the last, I was rather out of training.